*Dismal Ravens Crying*

Cyril Jolley returns from holiday to his newly promoted position of Detective Inspector. It is not an
elevation he appreciates, particularly as it means his
long-standing partner is promoted out of his area.

The robot-like efficiency of his stand-in has left
Jolley very little to come back to: except for an
anonymous note declaring that the three 'suicides' in
a nearby hamlet are three too many for coincidence.
Happily pushing aside the decision of choosing a new
sergeant, Jolley departs for the feudal-like village of
Chuters and its colony of ravens: and there meets
the devastatingly beautiful Dolores Bayger, who the
anonymous letter-writer believes to be the catalyst for
the deaths of the three men.

Jolley rapidly locates the author of the original note
and unearths a web of gossip against Dolores. Finding
nothing to undermine the verdicts of suicide, he uses
his influence to stamp out the whispering campaign
of hatred. Then Dolores appeals to him for protection
and Jolley discovers an obsessive labyrinth of violence
into which he is drawn, leaving him as both victim and
suspect.

David Fletcher's talents for depicting the dark side
of man, and for creating a tangible atmosphere, are at
their strongest in this compulsively readable novel.

# Dismal Ravens Crying

## David Fletcher

MACMILLAN
LONDON

First published in Great Britain 1989 by
MACMILLAN LONDON LIMITED
4 Little Essex Street London WC2R 3LF
and Basingstoke

Associated companies in Auckland, Delhi, Dublin, Gaborone, Hamburg, Harare, Hong Kong, Johannesburg, Kuala Lumpur, Lagos, Manzini, Melbourne, Mexico City, Nairobi, New York, Singapore and Tokyo

ISBN 0-333-51788-1

A CIP catalogue record for this book is available from the British Library

Typeset by Matrix, 21 Russell Street, London WC2

Printed and bound in Great Britain by the Camelot Press Ltd, Southampton

# One

His head was still full of Gundula Janowitz, for her recital had been the highpoint of his holiday. To have heard her live at last still made him feel unreal, like a child given an unexpected half-holiday. How many years, he wondered, purblind to the road, the countryside through which he passed, had he admired her voice, awoken so many times from grooves of black vinyl? More than he could count or cared to remember. And now, this summer, in a spartan Austrian hall, she had stood upon the stage before him and sung. He sighed, his mind still replaying a single phrase she had executed with unique grace.

Cyril Jolley smiled a self-mocking smile. Other men returned from holiday with a sense of anticipation, albeit possibly tinged with depression. But even a return to the same old routine had its compensations. Faces and voices and places missed. The countryside changed rapidly, became more beautiful. People aged or looked better because of the refreshing glass of your absence. As Eileen said, it was always nice to get home, be in your own place.

Jolley changed gear badly, making the car stutter. He clung almost desperately to the memory of Madame Janowitz, his only regret that here, back home, there was no one with whom he could share the experience, live the memory, make it real for someone else. He was a fool. He acknowledged the fact as he slowed, leaned forward, signalled his intention to turn right. The hedges had an overblown look. A few weeks of good weather and they lost that sharp English green, became dusty, rested in wait for autumn. We need some rain, he thought, and

7

immediately felt depressed. He was a fool to shut all this out, set his face against the reality of his return to work. It did not become a middle-aged, overweight policeman to moon like a love-sick adolescent over a soprano nearing the end of her illustrious career. It was undignified. And yet she had been so . . . wonderful!

His sigh filled the car, embarrassing him. Apart from anything else, he lectured himself sternly, such behaviour was unbecoming to Madame Janowitz and her art. He was pressing the memory of her into service, indulging in diversionary tactics. Fooling himself and everyone else. Eileen, for example, who had remarked on his keenness to get back to work, pointing out that he was early by a good half-hour.

It wasn't keenness; it was fear. And there the trouble lay, like a thick blanket of fog, obscuring all before his eyes. His promotion. He had left Oversleigh Police Station a month ago Detective-Sergeant Jolley and he was returning a full-blown inspector. There would be a fuss. He knew it, despite all the hints he had dropped, the growls of disapproval and warnings he had made to anyone who had dared to mention his impending 'eleva-tion'. They did not understand – except for Hughes, of course – that his promotion was a defeat. For years he had battled with Superintendent Teddy Tait of Passington, resisting all attempts to kick him upstairs. For years he had out-manoeuvred his lethally devious superior. But Tait had won in the end. And, to make matters worse, he had stolen Hughes, seconded him to Passington, leaving Jolley without a confidant, a friend, his right-hand man. But at least the Superintendent had let him remain at Oversleigh. There was some lining to every cloud, he thought. Even now he could be on his way to Passington . . . And then Hughes, for all his sterling qualities, could not tell Gundula Janowitz from a rock plant.

He hit the brake pedal hard, the car skating to a halt as the lights at Oversleigh Bridge changed almost unseen to red. Jolley rocked back in his seat. Fine bloody start that would have been. Newly promoted bobby jumps red light. He could be demoted for that. He smiled bitterly. Could he? Reduced to the ranks, even. Could they equip him with a rusty old bicycle and a pair of shiny new clips, dispatch him to pedal the beat in perpetuity? Well . . . He watched the lights carefully, depressed the clutch and drove smoothly over the narrow bridge.

In fact he was a little shaken by his lack of attention. Searching his mind, he found he could remember almost nothing of the journey. True, he had been making this run for years, knew it backwards, but even so . . . Perhaps he was too old for the responsibility. Perhaps his new sergeant – *when* he got one, *if* he got one – would have to do all the driving. Good. Then he could loll in the back seat and remember that exquisite phrase, note by limpid note, to his heart's content. Only the phrase was no longer there in his head, would not be retrieved to his ear. It was time, he concluded, to face a different kind of music.

He crept into his old parking bay at the rear of the police station and locked the car punctiliously, checking each door, even the boot against his own forgetfulness. Then, hunching his shoulders, he pushed through the swing door and walked down the dim corridor, past the canteen, the smell of bacon and more general frying strong in his nostrils. He avoided the main lobby by ducking up the narrow side staircase, panting as he climbed. With any luck he would reach his office, get safely behind his desk before any of them were aware of his presence in the building. From the safety of his own territory he could quash any fuss, any attempts at celebration or congratulation with a snarl or a show of busyness. There must be a hundred urgent matters awaiting his attention. Pausing at the foot of the last flight of stairs, Jolley knew this was a vain hope. Teddy Tait in his authoritative wisdom had provided Oversleigh with a caretaker during Jolley's absence. An excellent man, according to Tait, one Detective-Inspector Lethbridge of Cosby. Lethbridge, Jolley thought, climbing the last stairs, would have cleaned up everything that was going.

He butted the heavy fire door with his right shoulder, grimaced at the force of the impact which started a flash of pain down his back. The door swung open revealing the third-floor corridor and a gaggle of uniformed personnel at his office door. He stopped dead, too late to prevent the door crashing against the wall. He seriously considered backing off, making a run for it as surprised, eager faces turned towards him. He felt his own face set like concrete, minus its habitual smile. Sergeant Bentinck, the senior officer present, detached himself from the group and hurried towards Jolley. Behind Bentinck, the others closed ranks, shielding PC Doulton.

'Good morning, sir. You're early. Welcome back. Good holiday?' Bentinck spoke in a rush, none of his words given their proper weight of meaning. Jolley stepped forward, letting the door swing back behind him.

'Morning, Sergeant. Yes, thank you. What's going on?'

Bentinck barred his way, smiling. For a minute Jolley thought that they were going to have to indulge in an undignified shuffle, squeezing past each other. Then a murmur went up from the others and they broke apart. Doulton, red-faced, grinned at Jolley.

'All ready now, Sarge,' PC Neil said.

'Ah, good . . . Welcome back, sir,' Bentinck repeated, stepping aside. 'And many congratulations.'

They even began to clap. All except Doulton who, Jolley saw, held a screwdriver in his left hand and was desperately failing to stuff it into his trouser pocket. Jolley glanced at Doulton, unfairly making him the butt of his embarrassment.

'Haven't you got any work to do?' he demanded, but Doulton skipped aside, waving his screwdriver at the door.

## DETECTIVE-INSPECTOR C.I. JOLLEY

Jolley stared at it. It was lopsided, had a distinct list to starboard. Undoubtedly Doulton's cack-handed work.

'Sorry about that, sir,' Bentinck whispered in his ear. 'We'll get it fixed.'

'Thank you. Thank you all very much,' Jolley said in a voice that sounded ungracious even to his own ears. 'I'm . . . very . . . touched.'

A door banged at the far end of the corridor, behind the group of smiling, now rather embarrassed faces. A tall, lean figure advanced towards them, his step firm and light. Jolley heard PC Roscoe murmur, 'Ee-up. Here comes trouble.'

'Ah, Mr Jolley and . . . welcoming committee, I presume.'

The crowd parted to let Detective-Inspector Lethbridge through. He held out his hand, his manner perfectly correct, his face without expression. Jolley broke into a grin and pumped his hand with a warmth born entirely of relief.

'Mr Lethbridge.' The others began to melt away, all except Doulton who had to be tugged and prodded in the right direction. 'No doubt you'd like to make your report,' Jolley said, moving to his office door.

'If this is a convenient moment, yes.' He stared after the retreating men. 'There was no one on the desk five minutes ago,' he added loudly.

'There will be now, I can assure you.' Jolley opened the door and stepped into a blaze of sunlight, on to a strip of bright red carpet which ran pristine before his desk. 'What on earth . . . ?'

'It's customary,' Lethbridge said, ever the old hand, moving past him. 'One of the perks of the job.' There was a slight, patronising lift to the corners of his thin mouth, Jolley thought. He put a bulky blue folder on the desk.

'And the flowers?' Jolley queried, going around the desk to his old, familiar swivel chair. Six pink carnations and a frond of greenery adorned the neat, polished desk, in a glass vase.

'WPC Russell's idea, I believe,' Lethbridge said dismissively.

'Ah . . . I must remember to thank her,' Jolley said, thinking that he would like to throttle her. But Lethbridge first. 'Won't you sit down?' Jolley sat, took a certain mean pleasure in watching as Lethbridge looked around the room for another chair, carried it, straight-backed and workmanlike, with a torn rexine seat, to the strip of red carpet and sat, facing Jolley squarely. Naturally, he hitched the perfect creases in his grey pin-striped suit as he sat, exposing a few inches of dark grey silk sock.

'Been busy?' Jolley asked, eyeing the blue folder.

'Nothing to speak of,' Lethbridge answered, reaching for the folder. 'You didn't get much sun, I see. Weather's been marvellous here.' He opened the folder, snapped the ring binder apart and extracted the first report. 'Taking and driving away. Three cases, obviously related.' With a flick of his wrist he tossed the report towards Jolley. It was contained in a plastic envelope and was meticulously typed. Jolley touched the plastic gingerly but made no attempt to read. Instead he recalled Tait's fetish for written reports. Lethbridge was obviously a Tait man. Another report slithered in front of him. 'Break-in at the West Street Stores. Cigarettes and booze mostly. Seems not to be a local job. Retford are helping with inquiries. The computer showed certain similarities in tactics. Think it might be a peripatetic gang. You'll find it all there.' Without pause, he went on, 'Reported theft of turkey chicks from some farm in Brindsleigh.' Lethbridge's tone indicated that he considered this a complete waste of time.

'Odd,' Jolley said, taking the folder from him. 'Jack Smart's not the sort of chap to call us in for a peccadillo.'

'Apparently it's been persistent. Haven't heard from him the last couple of weeks, though. Oh, this may interest you. Ralph Amis. Solvent abuse. Apparently you handled some previous incident.'

'Indeed I did,' Jolley said, accepting the plastic en-velope from Lethbridge's fingers. 'In connection with that stabbing we had last winter. In fact, I promised Amis no further action.'

'Well, he's charged and booked now.'

'Why?' Jolley said coldly, letting his anger show.

'Because he didn't heed your warning. He broke your trust or whatever it was.' Meeting Jolley's angry eyes, he added, 'We simply had no choice. The boy's obviously a persistent offender.'

Jolley set the report aside. *He* would look into that.

'A couple of domestics, a public affray outside the Bridge Hotel. Three men charged. It's all there. Oh yes, and you can keep the folder.'

Jolley did not acknowledge this. 'And that's it?'

'Mm.' Lethbridge leaned back in his chair, hands clasped behind his head. 'I've got WPC Russell on to your filing, by the way. Introduced her to a new system. Much more efficient. You should chivvy Passington for an update on your computer link, too. What you've got is less than useless.'

'I'll give it priority,' Jolley said drily. He hated computers. 'Anything else?'

'No. I don't think so. You'll feel free to ring me if you have any queries.'

'You'll want to be getting back to Cosby,' Jolley said, standing up, 'where the real action is.'

'Any crime is action in my book, Mr Jolley. Even disappearing turkey chicks . . . ' At this he smiled and stood up. Jolley offered his hand aggressively, squeezed Lethbridge's cool, dry palm as hard as he dared.

'Thanks for looking after the store,' he said, the lack of sincerity in his tone making him feel ever so slightly guilty.

'Oh, it's been interesting. Well, I'll be making tracks.'

'I'll see you . . . off the premises,' Jolley offered.

'No need. I'm sure you want to tackle those reports and check your post. Good luck.'

'The same to you,' Jolley said. Bloody man, he thought, as the door closed behind Lethbridge and his confident steps faded down the corridor. He shuffled the slippery plastic envelopes together, dumped them to one side. WPC Russell could have the pleasure of fitting those back into their blue binder.

'Bloody cheek,' he said aloud and sat down again, his elderly chair creaking in protest and, he thought, sympathy. He stared into space for a moment or two, a smile spreading slowly over his face as he recalled the scene outside his door, the little ceremony of welcome and celebration. What amused him and made him feel that he really was back was Doulton's incompetence with the screwdriver. Privately, Jolley called Doulton 'the Dolt'. The lad was as thick as two short planks, but Oversleigh would not be the same without him. In a set-up like this you could carry, even enjoy a Doulton, whereas blokes like Lethbridge . . . He let the thought die unfinished, pulled his neatly stacked in-tray toward him and began to go through it.

The dove-grey folder was stamped twice: *Private & Confidential* and, lower down, *From the Office of the Superintendent, Passington City Constabulary*. This legend was repeated, in dye-stamped pale grey ink at the top of the handwritten note, clipped with a grey paper-clip, to four typed sheets. Affectation, Jolley thought. Colour co-ordinated bloody stationery now.

'My dear Jolley,' he read.

'Enclosed fullest details of the two recommended applicants for Hughes's post. The very best I can do, I promise you, in these difficult times. Both excellent bods, I'm sure you'll agree. Of course, the final decision is *entirely* up to you, and if neither should be deemed acceptable, I'll try my best to find you someone else, but good candidates are thin on the ground these days, as you know.

'I believe either candidate would benefit *enormously* from working closely with you and I know you'll bear this in mind, their future career prospects etc. etc., when making your decision.

'I've taken the liberty of arranging interviews for 4th September. Your girl will have the details. Correction.

14

Your girl *should* have the details. I gather from Lethbridge that efficiency is not a forte among Oversleigh office personnel. No doubt you'll crack the whip.

'Trust your leave was enjoyable. My best to the charming Eileen.

'Yours, etc.'

The signature was a florid scrawl of blue ink.

The bloody nerve of Lethbridge, criticising his staff to the old man! 'Your girl', indeed. He stared morosely at the note, the pages it hid. Oh, how he missed Hughes! He did not want anyone to replace Hughes. He did not want to train someone, get accustomed to them. He wanted someone who knew his ways, latched on to his thought patterns, fed him the right information at the right time and told him when he was being an imaginative fool. Damn it, he wanted someone who would indulge him and trust him and yet keep a wary eye on him. He wanted David Hughes. He wanted a partner, not some raw, jumped-up, upwardly mobile kid with blue folders and plastic envelopes and computer know-how. He had a sudden strong impulse to pick up the phone and ring Hughes, just to hear his voice, to discuss it all with him. He felt ashamed of this, recognised self-indulgent dependency when he saw it. Then he grew gloomy again at the almost certain knowledge that Hughes would be unobtainable anyway. Hughes was a high-flier now, based at Passington. He'd be out chasing some real villain, not wasting his time on missing turkey chicks and staff problems.

A light, polite tap on the door made him pull himself together. He closed the grey folder and called for his visitor to enter. WPC Russell came in beaming, carrying a cup of coffee and three chocolate biscuits on a pretty plate. Jolley beamed back at her.

'Welcome back, sir. We have missed you.'

'Really, Penny? I'd have thought you'd have been too busy with Mr Lethbridge's new filing system to have time for such emotional matters.'

The young woman looked uncertain for a moment.

Jolley could see her adjusting to his manner, sifting the evidence of his speech to see if he was teasing, angry or pleased.

'Oh, that,' she said, putting down the coffee and biscuits. 'I've been doing overtime trying to get it back to normal. I hoped you wouldn't notice.'

'I haven't. Mr Lethbridge told me.'

'There was no doing with him, sir. He wouldn't listen.'

'That's all right, Penny. As long as you can find whatever we need.'

'It'll soon be right as rain again.'

'Chocolate biscuits, I see. You're spoiling me.'

'Well, as it's your first day back— '

'And flowers. I believe I have you to thank . . . '

'Well.' She blushed becomingly. 'I thought, just this once.'

'Good thinking. Don't let flowers become a habit, there's a good girl.'

'Oh no, sir. Would you rather I— ' She reached nervously for the vase.

'Over my dead body,' Jolley said. 'It's just that . . . For high days and holidays, eh?'

'Right you are, sir.'

'Now, what have you got to tell me?'

'It's all in your tray, sir, except for this.' From the pocket of her skirt she pulled a folded piece of paper, torn from a shorthand pad. 'It's the times of the appointments for tomorrow. I'd have had it typed up and everything only the Super's office only just rang to confirm. DS Latham at ten and DS Glade at eleven. If that's all right with you, sir.'

'It'll have to be, won't it, Penny?' Jolley said, noting the 'efficiency' of the Superintendent's office. 'Mr Tait has spoken.' He glanced at the piece of paper. 'Which one do you fancy?'

'Oh, I don't know anything about them, sir. The folder,' she added primly, on her dignity, 'was marked confidential.'

'So it was. And you wouldn't peep, would you, Penny?'

'More than my job's worth, sir. Though that Mr Lethbridge would have done if I hadn't been quick. I had to keep it locked in my bottom drawer until this morning.'

'Thank you, Penny. It's good to be back.' He bit into a chocolate digestive, spattering crumbs on to the grey folder.

P.D. Latham and M.G. Glade. Both new promotions. Neither of them local. One seconded, the other requesting a transfer on personal grounds. Both young. Both well qualified. Neither of them Hughes. He closed the folder, shaking crumbs on to the floor, swigging the coffee which tasted weak and ersatz after what he had been drinking on the Continent for the last few weeks. Oh, he was back all right, with a vengeance. Latham and Glade. He would have to take one of them. If you were sensible, and Jolley was, you read between the lines of Tait's little notes. You ignored the promises and picked out the implied threats. What the note really said was: 'Take one of these or I'll lumber you with a uniformed disaster area.'

'To hell with it,' he said, and put the folder into his top right-hand drawer. Tomorrow was another day. Latham and/or Glade might surprise him. One of them might even *do*.

He shuffled through the rest of the in-tray's contents. All routine. All rubbish. A pile of letters, neatly clipped with ordinary, standard-issue paper-clips, of congratulation on his promotion. Local bigwigs. A few from local people he'd helped. A postcard escaped the clip, slipped picture side up on to his desk. He turned it over.

'Congratulations. I can't think of a better *policeman* to get promotion. Good luck. X Karen.'

Cheeky young madam, he thought, smiling broadly. Karen Ashburton whose dislike of the police – she usually used a more colloquial and less flattering noun – she had never concealed from him. By the same token she had never quite been able to conceal that she trusted him. His smile faded. And last winter, because he was too busy, too preoccupied, she had come close to death at the hands of a young man who had already killed once. It still made him shudder to think of it. But all that was in the past, he told himself, slipping the postcard into his pocket to show Eileen later. Karen was alive and well and sending him cheeky messages. What more could a despised old policeman ask?

At the very bottom of the tray was a smallish, cheap white envelope, clearly, if somewhat untidily, marked for his attention and *Private*. The biro with which it had been written had been leaky, the hand printing somewhat shaky. The ink from the faulty pen was smudged by much hand-ling. The postmark was Passington. Jolley held it, turned it over, regarded it with instinctive suspicion. The Post Office franking-machine had run amok, leaving a line of grey spots, some blurred printing on the back. But the postmark was clear enough. Carefully, using an old brass paperknife he had inherited from some previous occupant of this office, Jolley slit the envelope and took out two sheets of lined Lion Brand paper. Like the envelope, the message was printed. The shakiness of the letters was, he suspected, due to an attempt to disguise the hand. The words wandered away from the printed lines.

YOU WANT TO INVESTIGATE THE SUICIDS AT CHUTERS. THREE HAS GOT TO BE MORE THAN COINCEDENCE. IF YOUR DONT YOU ARE NOT WORTH PROMOTING. WHAT DO WE PAY TAXIS FOR? Jolley smiled at this. To take us from A to B, he thought, wondering where this would lead him. IF YOU WANT TO KNOW MORE YOU WANT TO SPEAK TO . . . He turned over. A telephone number was writ large. Of course the letter was not signed. Jolley closed his eyes for a minute, trying to translate the code before the three-figure number. It was local, he knew that much. But what did that mean? British Telecom, in its infinite wisdom, had carved up the area according to some weird and wonderful logic of its own. Brindsleigh, for example, came under Oversleigh, which was logical enough, but his own village, Clifton King's, shared the Cosby code although it was five miles nearer to Anderton. He gave up. There was, after all, one very easy way to find out.

*Three* suicides, he thought, opening his eyes. He remembered one, back in March or April. A married man had gone up into Chute Wood after watching *EastEnders* and had blown the top off his head with a shotgun. His own shotgun, properly licensed. Left a wife and two kids, lived in Chuters. But two more was, as the letter said, pushing coincidence somewhat. If there were two more.

Jolley reached for his internal phone, pressed 12 for WPC Russell.

'What's all this about suicides in Chuters?' he demanded.

'Sergeant Hadfield handled that while you were away, sir. He's not on duty— '

'But there are files, I suppose? Or has Lethbridge buried them?'

In her coolest, most reproachful voice, Penny Russell said, 'I'll bring them in straight away, sir.'

Two more suicides in a village of – what? two hundred and fifty, three hundred souls? – in four weeks? And nobody smelled a rat? It could not be. Impossible. Somebody, the writer of the letter possibly, had got it wrong. There had to be some other explanation.

And so, in a sense, there was. The files which WPC Russell brought in showed that the suicides had been spread over a longer time-span than Jolley had guessed. But they had all occurred in Chuters. Two were residents and one a temporary visitor who had lodged there, with old Mrs Pasque whom Jolley had known slightly all his life. That one's name was Antony Corr-Beardsley. He was aged twenty-seven. He had been employed as a field researcher by the Chute Foundation, which was a conservation and ecological research station or some such, set up by the late Lady Katherine Chute. Unmarried. He had blown his head off with a shotgun, borrowed with permission from the gun-room at Chute Manor. His death had occurred in the first week of August, while Jolley was on leave.

But David Brimble, aged nineteen, unemployed, had hanged himself from a tree in his own back garden some three weeks before Jolley's leave had commenced. Why had he not known about it? Because there were no suspicious circumstances. Because he had been busy with a spate of hijacked lorries and no doubt preoccupied with his promotion. The boy had been depressed for weeks. Dr Stoller of Oversleigh had prescribed 'mild anti-depressants'. His girlfriend had ditched him. He had no job. He had walked to the horse chestnut tree at the bottom of the garden at number 17 Chuters and had hanged himself with an old rope his father kept in the boot of his car.

Frederick Smith had been the first, back in March, as Jolley had recalled. With his own shotgun in Chute Wood. He had told his wife he was going for a walk. He often took a gun, apparently, to pot a few grey squirrels or rooks. Jolley wondered what Lady Katherine would have had to say about that? Perhaps the conservation programme she had instigated only extended to flora. He thought he'd read that somewhere. Anyway, the man had worked for the Foundation as maintenance manager. Lived in a cottage in Chuters, owned by the estate. Left two sons, thirteen and fifteen, and a widow. Had not seemed himself lately, according to his wife.

Jolley turned back to the first report. Antony Corr-Beardsley had seemed 'anxious'. Mrs Pasque thought he had been homesick. The landlord of The Clouded Yellow had thought him 'a bit down-in-the-dumps'. The Director of the Chute Foundation had thought him 'an excellent botanist with a bright future'. The Director did not, however, concern himself with his employees' private lives.

No suspicious circumstances. Just a coincidence. Was suicide catching? Was it an example to which others, depressed and lonely, were attracted? Had Fred Smith's terrible self-slaughter beckoned David Brimble and Antony Corr-Beardsley, shown them the way out?

IF YOU WANT TO KNOW MORE YOU WANT TO SPEAK TO . . .

Jolley picked up the telephone and punched out the row of figures printed on the second page of Lion Brand paper.

Jolley was destined never to forget that first experience of her voice, its sound. She gave the number in full, said, 'May I help you?'

He would never forget her voice but he would never be able to describe it accurately, to his own satisfaction, either. It was low, rich, dark, soft and yet with a hint of steel in it. Had she been a singer, she would have been a mezzo-soprano, possibly even a contralto, at least in colour. Perhaps a meld of Ferrier and Fassbaender or Baker and Baltsa.

'Hello? Who is there?' she said into Jolley's surprised silence.

He only knew that her voice touched some unsuspected erogenous spot in the base of his spine. It was much more than a shiver that ran up his back. His hand, holding the receiver, was suddenly wet. Unconsciously, Jolley pushed a finger between his neck and his collar, tugging at the latter which was suddenly too tight. At the same time he announced himself in a rather strangled voice, stumbling over his new rank.

'Oh,' she said, and then, with a husky little laugh, 'Have I done something terribly wrong?'

'That I couldn't say, madam. To whom am I speaking?'

'Dolores Bayger . . . Inspector. Should I call you that?'

'That will be fine. Are you the sole subscriber to this number?'

'Ye-es.' She made two musical syllables of the word, stretching it charmingly. What might be taken for hesitation was, he thought, humour at his pomposity.

'And your address is . . . ?'

'"The Stables", Chuters Village . . . ' Jolley wrote this down, frowning. 'Would you mind telling me what this is about?'

'It's not a matter I can discuss on the telephone, madam,' he said. He thought he heard her smother a laugh, but could not be sure.

'Well, in that case, you'd better come to tea. Shall we say four o'clock? I'll look forward to it.' And she put the phone down.

Tea? You don't ask a policeman to tea. It was only then that Jolley registered she was not British. It was a damn cheek in a way, he thought. She had robbed him of his rightful initiative. He should ring back and put her in her place. But he didn't. He would simply honour her invitation. In fact, he was rather looking forward to it. Almost ridiculously so.

Chuter's Village, now commonly and colloquially shortened and shorn of its apostrophe, had been built in the mid nineteenth century as a model village by Lord Robert Chute, to house his employees and 'deserving' persons. Gradually, over the years, it had declined. Successive generations had sold off parts of the property until all that remained, apart from the Manor House, were a few acres of neglected farmland and the famous wood which had inspired Lady Katherine's interest in conservation. This truncated version of the estate formed the basis of the Foundation which she had set up and funded from a trust. The village had survived, virtually as originally planned, as an anachronistic tourist attraction, a curious beauty spot.

Sociologically, the village had become a new mix of retired couples, drawn by its 'Miss Read' charm, and the odd upwardly mobile executive, brought to the area by the development and expansion of Passington. The Foundation retained a handful of the cottages to house its greatly reduced staff and leased others to retired or former employees of the Estate and their families. Two served as bed-and-breakfast houses, run by the wife of the pub's manager, catering mostly to the well-heeled parents of boys at Oversleigh School. Those cottages which had been sold off changed hands with a frequency that kept

22

the Oversleigh estate agents laughing all the way to the bank and provided a welcome source of local gossip.

This lack of stability among the cottage-owners did not surprise Jolley who had an irrational dislike of Chuters. It seemed to him, as he had often remarked, closer to 'Agatha Christie land' than 'Miss Read'. It was something to do with the unavoidable fact that the village was essentially unnatural. Other villages grew up in a random, haphazard way. Their visible geographical and architectural history reflected necessity, convenience and personal taste. Chuters was, for all its good intentions, artificial and, more disturbingly to Jolley, one man's ideal into which ordinary people were fitted, willy-nilly. Its very uniformity reinforced his impression of an institution. Lord Chute had possessed an ideal of the English country cottage which he had realised in stone and thatch, in uniform, semi-detached pairs, for his own purpose and, presumably, delight. To Jolley, these ideal dwellings had a louring, dour look. This was partly due to the lowness of the thatched roofs which beetled down disproportionately, overhanging the heavily leaded windows, frustrating sunlight. It seemed to Jolley, as he parked at the central village green, that the cottages surrounding it and dotting the lanes, were perpetually frowning. And there were too many trees.

Jolley did not dislike trees – on the contrary – but he objected to them being placed so close together in such profusion and in such close proximity to dwellings that they took away the natural light. All things considered, he reflected, Lord Chute would never have got planning permission for this lot today. It was as though the famous wood spilled over into or encroached upon the village. Nature, here, had a way of asserting itself. He slammed the car door and listened to the shocking loudness of the sound. That was another thing: Chuters was always quiet, too quiet.

That had struck him the first time he had visited the place, as a child, on a school study-trip. The village was a boon to local history teachers since it provided a living, visible example of Victorian philanthropy. Jolley, in common with a majority of the children in the county, had been bussed here to collect data, draw pictures, hear legends. Kids were naturally noisy, especially when rarely freed from the confines of the classroom, but he remembered how quiet they had been, following the teacher around, taking notes, whispering together in awe of the silence. There was something hushed and secretive about Chuters' silence, as though the inhabitants were holding their breath behind the dark, leaded windows, eternally waiting for something.

He shook himself mentally and turned instinctively towards the chapel-cum-schoolhouse, telling himself not to be so fanciful. It was a community of elderly people, for the most part. The young left in search of jobs and entertainment. Who could blame them? For the first time it occurred to him that Dolores Bayger might be elderly. Beautiful voices did not age. Look at Peggy Ashcroft, Siobhan McKenna . . . He had placed the accent as North American, possibly Canadian. French Canadian, he had thought, because that somehow accounted for the hint of husky exoticism in her voice. But he had imagined her as . . . well, youngish.

His feet crunched loudly on gravel as he came to the gate. He relinquished thoughts or fancies of her with a sort of relief. He opened the silent metal gate into the chapel ground. The chapel itself was inter-denominational, Lord Chute having been a godless free-thinker, more concerned to provide his workers with the chance of liquid refreshment than spiritual salvation. It had also, in its heyday, served as a school. It was a fine building, light and spacious in direct contrast to the cottages around it. Jolley, whose grasp of architectural style was meagre, thought it more eighteenth than nineteenth century in aspect. It stood now behind a carefully maintained and sparsely populated graveyard. The grass was neatly mown, the edges clipped to a geometrical tidiness that even Eileen, his beloved queen of the edging tools, would have

24

admired and envied. Gloomy again, he thought that it was no wonder so few of the inhabitants of the village had chosen to be buried here. For all its evidence of careful care, it was a cold place. Presumably though, when it came to meeting their Maker, the silent people of Chuters decided to hedge their bets and opted to be buried in properly sanctified Protestant or Catholic or Methodist ground. A soul might run a bit of a risk, if only of confusion, by being buried inter-denominationally.

Shades of Agatha Christie again, he thought. If only Miss Marple, preferably in the rotund and lovable shape of Margaret Rutherford, would pop up from behind one of the headstones . . . But, as far as he knew, Chuters was free of mysteries, had no history of violence or unnatural death . . . Unless, of course, you counted suicide.

Still, at least here the trees were kept to the perimeter, permitting the sun to penetrate. It warmed his back as, facing the chapel, he turned left, walking the length of its façade.

My God, he thought, coming to an abrupt halt, I had forgotten the ravens. Running down beside the chapel, where sunlight lost to dark shadow, he faced a long wood and wire enclosure, full of stumps and stunted trees, roosting places, covered with the white and grey lime of excrement.

'The bloody ravens,' he whispered aloud.

Another history lesson swam to the surface of his mind. This eastern edge of the county had once been the common breeding ground and natural habitat of ravens which had subsequently migrated west and north. One of the Chutes – his memory could not offer a precise name – had decided to keep them here, in ostentatious imitation, so Jolley thought, of the old legend about the Tower of London. And there, by association, was the source of his creeping dislike of these enormous, glistening black creatures. Another school trip, the obligatory one, to the Tower. He had been fourteen, maybe less, clutching his sandwiches and his bottle of dandelion and burdock, his precious store of spending money. Inevitably they had come, in crocodile fashion, to the ravens, had been told to spread out and pay attention, while Mr McKechnie recounted the legend and explained how their wings were clipped. A typical example of compromise, the young Jolley had thought even then. Even as the teacher spoke, a plump grey pigeon had fluttered down to the greensward, obeying the instinct of all London pigeons which associate people with food. He had witnessed, for the first and only time in his life, the phenomenon known as 'mobbing'. The ravens, scattered, peaceful, watchful, had suddenly surrounded the pigeon, rushed it, flapping and squawking, worrying at it. One, a massive brute had pounced and, right behind Mr McKechnie's back, in a matter of seconds, the pigeon had been killed. Blood stained its grey feathers. Entrails were drawn out like worms by blunt, black bills. Great, ugly black talons stapled it to the earth. Others fluttered up to feast.

'Look, sir, look. The ravens killed a pigeon.'

Jolley moved into the shadows beside the chapel, anxious to avoid the ravens, looking for a way out. There was none. A second aviary rose, blocking his way, adjoining the back of the chapel and stretching on away from him as far as the eye could see. Jolley turned smartly around, turned his back on beady eyes and the dry flap of feather. He hurried back into the sunlight and down the gravel path. It was not that he was exactly afraid of ravens, though the spectre of that unwanted slaughter had always stayed with him and still produced shudders. He liked birds, even ravens, in their place. It was partly their confinement he disliked, be it in roomy aviaries or by dint of clipping their feathers. Off in the wild they were all right. Imprisoned . . . It was actually, he thought, standing at the gate and looking across the village green, between the heavy trees, the whole bloody place. People thought he was eccentric in his dislike of the place, he knew. Even Eileen had chided him about it, telling him not to be so fanciful. She was right of course, he conceded, opening the gate. Snap out of it, he told himself. There was no reason to feel this sense of unease, of impending doom.

He began to walk deeper into the village, remembering why he was here. Three suicides, an anonymous note leading to a woman whose voice had set fantasies spinning in his head, a woman who had invited him, imperiously and incongruously, to tea. He was a middle-aged policeman with a job to do, not a kid to be frightened by ravens, oppressed by an atmosphere to which everyone else seemed to be impervious. He looked at his watch and then around him with a keener eye.

There was only one road into Chuters and the same one provided the only way out. This single road divided at the green, branched either side of the pub. Both were, in effect, cul-de-sacs, though Jolley recalled having been told that the left-hand fork, along which he now began to walk, ended in a footpath which led through the wood to Chute Manor. The very footpath, perhaps, which Frederick Smith had taken that night, his shotgun broken over his arm. What possessed a man, apparently hale and hearty, to leave a wife and children and walk into the wood and blow his own head off? The answer, Jolley knew, often lay within the bereaved family itself. Was the same then true of Antony Corr-Beardsley, David Brimble? Jolley sighed. He would have to talk to their families again, no matter what the Bayger woman could or could not tell him. 'The Stables' she had said. The houses in Chuters did not normally have names and he could not remember having seen any stables in the village. Perhaps she ran a riding school, was a hearty, horsy type. This brought a smile to his lips. There was no one about to ask for directions and his watch told him it was almost four o'clock. But it would only take about ten minutes to walk around the entire village and, provided her cottage was labelled, he could not possibly miss it.

In fact it lay a few hundred yards further up this road. Approaching it, the stable block was just visible over the back fence, a more recent brick and pantile structure set at right-angles behind the cottage. Or cottages, he corrected himself, for one semi-detached pair had been converted into a single dwelling. One door and thatched porch had been removed and filled in with matching but obviously unweathered stone. A young, white climbing rose had been planted to soften this scar but was still in its infancy. The conversion gave the house an individual lop-sided appearance that immediately appealed to Jolley. He stopped at the wrought-iron gate on which the name of the house was prettily worked. White standard roses, now in their blowsy second bloom, lined the off-centre path. He saw that the door stood open, into black shadow. The windows, too, had their casements wide and that on the ground floor to the left of the door dangled a length of long, white lace curtain out into the garden. He opened the gate. Trees behind the house and to the right of the garden shaded half of it, but he walked in sunlight to the door, looked in vain for a bell-push, raised his hand to knock. As he did so, he heard music sounding softly from inside. His fist waited in the air as he automatically anticipated the next phrase, the entry of the voice.

*Thy hand, Belinda . . .*

Jolley stood there, unaware of his raised hand, smiling, entranced by the music.

She was indeed shrouded by darkness.

'You must be Mr Jolley. Come in.'

He scarcely saw her, so quick was she, so deep the gloom in the little hallway after the brightness outside. He followed her instinctively, registering her scent, not noticing the implicit command in her tone. He followed her into a room that was both dusky and dazzling.

'Just a minute. Let me get the phonograph . . . '

He was struck by the old-fashioned term, saw her hand reaching out for the pick-up arm of the stereo system which stood black and gleaming expensively near the back window.

'No . . . ' he said, too loudly. She turned her head,

28

her very white arm poised over the turntable. He saw her eyes widen, the dark brows lift slightly in surprise. Then she shrugged, accepting. She moved her arm, indicating a small two-seater settle near Jolley. He sat in it cautiously, fearful that his weight would set it creaking, perhaps even snap its elegant, spindly legs. She sank into a matching chair beside the stereo, her face turned half away from him, the point of her chin cushioned on her palm.

*When I am laid, am laid in earth . . .*

His eyes moved from the strong slope of her jawbone to one long, black-covered leg stretched out towards him. Her white shoe was bright against the black floor. Black hair, glossy, swept back from her high forehead, fell down to her shoulders, partly obscuring her face. He could not read her expression. The pose, her stillness, was that of a dreamer, not an intense listener.

*May my wrongs create . . .*

Just below the knee some soft, silky material began. Lilac or violet, Jolley could not pin down the colour. The softness of the material enfolded the thigh of the leg that stretched towards him. Very long legs. A very rounded thigh. Her upper body was twisted slightly away from him, the arm raised to her chin obscuring her breasts. The sleeve of the violet dress fell back, showing the stark whiteness of her arm.

*No trouble in thy breast . . .*

Jolley looked away, made self-conscious suddenly by his naked inspection of her. A bowl of white roses stood on a small, highly polished table. Long lace curtains at the window. She was very still. Her scent was sweet but not cloying, reminded him, even though he did not look at her, of her vital presence.

*Remember me, but ah! forget my fate . . .*

He listened, following the curves of the melody in his mind, his eyes half closed. When the music finished, expired, she turned towards him and he met her eyes fully for the first time. She said nothing, but he understood that she was asking permission to stop the record now that the aria was finished. He inclined his head. She rose and lifted the stylus, filling the room with a bright silence. Jolley heard himself say, 'Tatiana Troyanos. In my view, the finest Dido on record.'

'You're obviously knowledgeable about music,' she said, picking the disc deftly but carefully from the turntable and slipping it into the grey sleeve. Jolley approved of such care, even as he was aware of the dark maroon-red of her nails.

'Not really so very knowledgeable. Music just happens to be a passion of mine, especially vocal music.'

'That's good,' she said, straightening from the shelf where she had carefully replaced the record. 'I like a man with passion. A man without passion is somehow . . . empty.'

She spread her hands to indicate a void. Jolley pounced gratefully on a flaw. Her hands were not beautiful. 'Now I must get you some tea . . . '

'I have a few questions— ' he began, half rising from the settle.

'Well, of course you have. But a cup of tea won't prevent your asking them, will it?' She smiled. It was dazzling. And then she was gone. Jolley sat again, felt foolish and clumsy. The bare boards of the floor had been stained black and were highly polished. Soft, obviously expensive rugs in pale colours, exotic designs, lay like islands on this black surface. The lace curtains at each window were deliberately too long, so that they pooled against the boards. Her scent remained, but softer now. He could smell the roses, saw that beyond the little table was a couch, two winged easy chairs facing an empty grate where more roses were arranged in a cauldron-shaped copper bowl. The rattle of an approaching tea-trolley startled him. He half rose again, perhaps to help. She ignored his crouching stance, if she noticed it at all. Jolley sat quickly, embarrassed.

'Plain, strong Indian tea. Is that all right?'

'Yes indeed.'

She placed the trolley between them, brought her chair

closer to it, into better light. Again Jolley rose, too late to help. He felt clumsy and unmannerly.

'Please sit down. Are you uncomfortable there?'

'No, no. This is fine. Thank you.'

'Milk but not sugar, right?'

'Right.' He tried to laugh but could not. She leaned a little over the trolley, lifted the silver teapot, pushing a heavy swathe of black hair over her left shoulder as she poured.

'I made cucumber sandwiches,' she said, with the air of a little girl in the confessional. 'Crazy, huh? I don't know what got into me. It just seemed . . . apt.'

'I haven't had cucumber sandwiches since . . . for years,' Jolley said lamely.

'I'll put your tea there, OK? Will you have a sandwich – or perhaps you don't like them?'

'Please.'

She handed him a plate, a real linen napkin and turned the plate of tiny, brown, crustless sandwiches towards him.

'And I got chocolate cake because it's my favourite,' she added.

On the lower shelf of the trolley he could see one of Webber's Bakeries largest and most delicious chocolate gâteaux awaiting the desecration of the knife. His favourite, too. Forbidden. He bit into the cucumber sandwich. She was studying him over the rim of her cup, her eyes laughing at him, he thought.

'Well, now . . . ' she said, leaning back slightly. 'Have I done something I shouldn't?'

Jolley felt himself smiling, reassuring her when he knew he had no right to do so. He swallowed the cucumber sandwich and lifted his cup, half hoping that his silence would unsettle her. In fact he was playing for time, trying to think how best to cover lost ground. She really was an astonishingly beautiful woman, he thought, and, angry with himself, pulled a photocopy of the letter from his jacket pocket and thrust it towards her. She took it, eyebrows

31

slightly raised again. She unfolded the stiff sheets. A small, troubled frown crossed her face as she read. When she had finished she looked up at him, the letter lying in her lap.

'Can you explain why somebody should give me your phone number in this context?'

'Yes,' she answered, with more resignation than sadness. 'Yes, Inspector, I think I can.' He noted her use of his rank and felt that he had made up some ground at least. He helped himself to another sandwich. 'Are you a local man?' she asked. Jolley could only nod. 'Then you will understand. Please don't get me wrong. I am an Anglophile, almost obsessively so. Hence the cucumber sandwiches . . . ' She almost laughed but could only manage a fleeting, self-mocking smile. Clearly the letter troubled her, Jolley thought, but he could find no hint of guilt about her. 'You'll forgive me, I hope, if I say that in some ways the British are very insular, not to say xenophobic. I guess it's more marked in a very small community like this. I'm not getting to the point, am I?' she said, reaching for her cup. The letter slid to the floor.

'Take your time,' Jolley said. He stood and picked up the letter from the shiny floorboards, crumpled it back into his pocket.

'I am resented here. That's the truth of it. Oh, it sounds so neurotic when I say it out loud. But I'm not neurotic, I assure you. I mean that people here regard me as a foreigner – which I guess I am – but also an outsider. They regard me, I believe, with suspicion and I conclude that that letter was a . . . natural expression of their . . . dislike of me . . . fear, perhaps? I don't know. I think someone was trying to hit back at me.'

'For what?' Jolley said, his policeman's mind overcoming the human impulse to agree and commiserate with her.

'For being . . . me.' She shrugged. 'For being an outsider, different. I guess I have to say rich. At least in comparison to some of my neighbours.' She paused, looking questioningly at Jolley. 'Have I offended you?'

'Not at all. We can be rudely insular, *are* very suspicious of . . . newcomers. I wonder you didn't choose to settle – if you *have* settled – in Oversleigh. I think we're a little more civilised there.'

'Ah, but I didn't fall in love with Oversleigh. I fell in love with Chuters.' She said it quite naturally, but with passion. 'And yes, I have settled here. I bought these cottages from the Chute Foundation . . . oh, I guess about two years ago. And I've lived here for eighteen months now. And I intend, in case you're wondering, to stay and fight my corner, no matter how many anonymous . . . complaints are laid against me.'

She could be, he thought, a formidable adversary. Something about the phrase 'fight my corner' conjured up an image of a lioness at bay, fierce, protective and incredibly beautiful.

'Perhaps this isn't a complaint,' Jolley said. 'Perhaps you do have information . . . information you're not aware you have, that might throw some light on the matter.'

'You mean you don't think they were suicides?'

'I . . . ' Jolley was momentarily thrown by her directness. 'What do you think?'

'I? I only know what I read in the local paper. I heard talk, when I was in Oversleigh, marketing. The people here don't gossip to me. I believed what I read and heard. I had nothing else to go on.'

'It doesn't strike you as odd that three apparently healthy, sane men, all living in one small village, should take their own lives in such a short space of time?'

'No. It didn't.' Jolley stared at her. Without asking, she poured him more tea, added hot water to the pot, and then refilled her own cup. 'You want me to explain that, don't you?'

'If you wouldn't mind.'

'I have a long experience of suicide. I know that no sane person commits suicide. I know that insanity has many forms. Much insanity is unrecognisable, appears to be its very opposite. I think we all have a little insanity within us. I think depression, that awful, black cyclical cloud that overtakes some of us, is a common form of insanity and that depression, of that extreme and often incommunicable kind, is a common cause of suicide.' She looked at him as one who has stated her case and rests. It was up to him to challenge her.

'Are you talking of yourself?' he asked, surprised by his own daring and how deeply her words had moved him. She laughed, shattering the mood, making him feel foolish.

'I don't think I've ever really been depressed in my life. Oh, maybe when I was sixteen and smothered in acne and the best-looking boy in school was unaware of my existence . . . ' Jolley frowned. 'I'm sorry,' she said, the gaiety leaving her voice, 'I didn't mean to sound frivolous. I'm very lucky. I know that. You see, I worked as a psychiatric nurse. I trained in psychiatry for a while. And above all I married a man who was clinically depressive. I am no stranger to suicide, Inspector, and although it may sound cynical, I don't believe it shocks me as it does other people. To grieve over it is, of course, another matter.' She turned her head aside, put a hand up to her face.

Jolley wanted to comfort her and yet she seemed intensely private, beyond his reach. He realised that he had wanted to know, ever since he had entered her house, if she was married. To avoid examining the feelings this knowledge awoke in him, he said, 'I'm very sorry.'

'Oh, don't be. These things are meant to happen. I believe that. And one . . . survives. It can't all be roses. Will you have some chocolate cake?'

Again Jolley was thrown off balance, had been about to ask more about her husband. Instead, with a sort of coyness that made him angry, he said, 'I shouldn't . . . '

'But you will. Good.'

She lifted the cake to the top shelf of the trolley and cut a wedge the size of which, had Eileen been able to see it, would have made her apoplectic. Dolores Bayger handed it to him with a smile of complicity. She cut herself a very thin slice.

'May I ask . . . Your husband— '

'Oh, he's alive. That is what you meant, isn't it? I'm sorry, I'm terribly direct. One of the many reasons I'm not liked around here, I guess. He's alive but in an institution. I could no longer cope, you see. It's a little like living with an alcoholic, only you spend your days hiding the aspirin in your purse and learning to chop 'erbs with a blunt knife.' A little shudder agitated her shoulders but she managed to turn it into a shrug. 'Are you married?'

'Er . . . yes,' Jolley mumbled through a piece of cake which suddenly turned to chalk in his mouth.

'Happily so. I can tell.'

'Did you,' Jolley said, swallowing and putting the plate down, 'know any of the deceased?'

'Oh, sure. All of them.' She ate, rolling her eyes with relish. 'That surprises you?'

'I got the impression you didn't . . . hadn't made friends.'

'I didn't say they were my friends, Inspector.' She waited for the reproof to sink in. Jolley busied himself with his napkin. 'I got to know Fred Smith when I first bought this house. He was responsible for repairs and stuff for the Trust and they are very particular about alterations. So he had to keep a check on me, make sure I didn't put a pool in the yard . . . garden . . . or remove the thatch or something crazy. He was a nice guy. I got on with him. I don't think his wife approved, though. She was always distinctly . . . frosty with me. And then young David, David Brimble – isn't that a sweet name? – he worked for me for a while. I wanted some conversion work done in the stables out back and since he was unemployed I asked him if he was interested. He was a nice kid. And then Tony . . . Well, I guess you could say Tony was a friend. He wasn't a local, you see. And we met socially, not through work.'

'How . . . socially?'

'In the pub, if you must know,' she said with a touch of impatience. 'I go there sometimes. It gets lonely here. I like a drink. Tony went there a lot. Well, let's face it, there isn't much else to do around here when you've finished marking

35

trees and counting bugs or whatever he did up there. And since we were both politely frozen out by the locals, we got talking. And, yes, I did invite him here. He came to dinner, for drinks. We even went to a movie once, in Passington and I am perfectly well aware that you will be told, if you haven't been already, that he was my lover, that I am little better than a whore and very probably that I seduced Fred and young David as well.' Her fork clattered on her plate. She thrust both away from her on to the trolley.

'I apologise,' Jolley said. 'I mean it.'

She took a deep breath, eyes closed, shoulders drawn up and tensed. She was perfectly still for a moment, then she let the breath out in a long sigh, shaking her head slowly from side to side.

'No. No, it is I who should apologise. I shouldn't let it get to me, the talk, the silence rather. Mostly I don't. It's not having the chance to defend myself . . . '

'And then along comes a clumsy policeman to ask leading questions.'

'You aren't at all clumsy. You're a very gracious person. You have a gracious spirit.'

Jolley's eyes slid from hers in embarrassment. He could almost hear Eileen laughing.

'They were just routine questions, I assure you. We have to follow up, even on letters like this one. Sometimes, rarely, they contain a grain of truth. Mostly they're just vindictive or a cry for help. A cry of grief, perhaps. A desire to damage someone else because the writer can't handle his or her own grief.'

'I know. I know.' She sounded grief-stricken herself. Her voice was low, almost moaning, and she rocked a little in her chair, her hands tightly clasped together in her lilac lap.

'I didn't mean to distress you.'

'I know that too. And you haven't.' She lifted her face to him. It was quite calm, even smiling. 'You are just doing your job and I want to co-operate. The trouble is, I'd rather enjoy your company than talk about sad things

36

and narrow-minded people. But it has to be done. So come on. Ask your questions. I swear I'll answer every one. And then we can enjoy our cake together.'

Jolley stood up, turned towards the window. Instinctively, he pulled the long lace curtain back inside, shook it so that it hung straight to the floor.

'Do you have any reason to think that any of these men might take their own lives?'

'No!' She sounded shocked. 'For one thing, I really didn't know them ... No, that's not accurate. Not truthful. Wait a minute.' He turned to look at her. She was sitting back now, hands gripping the slim wooden arms of her chair. She was concentrating hard, thinking something through. 'OK. Fred Smith, no. I really did not know him well. We chatted, but only about the house, the weather. He was ... he struck me as being a morose man. Not a bundle of laughs. But what did I know? Young David, sure, maybe I did think ... but *after* the event. I knew he was depressed about being out of a job. He didn't seem to have many friends. When he finished up here, when I paid him off, he said that he would miss coming here, that his days would seem empty without the work. But I didn't think anything of it then. No. Not at all.' She shook her head in emphasis. 'But when I read the report in the paper, well ... it figured. I was less surprised than I might have been. But I swear to you that if I had thought, I'd have done something.'

Jolley nodded. He believed her. And with the experience of her husband behind her, perhaps she *could* have done something.

'And Corr-Beardsley?' he prompted. 'You knew him somewhat better.'

'How nicely you put it. I knew him pretty well. His death was a complete surprise to me. He was homesick and lonely. He had doubts about his career direction, but I thought he was the sort of guy who'd sort things out. After all, he was only here for a limited time and his questioning about his job was, well, the sort of thing everyone goes through from time to time. There was nothing to make me suspect— '

'What sort of career problems?'

'He began to wonder if the whole Planet Earth concept was sound. I got the impression he had gotten into conservation for very idealistic reasons. Now he was older, more experienced and he was beginning to ask questions. But who doesn't? My guess was, he'd sort it all out once he got home.'

'Where was that? Do you know? I have very little information about him.'

'Kent, somewhere. I can't remember. He was a graduate of Kent University. He told me I should see Canterbury Cathedral. Somehow I never got around to it.'

'His death must have hurt you.'

'Of course.'

'Since you knew him. Since he was your friend.'

'I'm not going to confirm or deny what you're asking, Inspector. I believe he had some kind of . . . attachment, back home.'

'Did you go to his funeral?'

'No. I thought about it. I felt I might not be welcome.'

'I see.'

'Do you?'

'You thought you might seem, to his family and friends, like an intruder. You thought they might misunderstand.'

'I thought Scarlet Woman might look a little underdressed in mourning,' she said drily. 'Next question?'

Jolley returned to his seat, finished his tea.

'Why are you here?'

'Because I want to be. I told you. I'm an Anglophile. I had a tough few years back there. I felt I ought to get right away . . . '

'From America?' Jolley suggested.

'Yes. I was in the States then. Actually, I'm Canadian. I have a Canadian passport, all in order.'

'I don't doubt it.'

'Some policemen would.'

38

'I don't.'

'Well, now, you have my word for it.'

'Your husband is in America?'

'Yes. It was felt that I could no longer help him. I told you I couldn't cope. There was nothing to keep me there. My father had just died and left me a lot of money. I decided to come to Europe, but really I meant England. I thought I'd find an idyllic country cottage and lick my wounds. I also planned to work at my photography. I am a good photographer and you could even say that it is a passion of mine. That's why I needed work doing on the stables. I wanted a studio and a dark-room.' She waited, her face composed, giving nothing away, for the next question.

'Thanks. Is it . . . *Mrs* Bayger?'

'Ms, actually, but you English find that so awkward for some reason. Bayger is my family name. You can call me Dolores.'

'Thank you. I don't have any more questions.'

'So what do you do now?'

'Oh . . . routine inquiries. Try to trace the writer of the letter. I doubt we shall succeed, unless we get more, and somehow I don't think we will.'

'It sounds like you're playing hunches.'

'I frequently do.'

'So . . . ' She leaned right back in her chair, crossed her legs, flicked her hair back from her face. 'I am not to be arrested, or watched or regarded with official suspicion. Is that right? Tell me, Mr Jolley, am I a free woman?'

'One of the freest I've ever met,' he said, smiling at her.

She laughed warmly, from her chest. 'I like you, Mr Policeman Jolley. I like you very much. And you know what I'm going to do? I'm going to ask you and your wife to dinner. Will you come?'

'Certainly,' he said. 'With pleasure.'

'Then you'd better give me your phone number.'

Jolley took out his notepad and wrote it down, without

hesitation. His office number, the direct line to his desk. He also added his name.

'Thank you,' she said, taking it and glancing at it. 'Cyril.'

It was the first time ever he had liked the sound of his own name.

# Two

DS Patrick Donegal Latham was one of those men whose chins are constantly blue-black with stubble, a perpetual five o'clock shadow. Jolley found himself wondering how often he had to shave, if a beard would not be the answer. Somehow DS Latham did not look like one of those men who carried a natty little battery shaver wherever they went. He stared harder at the young man, an apparently attentive and certainly inviting smile on his face. Latham was slightly under-shot, his jaw consequently pronounced in appearance. He was neat and correct in manner, slight in build. He was not, despite his name, Irish. He had an Irish mother who had named him out of sentimentality. Yes, he had been brought up a Roman Catholic and still went to mass, albeit irregularly. He believed in everything in proportion.

'What do you think about capital punishment?' Jolley leaned back. His chair creaked. He brought the tips of his fingers together in front of his face, saw that his wedding ring was deeply embedded in flesh. It was then that he discovered the reason for his wandering attention. Latham's voice was soft, flat and monotonous. It positively encouraged the listener to switch off. The man's dark eyes were fixed uncomfortably on Jolley's. 'Sorry. Come again?' Latham swallowed, his prominent Adam's apple wrestling with his white collar.

'I said I believe capital punishment should be restored for certain crimes, including the murder of a police officer.'

'Especially the murder of a police officer?'

'Yes. If you like.'

Jolley did not. 'Do you think we should be armed, then?'

'No. I think that would be a retrograde step. The status quo represents an honourable tradition, respected by police and public alike. I do not think it would be a good thing to overthrow that tradition.'

'What about water cannon, CS gas, rubber bullets? Would you like to see those used in civil disturbances?'

Latham paused, swallowed, appeared to look at some autocue fixed behind and slightly above Jolley's head. 'I would not *like* to see them used under any circumstances but I do believe that every force should be so equipped and should not hesitate to employ such deterrents upon the instruction of a superior officer.'

'Unfortunately, our Chief Constable doesn't agree with you.'

'I would, of course, be happy to support the Chief Constable in his decision.'

'Even if you believe that decision to be wrong?'

'Yes, sir.'

'You're not married, Mr Latham.'

'No, sir, I am not married.'

'Courting? Engaged?'

'That is not at present on the cards, sir.'

'But you have thought about the special strain and difficulties faced by a policeman's wife?'

'I have considered it, sir, yes.'

'And what conclusion did you reach?'

Latham moved in his seat, uncrossed his legs, recrossed them, left over right. 'Obviously I could not marry a woman who could not handle the special pressures that face all policemen's wives, sir.'

How would you know, Jolley longed to ask. What about love, passion? What about when choice is impossible, is made for you because there is no one else imaginable in the world? Such a line of questioning was, he conceded, outside his remit. He turned to the c.v. before him, talked Latham through his career so far, his qualifications, special interests, which included rowing and science fiction. Latham could only confirm not add to this information. Jolley stood up and shook the young man's hand, promised to let him know as soon as possible.

Restless, Jolley stood at his office window, looking not down at the yard behind the station but up at the blue sky which showed as a narrow strip above the opposite roof-tops. It was a very dark, rich blue, cornflower-blue, almost. He felt that he had been hard on Latham, or perhaps that he had not tried hard enough. He knew that he would never be able to stand that dreary voice. You could do much with a man when you worked closely with him. You could modify his attitudes, develop his sense of humour. In the normal course of events he would unbend, learn to relax with you. Few situations were as artificial as the formal interview. But you couldn't change a man's voice. He couldn't see Teddy Tait shelling out for voice production lessons either, though the thought of indenting for some brought a happy smile to Jolley's face. Perhaps he should take Glade down to the Talbot for a pint. Except that he was on duty and that would set a bad example, quite besides giving Glade an unfair advantage over Latham. He grunted in response to the tap on the door, heard Penny Russell say, 'Detective-Sergeant Glade to see you, sir.'

'Thank you, Constable.' He turned, his mouth already shaping the automatic, routine words of welcome which were never to be spoken. It felt as though his jaw had snapped. In any other circumstances, Jolley would have categorised her at once as a 'trim little body', neat and compact and very femininely rounded. She wore her uniform with a smartness that indicated pride and pleasure. The set of her hat was rule-book perfect and it became her as it did few women, in his opinion. As he struggled to get his jaw under control, he thought that she would be a wow in the canteen.

'Er . . . sit down, Sergeant.'

'Thank you, sir.'

Her face was round with pleasingly pronounced cheek-bones, very large blue eyes. Her hair was either very short or severely scraped up and back under her hat. Jolley could only guess that it was blonde. She stared him down.

'I . . . er . . . see from your form . . . With promotion – congratulations, by the way – you've requested a transfer. From . . . er . . . Letchworth. What's wrong with . . . Letchworth, Sergeant?'

'Nothing, sir. I was very happy there. But my parents have moved up here and I felt I would like to be closer to them. They're getting on.'

'Admirable sentiments,' Jolley said, hitting his stride, 'in a daughter, but how would they fit in with the demands on a police officer?'

'There wouldn't be any conflict, sir. My parents are perfectly hale and hearty. If and when they're not, well, we'll have to make arrangements.'

'Oversleigh's a pretty quiet kind of place. A lot smaller than Letchworth. A lot of our work is rural . . . '

'I think it's only fair to tell you, sir, that Oversleigh was not my choice. I applied for Anderton and Passington. The Superintendent— '

'Directed you to me,' Jolley interrupted rudely.

'He suggested that the most suitable vacancy was here, yes.'

Oh, Teddy Tait had bowled some wicked ones in his time. He had played some tricks that had left even Jolley breathless, but this, to foist a woman on him . . . Jolley stared at her, temporarily speechless, images of revenge, black and dreadful, mercifully undetailed, obscured her round and pretty face.

'You're not going to take me on, are you?' she said.

'I beg your pardon?'

'I can see it on your face. Would you rather stop now?'

'I am fully aware, Sergeant, of the Equal Opportunities Commission . . . ' Jolley blustered, realising that he felt animated for the first time that day.

'And no doubt you are equally aware of the Police Federation's attitude to the Commission.'

Jolley wasn't, but he was not about to admit it.

44

'As far as I am concerned . . . we will conduct this interview as I would conduct any other. You will be considered on your merits, and nothing else.' He thought she was going to shout 'Liar' at him, and he would not have blamed her. Instead, she crossed her legs, an action Jolley studiously ignored, and seemed to relax a little.

'Thank you, sir. That's all I ask.'

He took a deep breath and stared at her paperwork. Why had he not noticed the two give-away names. She was a sexless M.G. Glade at the top, of course, but lower down, clear for any idiot to see, was spelled out loud and clear: Marion Georgina.

'You are very well qualified. Your promotion is well deserved.'

'Thank you.'

'Three years as a Detective-Constable. You enjoyed that?'

'Very much.'

'You took part in a number of operations, an active part. I see you've been commended on three occasions . . . '

'It took a while for me to be accepted, of course, but I'm sure my superior officers at Letchworth would confirm that I was a fully participating member of the team. I wasn't wrapped in cotton wool.'

'You've been issued with a firearm on occasions.'

'And used them.'

'Apparently you're a good shot.'

'I believe so.'

'Well, there wouldn't be much cause for that here.'

'I can live with that. I'm not a gun fanatic.'

If she wore make-up, it was very subtle. Perhaps a hint of pink lipstick, very pale. Something on the lashes but no eye-shadow. Healthy, she looked. Scrubbed clean, businesslike. He wondered how she looked in plain clothes.

'It seems to me,' he went on, shying away from these observations which, he knew, were said to be irrelevant but which, willy-nilly, mattered to him, 'that you could have done better for yourself if you'd stayed at Letchworth.

45

Your superior officers were keen to keep you . . . '

'I don't know about "better". Promotion is promotion. That's what I wanted. As I said, I have personal reasons— '

'Personal? You mean your family . . . ?'

'Partly.' She waited a moment, eyes lowered. Something made Jolley patient. He did not push her. 'There was another reason. I was involved with a man. He was married. There was no future in it. I wanted to make a clean break, so when my parents moved up here— '

'Would I be right in thinking that your promotion could have caused embarrassment, of a personal kind?'

'It could have done,' she said guardedly. 'But I think I could have handled that.'

'So I would be right in thinking that the man was also in the Force?'

'I don't think that's relevant, is it?'

'I could easily find out.'

'Wouldn't that be rather like breaking a confidence?'

'Yes,' Jolley agreed, smiling, 'it would.' She should smile, he thought. It was a cheerful face. Her mouth looked pinched now but was naturally generous. He wanted to make her smile. 'There's no doubt you can handle working with men, in a predominantly male environment. How *do* you handle it?'

'I treat them as equals, colleagues and I won't tolerate anything less in return. I can look after myself. I try to earn their respect, as a colleague, and I expect to be treated as an equal. The day I'm asked to do something I can't do, I'll resign.'

'Yet you are human enough to become involved with someone, be concerned about your parents . . . '

'So are a lot of men. If I may say so, you are thinking in stereotypes. I noticed you said my feelings about my parents were "admirable" in a *daughter*. Would you find them equally admirable in a son?'

'I hope so.'

'So do I.'

46

'You have a sharp tongue, Sergeant.'

'I need it.'

'And you don't hesitate to use it.'

'Never. Sir.'

'Very well . . .' He shuffled the papers before him. 'I see you are especially commended for your investigative abilities.'

'I enjoy putting two and two together, sir. Police work, as you know, isn't all physical action.'

'How do you feel about computers?'

'Useful aids, but no substitute for mental graft, in my view.'

'But it says here you took a course in computers . . .'

'As soon as I passed my driving test I gave up my bike. It's the same thing. If you've got a useful tool I believe you should use it to the best of your ability. But computers aren't magic and certainly no substitute for human intelligence, properly applied. Similarly, there are occasions when a bicycle is more convenient than a car.'

'So you've bought a new bicycle.'

'I plan to. If I get this job.'

'And if you don't?'

'I shall apply elsewhere. I intend to get a job and not just any job, either. Even if it means I have to go to John O'Groats.'

'What about your parents then?'

'We shall have to sort something out. They're not dependent on me nor me on them, I just happen to like their company.'

'Admirable sentiments for *anyone*,' Jolley said, his smile teasing her. She nodded in agreement. He was disappointed, had expected a smile. 'Well, now, anything you would like to ask me?'

'Yes, sir. Thank you. If I were to get this job, what would you consider to be the main disadvantage of my being a woman?'

Jolley started to get up and knew at once that she would see this as evasive action. Indeed it was, instinctive

47

and natural to him, but he remained seated. Tell her the truth then? He shook his head without realising he had done so until he saw her sharp, impatient frown. 'I would be worried about taking you into certain situations,' he said, reaching for another truth.

'Violence, you mean? I can handle myself. I don't take unnecessary risks, none at all if I can help it.'

'Violence is not that common, thank God. No, I was thinking more of . . . A lot of our work is very unpleasant . . . '

'I've had a junkie die in my arms. I've seen a kid with his head cut off by a passing train . . . '

'Yes, Sergeant, but that's— '

'Excuse me, sir. I threw up when I saw that lad. I've been known to burst into tears. I've been scared . . . witless. I've had nightmares and crises of conscience. But, as my record shows, none of that has ever interfered with my work. I think a lot of men have similar, no, *identical* reactions. The difference is, people aren't standing around waiting for them to react in an "emotional" way.'

Jolley thought that there must be an answer to that, but if there was it eluded him. He felt cross, suddenly. Precisely because she was a woman, he was allowing her to get the better of him. He hit back, conscious of what he was doing.

'Then it would seem, Sergeant, that you are an absolute paragon.' She compressed her lips. They looked pale, bloodless, and he decided against the lipstick. 'It would seem that only a fool would turn you down.'

'But you're not a fool,' she came back at him, a little colour enlivening her face. 'Therefore you know I'm not a paragon. I have to tell you how good I am just because you assume I'm not good enough. Not *able* to be good enough. It's a cliché, I know, but like a lot of clichés, it's true. Women in my position do have to try harder and we can't afford to be modest about our achievements. Not if we want to get anywhere.'

'Point taken,' Jolley said. He was damned if he was

48

going to withdraw the jibe about being a paragon. 'Any other questions?'

'That's the only one that matters. And since you've answered it, all I can say is – try me.'

'Do you think you'd like working here?'

She shrugged. 'How can I tell? I can't see anything against it. The problems are people, attitudes. And they're the same all over.'

'With that I would have to agree,' Jolley said. 'Thank you very much, Sergeant. I'll let you know as soon as possible.'

'Thank you, sir.' She offered her hand and gripped his with just the right amount of pressure. Rudely, Jolley turned his back as she made her way to the door. He was not going to be caught out looking at her legs.

Eileen Jolley was kneeling by the flower border at the back of the house when her husband's shadow fell heavily over her. She looked up, blinking.

'Whatever time is it?'

'I was hoping for a bite of lunch.'

She twisted the loose bracelet of her watch around so that she could read the dial. Ten minutes to one. She rested her hands on her knees, stared for a moment at the border, reluctant to leave it. She had intended to get it thoroughly weeded today.

'Give me a hand up, dear, will you?' She held out one dirt-caked hand. Jolley took it with a show of fastidious reluctance.

'Why can't you wear gloves like other women?' he grumbled, pulling her up. 'And you want to get that watch-strap fixed or you'll lose it altogether.' He turned and walked back to the house.

Eileen brushed her skirt down and made a face at his retreating back. Methodically, she collected her tools together, dropped them into an old plastic bucket she used for weeding. One glance at his face had been enough. Whatever it was, he had come home to take it out on her.

She scrubbed her hands in the little cloakroom just inside the back door, went through into the kitchen and, even though she was wearing old, stained gardening clothes, automatically tied an apron around herself. He appeared in the doorway. Eileen ignored him, took a lettuce from the refrigerator.

'I brought you a sherry.'

She heard the glass click on the table behind her.

'That's very nice of you.' She glanced over her shoulder, saw that he nursed a Scotch and water, quite a strong one for the time of day. 'A restaurant strike in Oversleigh today, is there?' she asked, slicing tomatoes.

'Don't be witty, Eileen, it doesn't become you.'

'You won't get much here ... If I'd had prior warning— '

'I'm not hungry anyway.' He walked out.

Eileen looked through the kitchen window. The sun slanted into this corner of the yard where they had laid old bricks and she grew a clematis. She decided they would eat outside and, opening the fridge again, that they would have wine. It might mellow him and then again it might send him to sleep. She told herself she didn't care either way, but this was not true. Still, she would have preferred to be left in peace to finish weeding the border.

They had ham with the salad, a glass of hock, last remnants of their holiday, outside at the round table.

'No potatoes?' he said, not looking at her.

'No time,' she answered. 'Have some bread.'

He took a slice. 'Wine,' he commented, touching the stem of his glass.

'I thought it might cheer you up.'

'I'm perfectly cheerful.'

'You're apopleptic.'

Eileen ate. He nibbled, sighing occasionally, helping himself to more wine. She knew that he did not taste the food. She took his plate away. 'Cheese? Or there's some ice-cream.'

'No. I'm full.'

50

She carried the plates inside, put the coffee on. Return-ing, she filled her glass again and sat for a moment or two, looking at him. He crumbled a slice of bread, tossed it into the yard for non-existent birds.

'Well? Are you going to tell me about it?' He looked at her with feigned puzzlement. She had often charged him with being a good actor. Today, she thought, he was a lousy one. 'That's why you came home, presumably. What is it?' He sighed and slumped a little in his chair. 'Darling . . . ' She reached across the table and touched his hand. 'You knew neither of them would be another Dave Hughes.'

'One of them's a bloody woman,' he mumbled.

Eileen burst out laughing, leaned back in her chair, watched him struggle to keep the smile off his own face.

'I'm sorry,' she said, wiping a tear of merriment from the corner of her eye.

'Oh, I can see it's funny, put like that. But funny or not, it doesn't alter the fact that I'm on the horns of a dilemma.'

'How's that?'

'Well, Teddy Tait's made it quite clear I'd better take one of 'em or God knows what he'll wish on me. And how, today, can I, in all conscience, turn down a woman? And if I take her on, I'll be the laughing-stock of the entire Force.'

'Of course you can turn a woman down. That's what equality is all about. Choose the other one, who is, presumably, of the preferred sex,' she said with heavy irony.

'Him? He's like a lay preacher with haemorrhoids. About as much go in him as the average rice pudding. And he's an incipient fascist . . . ' None of this was true of Latham and Jolley knew it, but he felt better for exaggerating.

'You didn't like him,' Eileen said, goading him.

'Let's say I didn't take to him straight off.'

'But he'd be better than a woman.'

'You see? There you go, putting words into my mouth, misinterpreting my motives. That's how it'll be all the

51

time if I turn her down. No matter how good my reasons, no one will believe them. Especially not her. Old Jolley's prejudiced, a stick-in-the-mud, that's what they'll say. And she'll create merry hell . . . '

'If all that's true I don't see why you'd be a laughing-stock if you took her on.'

'Because they'd say I was soft, scared of Tait, dancing to his tune. Oh no, there's no doubt about it, he's out to humiliate me and I'm damned if I can see how to thwart him.'

'That's nonsense,' Eileen said sharply. 'Teddy Tait's a difficult, devious man, I'll grant you, but he respects you. He knows you're one of the best. If he's wished this girl on you, as you say, it's because he thinks you can handle it.'

'Well, of course, I can handle it.'

'Well, then?'

He looked at her reluctantly, his fingers tracing patterns on the table. 'It's as I said.'

'Cy, you're projecting on them – whoever *they* are – your own fears. Or perhaps how you'd react if someone else took on a woman . . . ' She paused, giving him time to confirm or deny this, but he simply shook his head loftily, dismissing this idea. 'All right then. So what's really troubling you?'

He did not answer immediately. He finished his wine and stood up, put his hands in his trouser pockets and took a few steps towards the garden. 'It's a very . . . in a curious way . . . it's an *intimate* relationship, sergeant and inspector. You work very closely together. You have to. You spend a hell of a lot of time together. You have to know each other pretty well, you have to feel at ease . . . ' He turned round suddenly looking lost and frightened. 'Eileen, how can I talk to her? How can I be myself?' There was a certain relief in having said it, in admitting what really worried him and he knew that he could only say it to her, to his wife.

'You can talk to me, be yourself with me . . . '

'That's different. Damn it, I'm married to you. I've known you forever. We're partners . . . '

'And that's what you and Dave were, though in a different way, of course. Look, Cy, you're not a womaniser and you aren't afraid of women. You're a bit of a flirt, but you can easily control that. Besides, she might like it.'

'Don't be ridiculous. You see? I haven't even taken the girl on and you've got me flirting with her.'

'I just mean that women, on the whole, like a man to flirt with them. I mean it wouldn't do any harm. You could be yourself . . . '

'I don't flirt.'

'Of course you do. And nobody takes you seriously. That's why it's all right.'

'You're a hard woman, hitting a man when he's down.'

'You're not down. And you know it's true anyway. That's why you do it. If a woman ever did take you seriously— '

'What?'

Eileen grinned. 'I'd scratch her eyes out.'

He glared at her and turned away again. Eileen began clearing the table, carrying the dishes and glasses into the kitchen. She brought the coffee out on a tray.

'Have you decided then?'

'Certainly not.' He sat down opposite her and pulled his coffee cup towards him. 'I shall sleep on it.'

'No, you won't.'

'What do you mean?'

'You won't sleep. You'll lie there all night, tossing and turning, worrying yourself sick.'

Jolley feared this was true but was in no mood to admit it. 'So what do you think I should do?'

'Me? Oh . . . You know you don't like me to interfere in police business.'

'I'm asking you.'

'Well . . . ' She made a long pretence of considering it. 'I think you should turn her down, have the courage of your convictions.'

'But I don't have those sort of convictions. I think women should have equal opportunities. God, now you're making me out a chauvinist.'

'Nonsense, dear. You're not a chauvinist. You're just like most men. Equality is fine, women are wonderful, just as long as you don't have to do anything about it or them.'

'Is that really what you think?'

'Well, you did ask. I knew I shouldn't have said anything.'

He pushed his coffee away, slopping some into the saucer and stood up, patting his jacket pockets.

'Where are you going?'

'Back to work.'

'Don't you think you ought to have a little rest first? After all you have been drinking . . . '

'I am not a geriatric. I can handle a couple of glasses of wine and a weak Scotch and I am not just like other men.' He marched past her, around the side of the house and down the narrow little driveway to the high street. Eileen heard his car door slam, the engine start. She smiled and finished her coffee.

There was a package on Jolley's desk when he got back. Still seething, he might have swept it aside impatiently had it not been for the fact that it was elegantly wrapped in black and gold paper and that its flat, square shape almost certainly indicated that it was a record. He picked it up suspiciously, turned it over, shook it. There was no card. He was convinced it was a record and sat down, began to unwrap it carefully, prolonging the anticipation. He loved records, the shape and feel and look of them. In a record store he was worse than a kid in a sweet shop, according to Eileen. This recollection made him tear the paper clumsily. Jessye Norman stared up at him, her magnificent face partially obscured by a plain white card on which he read: 'A worthy rival to Troyanos, I think. D.B.'

He slid the card aside and pulled the record free of its wrapping, *Dido and Aeneas*. He held it, blushing. He read the card again, noting her bold, clear hand, and then slipped it almost furtively into his pocket. The torn paper he screwed up small and threw it in the waste-paper basket.

It looked somehow accusing, or embarrassing at least, so he buried it under more common office trash. He was panting a little, felt ridiculously pleased and touched. Tucking the record under his arm he went out and down the back stairs, humming quietly to himself.

Elinor Pasque must have been, by any conservative estimate, in her mid-eighties, but only a slowness of movement, an obvious stiffness of her joints, betrayed the fact. Watching her, Jolley thought that he had known her long enough to be able to ask her age without giving offence. At her age most women liked to boast of their longevity but there was something still so feminine and young about her that Jolley felt, after all, it would be an ungallant question.

She had insisted on making him a cup of tea, refusing his offer to help.

'It does me good,' she called from the little kitchen, which opened directly off her living-room, 'to move about. I'll just wait here while the kettle boils. You make yourself comfortable now.'

Jolley was comfortable in a deep, soft armchair beside a smouldering fire. It was a sign of her great age, he thought, that even on such a warm day she felt the need of a fire. It was a little too hot for him, but he liked the drowsy feeling it induced. The room was overcrowded, dark, but homely. Looking through the leaded back window, he could see sunlight on the field beyond her garden. Trees, though, shadowed the house on either side, making it cooler than the day actually was.

He rested back against the cushions, relaxing. Marion Glade and his wife's barbed tongue seemed very far away. He had parked outside *her* house, had glanced casually at it as he got out and locked the car, the record lying on the passenger seat. Door and windows had been fast closed, the lace showing like grey shadows behind the leaded panes. With a pang of disappointment, he had thought she must be out.

'Here we are, my dear. It takes me a while but I flatter myself it's worth waiting for.' Jolley stood up and took the tray from her rather unsteady hands, placed it on a little table beside her chair. She lowered herself gingerly into it with evident relief. 'I'll just let it draw,' she said, patting the white bun coiled tight at the nape of her neck. She was an elegant woman, he thought, had always thought. Her no doubt scrawny neck was disguised by an old-fashioned black velvet choker from which suspended a gold and pearl ornament. She wore matching earrings, a touch of red lipstick and her grey dress boasted pristine white detachable collar and cuffs. There was a faint scent of lily-of-the-valley about her. Her hands though, as she reached to pour the tea, were cruelly knobbed by arthritis. 'Darn it, I forgot to bring the biscuits . . . '

'Not for me,' Jolley said.

'No? Well, if you're sure. I'm not much of a one for eating between meals myself. Now, my dear, do you like sugar or sweetener? I ought to remember, but nowadays— '

'It's been years since we drank a cup of tea together, Mrs Pasque. Neither, thank you. I'm supposed to watch my weight.' She gave him a look that clearly suggested 'supposed' was the operative word. 'You're as trim as ever,' he said, accepting the cup from her hand.

'Even so, Doctor says I have to watch it. Mind you, when you don't do nothing day in and day out, you don't work up much of an appetite. Still, I have the sweetener things. Reminds me of the war. Saccharin. Horrible stuff.' She pulled a face as she stirred her tea, then looked across at him with sharp, dark eyes. 'Now, why have you come to see me?'

'A bit of business, I'm afraid.'

'That poor man. Funny, I had a feeling that wasn't done with. I said to that other chappie of yours at the time, I said, "Is that it, then? All over and done with, just like that?"'

'And what made you say that?'

'Oh, I don't know. It just all seemed so quick. One

minute he was alive, the next dead, and the day after it was just talk of his funeral.'

'Tell me about it.'

'I can't, my dear. I don't know nothing about it. Like I say, one minute he was alive . . . ' She sighed deeply and drank some tea, swallowing noisily.

'I was surprised to hear he lodged here. I'd've thought that was a bit much for you these days.'

'Oh no. He was no trouble. He had all his meals up at the Manor. They've got like a canteen place there now, you know, in the Great Hall. I shudder to think what Lady Katherine would think of that. So he was no trouble and besides, I like to have someone in the house, my dear, that's the long and the short of it. It's not the company but just knowing someone's there, in case.'

'I understand,' Jolley said. 'What was he like?'

'Oh, nice enough. Good-looking fellow. Nicely spoken. Educated, of course. Very quiet. No trouble. He wasn't what you'd call the cheery type. He wasn't like my Tom, always whistling while he shaved and always ready to have a joke, but I couldn't find fault with him. It takes all sorts, don't it, my dear?'

'Indeed it does. So you don't know why he might have . . . why he took his own life?'

'Bless you, no. It was a terrible shock when they came and told me. I never heard him go out, you see. He came in, much as usual. He used to spend a lot of time over the pub, didn't usually get back until closing time. That's just about my bedtime but, come to think of it, I had already gone up, so it must've been a bit later. "Good-night, Mrs Pasque," he calls. "You all right?" "Yes, thank you, my dear," I says as I heard him go into his room. There's a board squeaks in there. I heard him moving around like, and then nothing.'

'You sleep well, do you?'

'Mostly. And Doctor's given me some pills.'

'Did you take any that night?'

She frowned, looked slightly embarrassed.

'The truth is, I can't say. That's the trouble with getting old. You don't remember things, ordinary things. Maybe I did and maybe I didn't. But I slept through, that I do know.'

'You didn't hear a sound, a closing door, a shot perhaps?'

'Oh no, dear. If I'd heard anything like that, I'd've reported it straight away. No, next thing I knows is one of your chaps at the door asking does he live here and when did I see him last, and then this other one – Hadfield, his name was – he came along and said as how Mr Corr-Beardsley was dead. I had the pub send me over a tot of brandy I was that shook up.'

'It must have been very upsetting for you. I'm sorry.'

'Oh well, it was much worse for him, wasn't it?'

'How do you mean?'

'Well, it must've been, mustn't it?'

'You've no idea why?' She shook her head emphatically, finished her tea. 'Did he have any friends? How did he spend his free time, apart from the pub?'

'Well, being summer, they often worked evenings, out in the woods and that. As far as I know, apart from that, he went to the pub.'

'He didn't have any particular friends?' Jolley persisted. She regarded him gravely.

'I've heard talk, same as you have.'

'Oh? What talk?'

'Same as you've heard.'

'Now would I be asking you, Mrs Pasque, if I already knew?'

'Yes. You would. It's your way. You've heard about him and her . . . ' She gestured with one hand in the general direction of the village, but there was no mistaking whom she meant.

'Dolores Bayger,' he said.

'Mm. Something like that.'

'Well?'

'I can't tell you anything. I've heard what you've heard no doubt. But it's five years since I went further than my front gate or the bottom of the garden. I can't see her place from either, so I don't know who goes a-calling. And he never said anything. "Just going out, Mrs Pasque," he'd say and it wasn't my place to cross-question him, was it?'

'No, of course not. So what have you heard?'

'That they were carrying on. But you know as well as me that if a woman has a man in the house, even if it's only to mend her telephone, there's talk.'

'But Corr-Beardsley wouldn't have gone there to fix her phone, would he?'

She shrugged. 'Far as I know, he never did go there.'

'So who says he did?'

'Everyone. You just ask about.'

'So was there talk about David Brimble?'

'Yes.'

'And Fred Smith?'

She nodded her head. 'Like I said, if a woman's alone and a man's seen around her, especially if he goes inside . . . '

'So she hasn't got a very good reputation, Miss Bayger?'

At this, Elinor Pasque laughed, throwing back her head. 'No, my dear. Bless you, no. And that's one thing she has got in common with most other women in this village. Well, them without a man of their own, anyway.'

'Including you?'

'In my day. But if you want to know about that, you can go and dig around elsewhere. I was seventy-three when my Tom was took, so you draw your own conclusions.'

'They say there's many a good tune played on an old fiddle,' he grinned.

'And policemen,' she said, with an attempt at stiffness, 'shouldn't be cheeky.'

'Well, thanks anyway. And thanks for the tea. If you should think of anything— '

'I won't. If I had I'd've done so by now.'

'Well, I'd better be making a move.' He stood up reluctantly.

'Where you off to now, then?'

'Thought I'd have a word with Mrs Smith.'

'You'll have to go over to Pytchmarsh, then. She's still stopping with her mother. There's talk she never will come back.'

'Thanks. You've saved me a wasted journey.'

'The Brimbles are still here, though. You'll likely catch Mary at home.' She glanced at the old, heavy clock on the narrow mantel. 'You might even just catch him if you look lively. Otherwise, he'll be off to snooker.'

'You don't miss much, do you, Mrs Pasque?'

'Oh, I don't know about that, my dear. It's just that if you sit still long enough and keep your own counsel, people come and lay it all at your feet. You can see yourself out, can't you? You and Eileen come and have a cup of tea with me one day. I'd like that.'

'I'll tell her,' he promised. 'You take care now.'

'And you.'


Number 17 Chuters was on the same side of the village as Mrs Pasque's cottage, but higher up, past the pub, within sight of the dead end where the road was blocked by a wooden fence, the forbidding wall of the forest. Two beautiful horse-chestnut trees kept the Brimble's garden in perpetual shade. Nothing grew there but grass, meticulously mown, and a dotting of lilac bushes, some dark, ornamental conifers. Mr Brimble, identifiable by the snooker cue he carried in a narrow black sheath, was coming down the path as Jolley turned into the gate. A woman appeared at the door behind Brimble, a handkerchief held to her nose. She answered Jolley's query while the man stared at him, bemused.

'You've got plenty of time,' she told the man. 'You can spare five minutes.' The man turned and walked back into the house. His bald, polished-looking head came halfway up Jolley's chest. Uninvited, Jolley trailed him into the dark porch, left into a room identical in size and shape to that he had just been in, to that in which he had met Dolores Bayger. This one was thickly carpeted in dark orange and sparsely furnished. An ugly, modern sofa

60

was squashed against one wall, a drop-leaf table pressed under the back window. From the table, Mrs Brimble pulled a straight-backed chair and indicated that Jolley should sit, in the centre of the room. The handkerchief was still pressed to her nose.

'She gets hay fever,' Brimble explained, sitting on the edge of the sofa, balancing the cue between his spread knees. 'She's a martyr to it,' he added. The woman walked past Jolley to close the door. A sideboard stood to his left, under the front window. It contained a gallery of framed, formal photographs. The lives of three boys, frozen and catalogued from christenings to manhood. In the centre, isolated but surrounded, stood a full-faced colour portrait of a solemn-looking youth. Jolley felt certain this was David Brimble. The mother of this brood crossed the room again and sat hunched up in the corner of the settee.

'It's about our David,' she said, lowering the handkerchief to reveal a large, red and obviously sore nose. 'You're a policeman.'

Jolley nodded and introduced himself. Mr Brimble looked surreptitiously at his watch as Jolley explained that he just wondered if they had anything to add to the statements they had already made to Sergeant Hadfield.

'Sometimes people remember things, little things that don't always seem important at first, what with the shock and distress.'

'She's not over the shock yet,' Brimble said, nodding at his wife.

'I'll never be over it,' she announced, the last words muffled by the handkerchief.

'It's best left,' Brimble told Jolley. 'Nothing'll bring him back.'

'It's a tragedy,' Mrs Brimble said into the handkerchief.

'I know and I'm very sorry to distress you all over again. It's just that, well, as you know there have been three suicides in the village this year and I just wanted to make sure nothing had been overlooked.' It sounded lame, even to his own ears. The room depressed him. He wondered why he was bothering, where all this could lead. Brimble was right. There was no point in making them relive their tragedy.

'It's no coincidence, if that's what you're getting at,' Mrs Brimble said, frowning at him.

'Now, Mother . . . ' Brimble turned to her, spoke soothingly.

'Well, he can't think it is or he wouldn't be here. That's right, isn't it?' she demanded of Jolley.

'The fact is, we've received a letter, an anonymous letter, making that very suggestion. You wouldn't have written that letter by any chance, would you, Mrs Brimble?'

'Certainly not,' she said, sniffing, her eyes watering. 'Fetch me my pills, Dad.' She flapped a hand at Mr Brimble who rose obediently and went to the sideboard. 'I'd put my name to anything I wrote. I've got nothing to hide. And I wouldn't write it, neither. I'd stand up and say it, loud and clear. Speak the truth and shame the Devil. That's how I was brought up.'

'Now, Mother,' Brimble said again. She snatched the container of pills from his hand, wrestled with the top. 'She gets agitated,' Brimble said. She shook some little white tablets into the palm of her hand and raised them to her mouth. 'They're not proper medicine,' Brimble felt constrained to explain. 'Only homeopathic.'

'Shut up,' Mrs Brimble said, wielding her handkerchief. 'You don't know nothing about it. Anything the doctor gives you makes you go to sleep,' she told Jolley. 'These are natural.'

'They don't do no good,' her husband grumbled.

'Nothing does much good this time of year. Nothing does any good as far as you're concerned. *I* know what does me good.'

Jolley said, 'About David . . . '

'He was very low,' Mr Brimble said, like a record suddenly activated by a familiar stylus. 'He hadn't had a job since he left school. Not a proper job. A bit of casual on the farms roundabout . . . delivering papers for a bit . . . '

'What's that got to do with it?' Mrs Brimble demanded. 'He doesn't want to hear all that rubbish. He wants to hear why . . . '

'That is why, Mother.'

'Oh, clear off to your snooker. Leave me to tell the man in my own way. I can't think with you interrupting.'

Jolley was inclined to agree with her. He could not see himself making much headway in the face of this domestic squall.

'Yes,' he said. 'There's no need for you to stay, Mr Brimble. This is all quite informal.'

'Well, if you're sure.' He looked immensely relieved but the glance he bestowed on his wife was tinged with uneasiness.

'Quite sure. I'll call again if I want to check anything with you.'

'She's still upset,' he said, standing. 'You want to make allowances.' Jolley nodded, reassuring him.

'Snooker! That's all he thinks about,' Mrs Brimble said as he closed the door. 'If he's not off playing it he's glued to it on the television.'

'It's very popular,' Jolley agreed.

'Not with me it's not.'

'No, well . . . '

'He doesn't agree with me,' she said. 'You'd better understand that straight off. He'd have contradicted everything I said. He's soft. Always has been. He believes anything he's told. David was depressed, he says. Because he couldn't get a job, he says. Well, there's thousands out of work. He was all right. He wasn't work-shy, mind you. But he was all right. And then he says it was because that Tracey threw him over. Well, I warned him that was coming. She's only interested in money. She was just amusing herself with David till she found a lad with money to spend, a car. That's the sort she is. He was well shot of her. He wasn't depressed about that. Not my David. He wasn't depressed . . . ' Tears suddenly augmented the flow caused by hay fever. She pulled a clean handkerchief from

63

her skirt pocket, dabbed her face, blew her nose. Jolley listened to the sound of Brimble's car puttering away and regretted having let him go.

'Please don't distress yourself, Mrs Brimble, but if you could just tell me why, why you think David . . . committed suicide . . . '

'Did away with himself,' she corrected him. 'Driven to it.' She wiped her nose again. 'That's easy. I've been saying it all along, only nobody would listen. Especially not your lot. You'll listen, won't you?'

'Certainly. That's why I'm here.'

'I don't know who wrote that letter you said you got. True as God's my judge it wasn't me, but whoever it was knew what they were talking about. It wasn't no coincidence, not three of 'em. Stands to reason. No. Coincidence, my eye.' She sniffed, but with disdain this time, turning her face aside.

'Well, then, Mrs Brimble, what was it?'

She turned her eyes on him slowly. They were wide and red-rimmed. Her expression suggested that he must be mentally deficient.

'Didn't the letter say, then?' She sounded genuinely surprised.

'The letter simply said,' Jolley lied, 'that the three suicides were not coincidence and that we − or rather I − should investigate again.'

'It didn't mention her?' Disbelief forced her voice up to a nasal soprano.

'Who, Mrs Brimble?'

'Her, of course.'

'Who do you mean, Mrs Brimble?'

'That woman. The American. Bagel she calls herself, or something like that.'

'Bayger. Dolores Bayger. Is that who you mean?'

'Of course.'

'Now why should the letter mention her?'

'Because she was the cause of . . . what my David done to himself. And what others did, too. Well, you must know

64

that. You was over there questioning her long enough the other day.'

Ah, village life, Jolley thought. The lack of privacy, the constant speculation that so quickly became gospel. For a moment he was angry. 'You don't know why I visited Miss Bayger, but we both know it's none of your business,' he said firmly. Her glare became sullen, but she did not back down. 'Now if you've got something to say about Miss Bayger, you'd better just come straight out with it, but I must warn you— '

'Oh, I see . . . ' Mrs Brimble almost pounced. 'You're on her side as well. Well, of course you would be. You're a man.'

Every time, Mrs Brimble, he thought. Anyone would rather be on her side. Any side would be preferable to your anger, narrowness, petty gossip-mongering . . . He stood up quickly, snapping his thread of thought.

'I'm on nobody's side, Mrs Brimble. As far as I'm concerned there aren't any sides. There are just facts. And I am a busy man. So if you wouldn't mind— '

'I can't speak for them,' she interrupted, modifying her charge a little. 'Fred Smith and the posh feller, but I know, sure as eggs is eggs, she turned my David's head.'

Jolley stared at her. Mrs Brimble stared back, awaiting some eruption of understanding, some sign of disgust. Jolley wanted to reach out and touch her, explain to her that of course Dolores Bayger turned David's head, that women as beautiful and cultivated as she were destined to turn the head of any nineteen-year-old boy. But he knew it was futile. Disappointment settled on Mary Brimble's sore face. She rubbed the handkerchief across her nostrils, stared at a point on the floor.

'He was full of her,' she resumed stubbornly, but more calmly. 'Every day, dinner-time, evening, it was "Oh, Mam, you should see the way she's done that place up." I'd tell him he had no cause to go in her house. His job was to fix the stables like she told him to. "Why do you want to go in there for?" I said to him. It was always so he could fix something for her, or would he like a cup of tea? "She's like a film star, Mam," he used to say and I told him, "And since when did any good come of film stars?" But he wouldn't listen . . . ' Mrs Brimble bit her lower lip, twisted the handkerchief about the fingers of one hand.

'Are you saying David was in love with Miss Bayger?' Jolley asked gently, feeling some pity for her.

'Love . . . ' she said on an explosive breath. 'I don't know about love. He was besotted by her. That I do know. She bewitched him.'

'And you think that somehow contributed to his death?'

'Well, don't you?'

'I don't know, Mrs Brimble. I must admit that I can't see . . . Even if David was . . . shall we say infatuated with Miss Bayger? That hardly seems a reason for committing suicide.' She pities me, Jolley thought. Those cold eyes, that sullen mouth mark me out for a fool, incapable of understanding a self-evident truth. Or rather she doesn't see me at all, only her own certainty, her own vicious prejudice.

'She dropped him. Just like that.'

'His work came to an end,' Jolley tried to reason with her.

'It was more than that.'

'How? What more?'

'She led him on, used him, and then dropped him. That woman destroyed him,' she shouted suddenly.

'Now, now, Mrs Brimble— '

'Don't you "now, now" me. When she took up with that posh feller, after our David, it killed him. Inside, it killed him. She's nothing but a strumpet and she killed my son.'

Any other woman would have cried at this point, Jolley thought, but Mrs Brimble was the exception. She seemed to turn to stone, her face set, her body stiff and harsh in the corner of the settee. He turned away from her, looked at the army of photographs then out through the window at the plain, dark garden.

'It's my duty to warn you, Mrs Brimble, to watch what you say. You've no proof. There are laws in this country to protect a person's character, reputation. You can't just go around accusing people . . . '

'All I've said is the truth. You asked me.'

Was there a hint of fear in her voice? Jolley thought so. 'Even so, I'm warning you not to go around shouting these accusations from the roof-tops. If you do, you could find yourself in very serious trouble indeed. Do you understand what I'm saying?'

'Oh yes. You're protecting her. Do you know what I think? There won't be no justice in this country until we have women running the police. You men are all tarred with the same brush.'

Marion Glade's face swam in front of him, taunting him. 'Well,' he said, 'that's a point of view. Meanwhile, I won't bother you any longer.'

'You won't do nothing, either.'

'I shall continue my investigations,' he said. Mrs Brimble sniffed. 'I'll . . . er . . . see myself out.'

He paused for a moment in the hallway, listening. No sound came from the room. He walked down the path and out into the road again, certain Mrs Brimble's watery eyes were following him, cursing him. He began to walk quickly, to walk off the anger he felt. Of course her son's death was a terrible blow, had devastated an already meagre life, he guessed. No doubt she was a good and loving mother, but to fasten so viciously on Dolores Bayger as the sole and only cause of that death . . . What had the woman ever done? He could list her 'crimes' only too easily. They were transparent in the eyes of the narrow-minded people of Chuters. She was foreign. She was a newcomer. She was beautiful. She had an easy manner. No doubt she had made young David Brimble laugh . . . Yes, and paid him over the odds, Jolley would be prepared to bet. He crossed the green in front of The Clouded Yellow, his pace slackening a little. What he could not understand was why she put up with it. A woman of her intelligence should move somewhere more congenial. How could she love a place like this? A stone lay in his path and he aimed a vicious kick at it, but he had never been a footballer. The stone skittered sideways, mocking his efforts. God, what a rotten little world it was when a woman couldn't be beautiful and free and charming, kind enough to give a lad a job, the occasional cup of tea . . . Was it her fault that David Brimble might have glimpsed in her the possibilities of another world?

Jolley was slightly out of breath when he reached the car. He stood beside it, staring at her house, still closed, still empty-looking. He hadn't, he told himself, really expected her to be in. He walked on, past the house, turned and looked back at it. From this angle, he could see a corner of the stable roof behind. What had she said? A studio, a dark room. He retraced his steps quickly, opened the gate and almost trotted across the lawn on his right. A narrow path ran beside the house, ended in a tall wooden gate, set in the fence. Both were new, still smelled a little of wood preservative. The gate was fastened, bolted on the inside, he supposed. Without thinking, he reached over it, standing on tiptoe, his hands seeking the bolt. If there was one, it was cleverly out of reach. He stared at the wooden gate as though it alone was responsible for his anger, wanted to aim another of his ineffectual kicks at it. He turned back, feeling conspicuous now and foolish. Such behaviour would only reflect on her, for he had no doubt that his every move was being observed, remarked and would be reported. He slammed the gate shut behind him and got into his car.

The record still lay on the seat beside him. He reached into his pocket and touched the little white card with her writing on it, pulled it out and re-read it. Then he placed it carefully in his wallet, in a seldom used compartment where he kept other precious mementoes. As he turned the key in the ignition, he decided he would tell Eileen that he had ordered the record before they went on holiday, had collected it today from the Oversleigh Record Stores.

# Three

Eileen was quite right. He had slept badly, had not slept at all until the small hours. His thoughts had turned as much on Dolores Bayger as on the problem of Marion Glade. He sat at the breakfast table, hunched over his newspaper. Eileen knew better than to ask. Humming to herself, she fetched the post and sorted it, pushing a few envelopes across the table. Jolley looked through them then at the larger pile beside his wife's plate. She was spreading Flora on her toast and was, irritatingly, in no hurry to open her mail.

'How come you always get more post than me?'

'I write more letters.'

'All I ever get is bills.'

'Well, you will insist on having them, dear. I've told you I'm happy to take care of them.'

'You're welcome to them.' He pushed his meagre pile of envelopes back towards her.

Eileen bit into her toast, put on her reading glasses and looked at his post. 'Those aren't bills,' she said casually. 'They're circulars.' She turned her attention to her own letters, apparently unaware of Jolley's glare. 'Oh, look. That's nice.' She held out a postcard to him. He stared at the picture of a modern building half-hidden by tropical-looking shrubs and trees.

'Very nice,' he said and shook his paper.

Eileen sighed heavily. 'It's from Karen,' she said. 'She's got a place at Falmouth Art School. She's going to be staying there. She sends her love.'

'Good,' Jolley said, 'That'll do her good.'

'Which reminds me,' Eileen said, opening a letter. 'I'm going to enrol for my evening class today, so remember I'll be busy on Wednesdays from now on.'

'What evening class?' This was the first Jolley could remember having heard about it. He stared at Eileen over his newspaper.

'Pottery.'

'You don't know anything about pottery.'

'That's why I'm going to class, dear, to learn.'

'You're not interested in pottery.'

'I am. Very.'

'You've never done it before.'

'True.'

'I expect it'll be full up.'

'Well, if it is, I shall take something else.'

'Like what?'

'Water-colour painting.'

'You'll be going to art school next.'

'Probably.' She began to read her letter.

Jolley, making heavy weather of it, poured himself some more tea. 'Who's idea was that?'

'What, dear?'

'I said, who's idea was that?'

'Mine, of course. Though Audra got me the literature.'

'She going?'

'No.'

'Sensible girl.'

'She's busy with the choir.'

'What choir?'

'You know perfectly well.'

Jolley could not deny this. He was still, he supposed, in the dog-house for having burst out laughing when his only daughter had announced she was going to join the Oversleigh Choral Society. He had a very low opinion of his daughter's voice, even though he had not heard it for many years. 'I'd better be off,' he said, not moving.

'All right, dear. James and Nigel send their love.'

'Is that from James?'

70

'Mm. They might come down for a few days at half-term.'

It still surprised Jolley that his son and his male lover were so easily referred to as a couple, that it did not really embarrass him that two grown men should send him their love. What surprised him most of all was that he liked Nigel and enjoyed his company. He liked him, he thought, brooding, a hell of a lot more than he liked his son-in-law.

'Let's have a look,' he said.

'I thought you were going? You can read it tonight. James has sent some dates for Opera North's winter season. You'll need to study them carefully. Off you go now or you'll be late.' She lifted her face to him, awaiting his kiss, squinting a little through her spectacles. Jolley dutifully kissed her and she went happily back to her letter.

It looked like rain. Eileen said they needed it for the garden. Jolley grunted with bad temper. Art classes. Come the bad winter weather and she'd never want to go. If she did go he'd be on tenterhooks the whole time imagining her in some icy accident. He blamed her for not asking what was on his mind, then felt relief that she had not as the image of Dolores Bayger floated before his eyes. Eileen had not asked about the record, either, or commented upon it. Of course he would have to thank Dolores Bayger . . .

It was at times like this that he missed David Hughes especially. Hughes would have understood his dilemma *vis-à-vis* Tait, would not have contradicted him or made excuses for the Superintendent. He knew perfectly well what Hughes would have said.

'You? Work with a woman? Don't be so daft.'

But, of course, if Hughes were there Marion Glade would not be a problem. He would not know of Marion Glade's existence and could laugh with Hughes when Tait had succeeded in dumping her on some other poor fool.

He drove through Clifton King's, away from Oversleigh, quickly coming to open country, the clouds thickening all

71

the time. And Hughes would understand about Dolores Bayger. What was there to understand? he thought guiltily. He meant that Hughes would have appreciated her beauty, would have been impressed by her manner, style . . . And Hughes would have sent him up rotten for receiving presents from strange, sexy women . . . Yes, definitely, he needed Hughes.

A few minutes later he joined the main Anderton road and got stuck behind a container lorry, dawdled along impatiently. There was a classic case in point. If by any remote chance he should find himself working with Marion Glade, he could not discuss Dolores Bayger with her. He could not ask Glade about her love life, as he did Hughes, could not make admiring jokes about Cheryl Dangerfield – 'Give me the field and I'll risk the danger' – could not, in a phrase, *talk* to her.

At the Nusford intersection, where the traffic backed up from the lights at the narrow bridge, a sort of complement to that which spanned the same meandering river outside Oversleigh, Jolley squeezed free of the traffic, sped along B roads again. The last time he had been to Pytchmarsh, Hughes had been with him. They had eaten excellent cheese and onion sandwiches washed down with good ale at the pub there, mulling over the case. Memories. He supposed it would always be like this now, every place, every day bringing up some new old association, underscoring the value of Hughes, their special relationship.

A few spots of rain exploded on the windscreen as he entered Pytchmarsh, but they came to nothing. He didn't like Pytchmarsh any more than he liked Chuters, though it could not be more different. It was a long, straggling village, built either side of a narrow road which included a very nasty blind bend at one end. The heart of the original village remained more or less intact, but most of the place was new development: brick bungalows, Bradstone houses, a mini-council estate. Approaching the dangerous bend, he slowed and looked to his left at a drab, discoloured

Snowcemmed house surrounded by old cars and patrolled by Dobermanns. Jed Haythorne wasn't too fussy where he got his cars from or how he patched them up. That was what had brought Hughes and Jolley to Pytchmarsh a couple of years back. Now Haythorne's yard had spread like a cancer into the field beyond where a caravan rested, a hand-lettered cardboard sign saying 'OFFICE' taped to its side. Jolley leaned on the horn and took the bend steadily. The sound of the horn set the Dobermanns barking on their rattling chains.

The council estate had won some sort of prize back in the sixties, although Jolley had never understood why. The houses were grouped in four rectangles, each with a bald patch of communal grass at its centre. They were joined by a single access road, from which fed drive-like entries to each block. The houses were built in terraces and semi-detached pairs. One terrace had orange front doors, the other cobalt blue. These same colours alternated on the semis, somehow making the whole place more rather than less depressing. He parked behind a van with one flat tyre and its back doors held together by twine. Probably one of Jed Haythorne's he thought, peering out to locate number 9. It was one of the terraced houses with an orange door and a profusion of looped and scalloped net curtains.

Three rose bushes struggled in a diamond-shaped bed in the approximate centre of the 'lawn'. Two skateboards and a football, a tennis racquet minus most of its strings, littered the cracked concrete path. Jolley felt rather than saw the net curtains twitch as he pressed a bell that did not sound. The door was opened anyway.

'Yes?'

'Good morning. Inspector Jolley, Oversleigh Police.' He showed his spanking new identification, holding it steady so that the heavily bespectacled woman could peer at it. 'I'm looking for Mrs Smith, Belle Smith.'

The glasses, thick as the bottom of wine bottles and set in a heavy, upswept blue frame, shifted from his identification to his face. They dwarfed the rather gaunt face which was topped by a pink chiffon scarf drawn over a multitude of plastic rollers around which bottle-blonde hair had been teased.

'She's not here.'

'Are you expecting her back?'

'Yes.'

'May I wait?'

The woman considered this, looking him up and down. 'All right.'

'She won't be long then?' He squeezed his bulk past her into the narrow hall.

'In there,' she said, pointing to an open door. 'No. She's just gone up the school.'

'Trouble with the boys?' Jolley asked, thinking it an understandable likelihood when you considered that they had lost their father and been uprooted all in the space of a few months.

'No. Not that it's any of your business. She's gone to see about a job.'

'You must be her mother.'

'As if you didn't know.'

'Mrs . . . ?'

'Keene. You can sit there if you can find room.' She pointed to a settee on which a large and overflowing plastic basket of clothes awaiting ironing stood unsteadily. It slipped as Jolley's weight depressed the other end of the sofa. A pair of brightly patterned boxer shorts fell to the floor. Mrs Keene scooped them up, lifted the basket on to her hip and stomped out of the room with it. Jolley stared around him. It was an ordinary, very clean living-room, made untidy by the clutter of teenage boys. Records and comics were scattered about, a pair of scuffed trainers lay beneath an easy chair. 'Want some coffee?'

Startled, Jolley swivelled to his right. Mrs Keene's face was framed by a serving hatch. Behind her, a cluttered kitchen showed.

'That would be very welcome. Thank you.'

'Milk and . . . ?'

'Just a little milk, please.'

'What's all this about then?' Jolley did not immediately know how to answer, whether to be formal and repeat that it was the daughter he wished to see, or to avail himself of the chance to gather what might be useful information. 'You can tell me. I'm her mother. We've got no secrets between us.'

'I'm sure not.'

'It's about poor Fred,' she announced, withdrawing from the hatch. Moments later a mug was pushed through and again she disappeared. Jolley picked up the mug and stood, back to the hatch, nursing his coffee. Mrs Keene came into the room. 'Don't go upsetting her, that's all.'

'What makes you think it's about the late Mr Smith?'

'Because there's nothing else it could be about. The boys are as good as gold. *I* see to that. And Belle's hardly been out of the house since she came here. Beside, it's unfinished business.'

'Oh?'

'Well, you tell me it isn't then.'

Jolley burned his lips on the scalding coffee, put the mug down quickly.

'I am making a few more inquiries, yes. What can you tell me about your son-in-law's death?'

'You don't wrap it up, do you? You mind you're a bit more gentle with Belle.' Jolley said nothing. 'He killed himself. You know all that. What you want to know is why he did it.'

'I would be interested.'

'Took you long enough. But I told her you'd get around to it eventually.'

'Why do you think we should be looking into it now? There were no suspicious circumstances.'

'Oh no. Only two more poor buggers gone the same way. I thought one of you'd spot that eventually. Anyway, there's bound to be talk.'

'What sort of talk?'

'About her, of course.'

75

'Her?'

'Dolores Bayger.' She pronounced the name with a sort of disgusted venom. He felt his mind close at this, but he gave her full marks for directness, unlike Mrs Brimble. 'You know who I mean?' she said, surprised by his silence. He nodded. 'She's why he did it. She turned his head, led him on and then told him to sling his hook. Bloody men,' she added bitterly. 'I know. Same thing happened to my hubby. Only he went off with his tart and married her. 'Course, Fred wasn't good enough for *her*. She was just amusing herself. And when someone else came along . . .' She snapped her fingers.

'Do you think your son-in-law had an affair with Miss Bayger?'

'Probably. I don't know, if that's what you mean. But if he didn't, it wasn't for want of wanting. Maybe she just likes to tease 'em. On the other hand, maybe she flops on her back straight away. It don't matter much. She made my daughter a widow, left my grandsons without a dad. That matters. And if there was any justice, she'd bloody well pay for it.'

'Those are big claims, Mrs Keene. It's my duty to warn you that if you can't substantiate— '

'Oh, don't give me all that bullshit,' she said crossly. 'I know you can't touch her. I know I can't prove anything. But I know what I know. He was a different man the moment he met her. Fred was a steady bloke, a good husband and father. He wasn't anything to write home about, no Robert Redford. Belle could've done better for herself, but she could have done a hell of a lot worse, too. Then he met her and went to pieces. I want her to pay for that.'

'How did he change?' Jolley asked, ignoring her last remark, but adding it mentally to the blockade of hatred that seemed to surround Dolores Bayger.

'He was like a bear with a sore head, restless, fed up, gloomy. Haven't you ever seen a bloke when he's sniffing after some woman? You must know what it's like.' Jolley

76

was profoundly glad that she did not pause there, apparently expected no confirmation or denial from him. 'And he took no interest in Belle, if you understand me. He was hardly ever home and when he was he never laid a finger on her. Then, when she took up with that Brimble boy, he shot himself. Now you know.'

Jolley tried the coffee again. It was strong and bitter, but cool enough to drink. 'Your daughter agrees with you about this?'

'Of course she does.'

'I find it difficult to believe— '

'Then you haven't met her.'

' . . . That any man would kill himself over a . . . casual affair . . . if that . . . Fred Smith doesn't sound an unstable man, nor a particularly romantic— '

'They'd have burned her for a witch a few years back,' Mrs Keene interrupted. 'Now the most we can hope for is that she gets drummed out of the village.'

'You think she has some sort of power?' Jolley said, trying to laugh it off.

'Over men, yes. You can't be as innocent as you sound. Don't you know anything about women?'

'It'd be a foolish man who claimed that he did,' Jolley said, with feeling.

'Well, you take it from me, then. There's some women make a career out of it, so to speak. There's some women who can't leave any man alone. Oh, I don't mean bed necessarily. I mean power. They like to get 'em worked up, have power over them. You take a tip from me. You go and see her. You go and see for yourself.'

'I've already met Miss Bayger,' Jolley said stiffly, 'and I'll tell you something else, Mrs Keene . . . ' He slid his hand into his pocket and pulled out a fresh photocopy of the letter, held it, folded, towards her. 'I think you wrote this.'

'I don't know what you're talking about.'

'You haven't looked at it yet.'

'I don't need to. I never wrote nothing.'

'Please, take a look at it.'

'I don't want to.'

Jolley turned away to put his coffee mug down by the hatch. He picked up a pad of Lion Brand paper as he did so.

'Here, you can't go picking up things. Put that down.'

'Why? You afraid I might find the imprint of that letter on one of the pages? You can you know. A bit of light, a microscope . . . ' He flipped the pad open, lifted the top sheet, raised it towards the window.

'Where's your warrant?' Mrs Keene stood up.

'I don't need a warrant for this.'

'Give it here.' She lunged towards him. Jolley held the pad high, thrust the photocopy at her.

'You don't even know, Mrs Keene, what I'm talking about. Why are you so agitated about something?'

There was a sound at the front door and she glanced nervously behind her, then approached Jolley again.

'Give me the pad. Now. Quick.'

A younger woman appeared in the doorway, her face frozen in surprise. Her clear, quick eyes took in the situation. Jolley smiled politely.

'What's going on here? Mum? Are you all right?' She ran to her mother, touched her shoulder.

'Mrs Smith, I presume?' said Jolley, lowering the pad to his side. 'I was just asking your mother about this.'

Belle Smith stared for a moment at the folded sheet of duplicating paper, then took it from him with a worried, nervous glance at her mother. Mrs Keene turned away, sat heavily, staring at the unlit electric fire.

'Read it,' Jolley said and watched her as she unfolded the paper, scanned it.

'Oh, Mum . . . Mum, you didn't— '

'What if I did? Somebody had to make them do something. I couldn't see you suffer and her get off scot-free. I had to make them do something . . . ' Mrs Keene fumbled her glasses from her nose, dropped them in her lap. Half-blind without them, blinded by sudden tears, she covered her face with her hands. Belle Smith dropped to her knees beside her, put her arms gently around the sobbing woman.

'Oh, Mum, Mum . . . It's all right. Don't. Please don't.' Her mother collapsed against Belle, burying her face in her shoulder. 'Could you . . . ' Belle Smith said in an uncertain, wavering voice, ' . . . could you wait outside for a minute, please?'

'Of course,' Jolley said. He put the pad in his pocket and went out into the hall, closing the door almost completely behind him. He listened shamelessly at it but heard nothing more than the weeping and the daughter's soothing words. He stared at the picture on the wall, a cheap, orange-dominated reproduction of some Victorian cottage garden. A row of clothes hooks held the usual collection of anoraks and showerproofs. There was nothing else to see in the hallway. Jolley studied the pattern on the stair carpet, overlapping circles of dark green, light green, lemon yellow . . .

'I'm sorry about that,' Belle Smith said in a whisper, closing the door. 'I don't think she's up to talking much for a bit.' Her eyes pleaded with him. They were large, clear, grey eyes set in a younger, fuller version of her mother's face. If it weren't for the lines of worry, the general care-worn cast to her face, Belle Smith would have been an attractive woman. Still was, Jolley corrected himself.

'It's you I want to talk to. Can we . . . ?' Jolley looked down the hall.

'Best go outside,' she said. 'Go for a bit of a walk.'

'What about your mother?' Jolley asked suspiciously.

'She'll be all right. Oh, she won't run away or anything like that. She just needs to collect herself, put her face on. Go on . . . ' She nodded at the front door. Jolley went up to it but did not turn the Yale lock. He heard Belle Smith say, 'I'm just going to walk around the block, Mum, with the policeman. All right?' Jolley opened the door and stepped out on to the concrete path. It was

79

overcast but dry and he was suddenly glad to be out of the house.

'She's going to do her face and put the kettle on,' Belle Smith said, belting her peach-coloured raincoat. 'Shall we walk along the road?' She meant the road that encircled the estate. Jolley agreed and they moved off, Jolley shortening his stride to accommodate Belle.

'I don't know what to say,' she said.

'Do you believe what your mother says about your husband's death? I'm very sorry about that, by the way,' he added, embarrassed.

'Thanks. Yes, I do. Well, up to a point, anyway. But that doesn't excuse her, does it? Oh, she's not the sort to write anonymous letters. She's been under so much pressure. She was very fond of Fred, and then having us here—'

'What do you mean, "up to a point"?'

Belle Smith looked at him, trying to assess from his expression what his flat voice did not convey.

'I suppose I mean that I'm not so one hundred per cent sure as Mum. But even if I was . . . I know it's no good raking it all over. You can't do anything, can you?'

'You mean you don't hold Dolores Bayger responsible?' Jolley asked, warming to her.

'Fred was responsible, wasn't he? He pulled the trigger, not her.'

'True, very true,' Jolley agreed. At last, he thought, a bit of common sense.

'Fred *did* change after he met her . . . I suppose Mum's told you all this?' He nodded. 'He was different. I thought he was . . . in love with her or . . . something . . . ' These words cost her dearly, still pained her. 'Perhaps I don't want to believe it, even now. Perhaps that's why I don't really hold her responsible. But there is nothing else to explain what he did. There were no money worries. The kids were all right. We were very happy till she came along. It was like he . . . I don't know how to put it,' she said despairingly.

'Try,' Jolley urged her.

80

'Well, like he'd . . . like he'd caught a glimpse of some-thing . . . magic . . . Like he couldn't ever settle down again after . . . I mean *her*, I suppose. I couldn't reach him. It was like there was a sheet of glass between us.'

Jolley thought she put it very well. He knew at first hand what she described, this ability of Dolores Bayger to suggest or indicate another world . . .

'You must have felt very lonely,' he said.

'It was the boys I worried about. And Fred. I knew he was suffering, whatever caused it, but I never thought it would come to that.'

'That's all very helpful,' Jolley told her. They walked on in silence for a while. A few spots of rain fell. Jolley suggested that they turn back.

'What are you going to do about Mum?'

'It's a serious offence, you know, writing anonymous letters, blackening an innocent woman's character.' The glance Belle Smith shot at him made him regret the word 'innocent'. 'However, I accept she's been under a strain. Even so— '

'She won't do it again. I'll see to that. It's not like her, really it's not. And she didn't really want to get at that woman so much as to help me and ease her own feelings. I think now that it's all come out, well, in a way, it's over, if you know what I mean.'

'I think I do. And what about you? Are you going to stay here?'

'I think so. I can't face going back there, not yet anyway. I don't know if they'll let me keep the cottage now that Fred's gone . . . '

'I think perhaps your mother needs you anyway,' Jolley said. 'The boys are all right here, are they?'

'Oh, they like it here. They're still upset. Confused, really. They don't say much. Terry plays up a bit, but that's only to be expected. I think we'll stay on, for a while yet, anyway.'

She let them back into the house. Mrs Keene had pulled the rollers from her hair, brightened her face with

81

make-up. She stared dully at her daughter who took her hand.

'It's a very unpleasant thing, you know, Mrs Keene, writing anonymous letters, accusing people . . . '

'I didn't accuse her. I just pointed you— '

'Shh, Mum,' Belle Smith interrupted. 'Just listen, Mum, please.'

'It amounts to the same thing. You could be said to have wasted a lot of police time, *my* time. However, your daughter assures me that this is uncharacteristic behaviour and that you've been under a lot of pressure lately. Can you give me your word you won't do anything like this again?'

After a long silence, during which she obviously struggled with herself, or her resentment, Mrs Keene said, 'Yes.'

'And no more talk, either,' Jolley warned her. 'I don't want to hear any more rumours about Dolores Bayger. If I do – and believe me not much gossip goes on without me getting to hear about it – I shall know where it started. Do I make myself clear?'

'Mum?' Belle Smith prompted her.

'Very clear.'

'Good. Because I can charge you whenever I like and I'm not going to let the matter drop.' Belle Smith stared at him in worried surprise, her mouth struggling to form words. 'I'm going to leave it pending. If you behave yourself, in time, I may forget all about it. But one peep, one scrap of paper, and I'll be over here and come down on you very, very hard indeed, Mrs Keene. Do you understand that?'

'Yes.'

'Thanks very much, Inspector,' Belle said with relief.

'It's blackmail,' Mrs Keene said, her eyes outlined in blue shadow, flashing behind her glasses. 'That's what it is. Only you can get away with it.'

'She doesn't mean that.'

'Oh yes she does. And she's right, up to a point. However, unlike most blackmailers, you can trust me, Mrs Keene. You keep a curb on your tongue and I'll forget all about this.' He pulled the writing pad from his pocket and laid it on the table. Both women stared at it. A flush crept up Mrs Keene's neck. In his pocket, Jolley felt the top two sheets he had torn from the pad, crisp beneath his fingers. 'Remember what I say. And now, good morning to you.'

Jolley swept through the main doors of Oversleigh Police Station and bore down on the desk like a man with a mission. Sergeant Hadfield, who was poring over some papers with Police Constable Roscoe, looked up and smiled.

'Ah, the very man. Couple of things for you, sir . . . '

'Hadfield, when you "investigated" those suicides at Chuters, did you bother to ask any questions at all? Did you interview anybody? Did you, in a word, do your bloody job, man?' Jolley thumped the counter with his fist, making Roscoe jump.

Hadfield looked confused, then wounded, then sullen. 'I went by normal procedures, sir . . . '

'You didn't think it odd that three men—'

'Yes, sir. That crossed my mind. But there wasn't anything to suggest they weren't three quite independent acts, sir.'

'And I suppose you never heard the name Dolores Bayger?'

Jolley saw the broad grin that split Roscoe's face. He chose to ignore it, but he would remember it.

'Oh, that, sir . . . ' Hadfield seemed to relax.

'Yes, Sergeant, *that*!'

'Just idle gossip, sir. I didn't think it worth while bothering with, sir. We all know how people talk, especially in Chuters.' He glanced at Roscoe for confirmation and received it.

'It should have been in your reports, all of this. And for your information, that is not idle gossip, that is harassment and defamation of character. That woman is being hounded and slandered. I wouldn't be a bit surprised if we didn't receive a formal complaint before long and, when we do, I shall want to know why there is nothing in your reports.' He swung round and marched away from the desk.

'Sir? Before you go up, sir— '

'Yes? What is it?' He spoke with his broad back to the desk, all quivering impatience.

'As a matter of fact, sir, there is a complaint from Chuters . . . ' Jolley turned around and went slowly back to the desk. 'It's all here, sir.' Stiffly, Hadfield handed him a report sheet. 'I thought you'd want to see it, sir.' Jolley cast an eye over the report. 'Someone hanging about, sir,' Hadfield went on nervously. 'Do you want me to— '

'I'll deal with it, thank you, Sergeant.'

'And the Superintendent's been on, sir. Three times. He doesn't seem best pleased . . . '

Jolley silenced him with a frown, turned and walked to the foot of the stairs. He heard Roscoe start to say something and Hadfield 'shush' him, bundle him through the swing door into the office behind.

'And don't leave that desk unmanned,' Jolley bellowed. 'I've had complaints about that from Mr Lethbridge.'

'Yes, sir,' followed him faintly up the stairs. He felt better. He had nailed his colours to the mast. He felt ready to face anything, even Superintendent Tait.

'Ah, Jolley . . . ' he purred, as soon as Jolley was put through to him. There was no mistaking the deliberate softness of the tone, the steel of impatience just audible beneath it. Jolley grinned from ear to ear.

'I understand you were trying to reach me, sir,' he said, affable, formal.

'I had rather expected to hear from you,' Tait said coldly.

'Sorry, sir. I had to go over to Pytchmarsh first thing. Matter of a poison pen letter. Nasty business. Could have repercussions, I'm afraid. But I was quite successful— '

'Just the sort of thing,' Tait interrupted, raising his voice, 'that your deputy could handle if you had a deputy.'

'Yes, sir. I was just going to see about that. I've just walked through the door, sir. And there's a reported— '

'You're obviously a very busy man, Cy,' Tait said, changing tack, 'Obviously you need help, urgently.'

'Oh, we can manage, sir. Don't you worry about us. I'm sure you've got— '

'A lot on my plate. A very great deal on my plate. And it will lighten my load considerably to know if you have reached a decision on those two excellent candidates I was able to send you. May I remind you that you are not the only officer crying out for staff? If you feel you can dispense with the services of either DS Latham or DS Glade, I should be glad to know. In fact, I would regard it as a personal favour, since there are other officers clamouring for their services.'

'I'm sorry, Teddy,' Jolley said, letting his smile warm his voice, 'it quite slipped my mind. You know how it is once you've reached a decision. You just put it out of your mind.'

'You have made a decision, then, Cy?' Tait purred again. Jolley could see his bared teeth, cold eyes.

'Oh, didn't I say? Yes. No problem.'

'Then perhaps you'd— '

'I shall be delighted to take DS Glade on to the staff as soon as possible.' Laugh, you bastard, Jolley thought. Just you dare laugh . . .

'An excellent choice, Cy. I congratulate you. And your . . . er . . . foresight, your . . . progressive attitude, will not go unnoted, I can assure you. Now, if you would just complete the necessary paperwork . . . '

'Good as done, Teddy. And I'll telephone Glade myself later. Put her out of her misery.'

'That would be very thoughtful.'

Jolley put the receiver down, laughing to himself. Well, old son, you've done it now. But it was worth it, just to hear the contained shock in Teddy Tait's voice, just to hear the wind whistling out of his sails. He picked up the report. Marion Glade could sweat a little longer. He did not want to speculate what the reaction in the station would be when news of his decision got round. Time enough for that.

There were two separate and independent reports of a man seen hanging around Chuters late the previous night. A Miss Ann Green had been startled by a man near the chapel gate and had run for her life. Her father had telephoned the station early this morning to report the incident.

Ronnie Birchall, landlord of The Clouded Yellow had seen a man 'hanging about the green' about midnight, as he was locking up. He had mentioned this to his wife who had checked for herself. She, too, had seen a man, 'lurking under the trees on the green'. At her request, Mr Birchall had rung the station. PC Neil, accompanied by PC Withers, had been diverted to Chuters in their patrol car and had made a circuit of the village at about 12.40a.m. They had seen nothing suspicious.

And there the matter would have rested, Jolley thought, had it not been for Mr Green's late call. Someone had better have a word with Miss Green. A perfect job for a woman, he thought cheerfully. The girl, if still scared, would be more likely to open up to a woman, to Marion Glade, for example. He took the application form from his in-tray and quickly completed and signed his portion, deliberately keeping his mind blank. He pressed 12 on the internal telephone.

'Penny, could you come in here for a minute?'

'Shall I bring my pad, sir?'

'No. Not now.'

When WPC Russell came in, he handed the forms to her and told her to get them off straight away.

'It's all right,' he added. 'You can look.'

She blushed a little, then studied the forms. 'Oh,' she said.

'Well?'

'I'll see to it right away, sir.'

'Aren't you pleased?' he asked, frowning.

'It's nothing to do with me, sir. I'm sure ... I mean as long as *you're* pleased ... '

'Where's your feminism, girl? I would have thought

86

you'd have been over the moon. A blow for equality and all that.'

'Yes, well . . . To tell you the truth, sir, I don't much like working for women. They can be very bossy, sir. Anyway, I'd better get these off.'

Bloody women, Jolley thought as the door closed behind her. He'd sort of been counting on Penny Russell's support – or did he mean approval?

Bold as brass, he thought as he strode up the path and banged loudly on her door. Regular, well-advertised visits from him would soon close their mouths. The good people of Chuters could spread the word to Pytchmarsh and Passington as far as he was concerned. They'd soon realise that anyone maligning her would have him to deal with. His presence was protection in itself, by virtue of his office.

The door did not open to his knocking. He stepped back, looked up at the house. It did not have the closed, deserted appearance he had noted the other day. A couple of upstairs windows stood open. But she did not appear at either of them. She did not answer. He was about to leave, reluctantly, when he remembered the gate at the side of the house. It was not visible from where he stood but, by crossing the lawn and turning down the side of the cottage, he came to it. This time it opened at a touch and swung silently inward. It gave on to a yard, fenced on one side to a height of eight feet at least and bounded by the stable block on the other. The back door of the house was open. The yard had been tarmacked, was black, felt almost rubbery. The stables had a pantiled roof and only one door, a stout, black wooden door, tight-closed. The windows and original stable doors had been filled in with thick planks, almost blocks of wood, placed seamlessly edge to edge and cut to the shape of the original apertures. They, too, were painted matt black. David Brimble's work, he supposed. He had evidently been a handy lad, knew a bit about wood, Jolley thought and started to cross the yard to inspect his handiwork more closely.

A sound stopped him. He had not registered what stood at the far end of the yard. Now, as he did so, narrowing his eyes a little against the overcast gloom, he felt eyes on him, heard the angry 'pruk-pruk' call of ravens. His eyes made out the shape of the aviary, the moving, glossy black feathers behind the netting. It was overhung by trees, a sort of wood behind the aviary. He presumed this must be a continuation of the aviary in the chapel ground, which meant that it must be big enough to hold hundreds, thousands . . . He made out the shape of gnarled roosting branches, heard the slow flap of large, dry wings, a sound that suggested all the time in the world, a terrible patience . . .

Another sound made him swing round, startled, his heart thumping unpleasantly in his chest. She backed out of the heavy door, did not see him. She had a bulky, black leather photographic bag slung from her left shoulder. The strap pulled her white shirt away from her neck, showed the perfect slope where it melted into her shoulder. Her hair was piled up and pinned. How vulnerable is the nape of a woman's neck, he thought. Black trousers made him aware of her height. She was almost as tall as he. He heard a lock close smoothly, he thought automatically. Then she turned around.

'Oh!' The bag slid from her shoulder. She caught it deftly, swung it up in her left hand. 'What on earth are you doing here?' Her face was very pale and not just because she wore no make-up. Even her lips looked cold and white.

'I'm sorry . . . ' he said, wanted to say that he had been equally startled by the ravens.

'Shit! I must've left the gate . . . ' She passed by him quickly, locked and bolted the gate.

'I did knock,' he said. 'I thought you might be out here . . . '

'You'd better come in.' She passed him again, without

a glance, and went into the house. She waited for him beside the open door, her right hand opening and closing impatiently. He went into a large, clean kitchen. She closed the door behind him and locked it.

'I really didn't mean to frighten you. You seem upset.'

She swung the bag on to the table, stood with her head bowed for a moment then looked up at him, her smile dazzling.

'No. Forgive me. It's just that . . . Oh, why not admit it, Dolores,' she said, swinging round to the sink, lifting an electric jug kettle from the work surface. 'I'm neurotically private about my work. Out there,' she nodded through the window at the yard, the stable block, 'is my private domain. My secret garden. You know what I mean?' She flashed him another smile over her shoulder while she filled and switched on the kettle. 'Also,' she went on, still moving, busying herself, 'I am very security conscious. I have a lot of very expensive equipment out there. As a policeman, I guess you'd approve.'

'Very much so. I really shouldn't have intruded.'

'No, no. You just caught me off-guard. I was miles away . . . '

'I was a bit thrown myself, by the ravens. Otherwise I'd have called out. I intended to— '

'Announce your presence?' she laughed, tossed a clean tea-towel from a baking-tray and lifted it towards him. 'I made some brownies this morning. I must have known you were coming. Try one.'

He took one. The kettle began to sing. 'Don't they bother you? The ravens?'

'No. Should they?'

'No . . . no . . . Mm. This is delicious.'

'Actually, I've gotten quite interested in them. I'm trying to photograph them. They're part of the deal.' She spooned tea from a lacquered caddy into the silver pot, her back turned to him. 'They're mentioned in the deeds. I can't move them. My property stops at the start of their cage. It was one of the many things the Foundation was very firm about. I said "OK" but I insisted they had to get access to them from the other side. For feeding and whatever they do with them. I felt at first I'd feel overlooked, but now . . . ' She shrugged, switched off the kettle, poured boiling water into the pot. 'They're the devil to photograph,' she said, turning round and leaning against the sink, her arms folded over her chest. 'You need light and they don't like lights. Not yet anyway. Brownies are good, huh?' she said with a sudden change of subject.

'Very.' Jolley licked crumbs from his fingers.

'Have another.'

'Er . . . no, thank you.' He patted his stomach, drawing self-conscious attention to his weight.

'So, what brings you here?'

It took him a moment to recollect. 'I've discovered who wrote that letter.'

'How clever of you. Tell me.'

'I'm afraid I can't.' She pulled a face of childlike disappointment. 'But there won't be any more. And I think you'll find that you are . . . shall we say less interesting to the local populace?'

'You scared 'em off, you mean. Well, I thank you.'

'I may have dropped the odd hint . . . '

'I'm indebted. And very, very grateful.'

'It's my job.'

'Oh . . . But you didn't have to come to tell me.'

'I thought to show my face, or rather to be *seen* to show my face would reinforce the verbal warning.'

'Well, I'm glad anyway. Shall we go through or do you like slumming in the kitchen?'

'I love it. And it's scarcely slumming.' He looked around the yellow and white, expensively appointed kitchen.

'OK, then you get to drink out of a mug and eat brownies straight from the baking-sheet.' She fetched the mugs, poured the tea. 'But you can sit down.'

'I'm quite comfortable, thanks. There are two other things . . . '

'Two? My, you have been busy.'

'We've had reports of a man hanging around the village, late last night. Did you see anything?'

'No.' She shook her head, not at all alarmed.

'It was probably nothing. Certainly nothing to get worried about.'

'But you thought it might be someone spying on me, checking to see who I was entertaining.'

'I didn't, as a matter of fact. But now you mention it . . . ' It seemed a distinct possibility and, if it was true, he'd throw the book at the culprit.

'Well, if that was the case, he was a very disappointed man. I worked last night, all alone as usual, and went early to my bed.'

'There's probably a perfectly reasonable explanation. I doubt that it will happen again.'

'I don't care. I feel as safe as Fort Knox now I've met you.'

'Even so, lock up well.'

'I always do. I am glad I met you, Cyril. I may call you Cyril?'

'Of course.'

'I'm glad that letter was sent to you.'

'Well, as I said, that's all taken care of. And finally, but by no means least, I must thank you for the record.'

'You like it? Really? Don't you think it's just wonderful? I thought you might be mad at me. It was an impulse. Pure impulse. And then I thought that maybe you might think it, well, indiscreet.'

'If it was, it was charmingly so.'

'You really like it?'

'Oh yes. I have reservations, of course, about the Leppard version . . . '

'Oh, sure. But Norman? Isn't she just gorgeous?'

'Absolutely gorgeous,' he agreed.

'You know, Cyril, I think the thing I've missed most living here is not having anyone to talk music with. To share . . . We must have a real record session sometime. I'd like that. But we must do things properly. Can you come to dinner Wednesday, next Wednesday? You and your wife?'

'I'd be delighted.'

'Good. About eight?' He nodded his head. 'And if you're really good, I'll show you some of my work. You may not realise it, but that is a big compliment. I'm very choosy about who sees my work.'

'I appreciate it. I only hope I'm up to it.'

She put her head on one side, considering him. 'Oh, you will be. I'm never wrong about the people I choose. That's why I choose so few.'

'I'm not an expert,' he reminded her.

'Neither am I. That's why I get so nervous about showing my pictures. But you'll be gentle, won't you?'

'Very gentle, I promise.'

She smiled at him, her eyes on his. 'And now I'm going to have to throw you out. Will you forgive me? I've got a thousand things to do.'

'Of course. I'm sorry I just barged in . . . '

'Any time,' she said. 'I really mean that. My door will always be open to you, Cyril.'

# Four

Andrew was just rattling up the grille of the lounge bar in the Talbot as Jolley, feeling rather pleased with himself yet somewhat awkward, held the door for Marion Glade. He was pleased with her, too. He had not pressed her in her first week, had told her to familiarise herself, which she had accepted without demur. Jolley had kept a deliberate distance, but her reports on her interviews with Ann Green and the Birchalls had impressed. 'Cogent' was the word he rolled around his tongue, prepared to use when he congratulated her. Very much to the point, those reports. Then again, perhaps some of his new-found warmth towards his Sergeant derived from the fact that her reports put his mind at rest. When you added it up, put it together with the blank drawn by PCs Neil and Withers, it seemed that the mysterious man seen lurking around Chuters had been, at least, a passing phenomenon. Neither Ann Green, Ronnie Birchall or his wife had seen much, a silhouette, a shadow on the green. And despite regular patrols, augmented, Jolley did not doubt, by increased vigilance on the part of the Chuters residents, there had been no further sightings. A village man out for a midnight stroll, possibly a passing motorist pausing to stretch his legs in a quiet place. There was, whichever way he looked at it, no cause to suspect any danger to Dolores Bayger.

''Morning, Mr Jolley. Your usual?' Andrew already had the glass under the pump, his eyes straying to Sergeant Glade.

'Thank you, Andrew. And good morning.'

'And for the lady?' the young barman said, smiling at her.

'Lager and lime, please. A half.'

'Andrew, this is my new sergeant, Sergeant Glade. Andrew is probably the best barman in town,' Jolley told her, 'and a very shrewd judge of character.'

'Pleased to meet you.'

'And you, miss. Hope we shall see a lot of you in here.' Andrew's glance at Jolley was approving, said something like, 'Lucky old devil.'

There were advantages to working with Marion Glade which Jolley had not expected. For form's sake, though, he frowned at Andrew.

'Will you be lunching, Mr Jolley?' the barman inquired innocently.

Jolley considered. Marion Glade followed his glance through the glass door to the spacious dining-room, which sparkled with solid silver and fine napery.

'What do you say, Sergeant?'

'Bit pricey, isn't it? Do you usually eat here?'

'Not every day,' Jolley said defensively, paying for their drinks. 'But now and again funds run to it . . . ' He picked up his pint of real ale. 'We'll let you know, Andrew. Shall we?' He nodded towards a corner table. Marion Glade led the way.

'I'd rather go where you normally eat,' she said sitting, smoothing down her denim skirt. 'Still familiarising myself, you see.'

'The Coffee Cavern,' Jolley said, feeling a tinge of disappointment. He was very fond of the Coffee Cavern but the cuisine was not in the same league as that of the Talbot. 'Cheers,' he saluted her. 'The Cavern it shall be then, but you're missing a treat.'

'Some other time, perhaps,' she said, taking a drink. Jolley was about to say that he and Hughes had kept the Talbot in reserve as a treat when they had something to celebrate or were feeling particularly low, when he realised this would be tactless. 'There are a couple of things,' Marion Glade went on, 'I'd like to discuss with you. Those missing turkey poults . . . '

94

'Ah, yes . . . ' Jolley had told her to look into that out of mischief, guessing it would be time-wasting and certainly not worthy of her talents. Now he felt slightly guilty.

'I saw Mr Smart, as you directed. There have been no further thefts, as we thought. Mr Smart is pretty sure the culprit was a young boy he employed during the school holidays. Apparently the lad is very keen on animals' rights. Mr Smart reckons he was "rescuing" a few, not to fatten up for Christmas, as we thought, but for humanitarian reasons.'

'Jack Smart's farm is meticulously run, surely?'

'Oh, absolutely. But he does breed for slaughter and it seems the lad was a bit of an idealist.'

'Name?'

'I didn't inquire, sir. Mr Smart didn't want to pursue the matter.'

Jolley liked her tact. What a policeman did not know he or she could not act upon. 'Good.'

'And he was most apologetic for bothering us.'

'I hope you told him that's what we're here for?'

'Words to that effect, sir. Now about this other business . . . '

'The Phantom Prowler of Chuters, you mean?'

'No, sir. These suicides you've been looking into . . . '

'Yes, Sergeant?' Jolley had deliberately kept that one to himself, instinctively resented her uninvited interference.

'You told me to familiarise myself, sir, so I've been looking through the files. Three things struck me— '

'Did they indeed?' Jolley's displeasure showed in his voice, but if Marion Glade noticed it, she ignored it. Probably too taken up by her 'findings' or whatever they were, Jolley thought bitterly, to notice anything.

'First, none of the people you've been to see expressed the slightest surprise that you should still be asking questions. I would have thought they'd assume, with some justification, that the cases were closed.' This was true.

Jolley was not sure, though, that he had noticed it himself. 'It struck me as odd. Of course, you can always argue that suicide is never "finished" as far as the relatives are concerned, but even so . . . it was as though they were expecting some further action, as though they weren't satisfied in their own minds . . . And then there was something very odd I noticed— '

'Excuse me . . . Jolley turned in his seat, held up his empty glass. 'Andrew, when you've got a minute. What about you, Sergeant?' She looked at her glass, barely touched.

'I'm fine, thank you.'

Andrew brought a second pint to the table.

'You were saying?' Jolley invited, bracing himself, when Andrew had walked away.

'There was no mention in any of the reports as to where Antony Corr-Beardsley's body was found. I expect you spotted that and no doubt there's some perfectly ordinary explanation . . . ' She paused, looking at him with her very clear eyes. The truth was he had not spotted it. He felt something that might be called a blush starting at the base of his neck.

'Go on,' he said.

'Naturally, I wouldn't necessarily expect to find any mention of it in *your* reports, but it should have been in Sergeant Hadfield's and it isn't.' Jolley thought that he would do something dreadful to Hadfield – but what? 'So I took the liberty of asking him. I'm afraid he hasn't got an explanation. An oversight is the best he can manage.' Damn her, did she think she was responsible for discipline as well? 'Not that it is important at this stage, but . . . when I asked Mr Hadfield he said the body was found in the ditch, or rather half in the ditch, half on the verge, outside "The Stables".'

'Was it indeed?' Jolley heard himself say and could have winced at his own play-acting. Lovelorn, then, had Corr-Beardsley made Dolores Bayger a sick present of his death? The girl had something, had spotted something he should have been on to but all he could think about, all he cared about, was the possible effect on Dolores. He took refuge in his new pint.

'It's probably not significant in itself,' Marion Glade went on, 'but since the owner of the house is mentioned so often in your reports . . . well, I thought you might be interested.'

'Thank you very much. I'm afraid Hadfield was a bit out of his depth. I should have been much more vigilant.'

'That wasn't my point,' Marion Glade said defensively. 'Anyway, you weren't even here. That was down to Inspector Lethbridge.'

'Even so . . . ' Jolley said.

'I wasn't trying to catch you out, sir, nor Mr Hadfield. I felt I ought to familiarise myself with the case and naturally it's my duty to report anything I've spotted direct to you.'

'I appreciate it,' Jolley said too quickly, even a little coldly.

'It sounds as though you resent it,' she told him frankly. 'Which I'm afraid means you won't be exactly pleased with my third point.'

'You mean there's more? My goodness you have been busy.'

'That's what I'm employed for, isn't it?'

Jolley knew there was no safe answer to this. He lifted his glass, playing for time.

'Drink up,' he said. 'It's time for lunch. The Cavern can get very crowded at this time of day. You can tell me your third piece of information while we eat.'

She took one swallow of her drink and picked up her shoulder bag. 'Right, I'm fit.'

'You haven't finished your drink.'

'Oh, I'll leave that. I'm not a heavy drinker.'

'No,' Jolley said. 'So I can see.'

The Coffee Cavern, situated at the corner of South Street and Oversleigh Market Square, traded on two floors. The lower, which employed rough plasterwork to create an impression of a cave or grotto, enhanced by cheap Italian prints – some of which, however, had a distinctly Hispanic look – was a glorified snack bar. The upper floor housed the restaurant proper and retained the look and ambience of an English tea room, circa 1950. Leading the way up the steep, dark stairs, Jolley was confronted at the top by Cheryl Dangerfield, she of the noteworthy legs and fabulous bosom, the latter today ensconced in a lime green, scoop-necked T-shirt.

'Oh, Mr Jolley. How lovely to see you,' she greeted him effusively. 'Inspector, I should say now, though, shouldn't I? Oh, we were ever so pleased, all of us, to hear about your promotion. That's really lovely. And not before time. Table by the window, as usual? And did you have a nice holiday? It seems ages since we've seen you.'

'Thank you,' Jolley said, following her across the room and assuming that those two words would serve to answer her entire speech. As he pulled out a bentwood chair from beneath the formica-topped table, Cheryl noticed his companion.

'Oh, hello, dear,' she said warmly. 'This table all right for you, Mr Jolley?'

'Yes, thanks. Cheryl, this is my new sergeant, Sergeant Glade . . . '

'Hello, Cheryl.'

'Oh! Hello.' Slightly surprised, Cheryl tucked her order pad under her left arm and tentatively shook Marion Glade's extended hand. 'Oh, she's a far cry from Dave Hughes, isn't she?' Cheryl said, laughing. 'Much prettier, anyway. Have you heard from Dave? How's he getting on?'

'No,' Jolley said shortly, turning his attention to the Market Square below. It rankled that he had not heard from Hughes and he knew he was cowardly in not making the first move.

'Oh, I shall miss him,' Cheryl said, placing cutlery wrapped in paper napkins on the table and straightening the centrepiece of condiment bottles. 'He was a real laugh was Dave, wasn't he, Mr Jolley? He used to have me in stitches. Anyway, I hope you'll be very happy, dear,' she told Marion.

'Thank you.'

'What've you got for us today, then, Cheryl?' Jolley asked, anxious to divert her from her reminiscences of David Hughes.

'Well, the special's lasagne,' she said, then lowered her voice, 'but I wouldn't if I were you. Cook's not really up to it. I mean, it's all right, but, well, don't say I didn't warn you.' She pealed with laughter.

'What do you recommend?' Marion asked.

'Well, we've got a nice quiche and the plaice is lovely, fresh in this morning. And of course you can't go wrong with a salad.'

'I'll have the plaice, then,' Marion said.

'Chips and peas and a slice? Nice cup of tea?'

'No bread, thanks. And just a glass of water.'

'Good girl. Watching your figure, eh? I should know, but in this job it's one long temptation, eh, Mr Jolley?'

'I'll have the quiche,' Jolley grunted through her laughter.

'And salad?'

'And chips.'

'Now you know what Mrs Jolley says . . . '

'Yes, but Mrs Jolley won't know because you won't tell her, Cheryl, will you?'

'Oh, you. He's a devil is Mr Jolley,' she told Marion. 'You'll have to watch him.'

Jolley studied the view. Being early-closing day, the square was already emptying, taking on that mid-week, deserted look.

'Nice woman,' Marion said as Cheryl bustled away. 'Indeed everyone round here seems very nice. I don't think I've met a soul this last week who hasn't wished me well.'

'Mm,' Jolley agreed, staring at the handsome façade of Donne House, trying not to remember too precisely

99

that last winter a young man had been stabbed to death right outside it. That was the last big case he and Hughes had worked on together, little knowing that it would be the last.

'You miss Hughes, don't you?' Marion Glade said, scattering his thoughts.

'Well . . . We worked together for a long time.'

'It's all right,' she said. 'I wouldn't expect you not to. And I know I can't replace him. Obviously. I'm not going to try, either. But I hope, well, I hope we'll work together for a long time, too.'

Jolley knew what she was trying to say and he did appreciate it, but he was not ready, yet, to respond as he knew he should. It still felt *odd* to be sitting with a young woman. He felt as though he ought to be playing host or socialising, or questioning her. It was difficult to remember that this was work, a routine lunch between colleagues. It just didn't feel right. Not yet.

'So,' he said, pushing these uncomfortable thoughts aside, 'tell me what I'm not going to like.'

'Very well. I made some inquiries of my own.'

'You did, did you?'

'I got on to a friend in Kent— '

'About Corr-Beardsley, of course.'

'Right. Look, if you'd rather— '

'No, no. Since you have been to all this trouble, I might as well hear what you've got to say.'

Marion said nothing but waited while Cheryl served their meal, smiling and checking that they had everything they wanted.

'This quiche is made by a local woman,' Jolley said. 'An excellent cook.'

'I'll try it next time.'

'Now, let me get this straight. You got on to the Kent police and asked them what, precisely?'

'To check a few things about Corr-Beardsley. All off the record. There's nothing official. As I said, I have a friend in Canterbury— '

'A police officer, I presume?'

'Yes.'

'And what did your friend turn up?'

'Corr-Beardsley came from a good family, well known in the area. Father's a JP, mother does a lot of charity work. A sister reading law. Corr-Beardsley was very close to her, apparently. He was a bit of a late developer. Read history at university, didn't settle to a job, spent a year or so travelling all over. That's when he got interested in conservation. He was in New Zealand when there was a big fuss over a rain forest . . . Then he went to South America— '

'What does all this have to do with his death? Besides, your fish is getting cold.'

Marion Glade ate for a moment or two, swallowed some of the glass of water Cheryl had brought her. 'Just background. He was unsettled, that's the point. Still unsettled, I mean. And he had a girlfriend of fairly long standing. The family confidently expected an engagement to be announced when he got back from Chuters.'

'He was here for three months, yes?'

'According to his contract, yes, but he only did two, barely that. However, he broke off with his girlfriend while he was here.'

Jolley's heart sank. He felt that he knew what was coming and he did not want to hear it.

'These things happen,' he said. 'Did he let the girl down gently?'

'I couldn't say,' Marion Glade answered. 'He did the gentlemanly thing, I suppose, went down to see her, to tell her in person. No "Dear Joan" letter . . . '

'That was considerate.'

'He did write to his sister, though, quite often and frankly. He told her he was ending the relationship with the girl because he was in love— '

'That also happens,' Jolley interrupted.

'He said he was in love with Dolores Bayger.'

The quiche seemed to turn to sawdust in his mouth. Even the chips – one of the Coffee Cavern's invariable delicacies – looked suddenly unappetising. *There's some women who can't leave any man alone . . . They like to get 'em worked up, have power over them . . . They'd have burned her for a witch a few years back . . .* Jolley pushed his plate away impatiently.

'Something wrong?'

For a moment he saw the sour face of Mrs Keene opposite him, the light glinting on her outsize spectacles. He blinked and Marion Glade's face, wearing a worried frown, replaced it.

'I think I'm becoming a little tired of all roads, all lines of inquiry leading to Dolores Bayger,' he said.

'I just thought you should know.'

'But what do I know? Corr-Beardsley came up here, met an attractive, charming woman, fell in love with her and when he found it was no dice, he took his own life. Tragic, I grant you. But you said yourself he was unsettled.'

'Unsettled, not unstable. And then there's Fred Smith and David Brimble— '

'It's all just gossip. When you've lived here a while— '

'All communities gossip. It doesn't matter where you are. What's odd is when you keep hearing the same gossip, over and over. You said yourself, all lines of inquiry lead to Dolores Bayger.'

'Coincidence. Not even that. She's an attractive woman, a stranger and that means she's a sitting target for idle gossip.'

'I wouldn't call Corr-Beardsley's disclosure to his sister gossip exactly.'

'All right. I except Corr-Beardsley. Then what have we got? A coincidence— '

'Excuse me, sir, but I thought it was the coincidence of three suicides in one small community that attracted your attention to the case in the first place.'

'That and an anonymous letter.'

'And now we have two coincidences. First the deaths themselves and now the Bayger connection.'

'That sounds like the title of a bad film.'

'I'm merely pointing out— '

'And I'm telling you that Miss Bayger just happened to be there.'

'She knew all three men.'

'Two of them through force of circumstance. She *had* to deal with Smith when she bought her house. Damn it all, she was trying to do Brimble a favour by giving him a few days' work and she insists that Corr-Beardsley was no more than a friend. She had a few drinks with him. He was lonely, far from home, as is she.'

'Then you're satisfied,' Marion said, not making a question of it. She finished her meal. Jolley watched her, fighting to keep his temper under control.

'Apple pie, trifle, summer pudding?' Cheryl took away Marion Glade's plate. 'Oh, Mr Jolley, you've hardly eaten a thing. Was it all right?'

'Fine. Not hungry.'

'Just coffee for me, please,' Marion Glade said briskly.

'You'll have some trifle, Mr Jolley?'

'No. Just coffee.'

'Well, Mrs Jolley'll be pleased anyway. I'll be sure and tell her next time she comes in. That is if you're not sickening for something.'

'No, Cheryl, I'm fine. Just not hungry.'

'Well, that's not like you,' she said, going away, shaking her head over Jolley's plate.

'Give me,' Jolley demanded, unable to leave the matter there and unwilling to play his final card, 'one good reason why I should not be satisfied by Miss Bayger's version of her relationship with Corr-Beardsley?'

'It doesn't tally with his.'

'Two people very seldom view a single situation identically. You should know that, Sergeant.'

'I mean that a woman, any woman, would know if a man felt that strongly about her. She'd know long before it got to that stage, even if he hadn't declared himself. And a man who feels that strongly *would* declare himself.'

103

'Are you talking about "female intuition"?' Jolley made no attempt to keep the scorn out of his voice.

'No. Common sense. By all accounts Miss Bayger is an intelligent, sophisticated woman. All I'm saying is she'd know, or at least have a pretty damn good idea, how Corr-Beardsley felt.'

'And what if she did?'

'She would handle the situation with kid gloves which, quite obviously, I suggest, she did not.'

'You can't know that.'

'The man killed himself, outside her house. There must have been signs. She must have known it was on the cards.'

*I have a long experience of suicide . . . Much insanity is unrecognisable, appears to be its very opposite . . . His death was a complete surprise to me.*

'Miss Bayger is a married woman. No doubt she told Corr-Beardsley that. How can she be held responsible for his death?'

'Really? I don't remember that in your report.'

Jolley looked down at the square. The shops already had their blinds up. Two girls wearing pink overalls, the uniform of the local supermarket, were climbing into a car, laughing together, presumably in anticipation of an afternoon off.

'Not everything goes into a report, Sergeant Glade. You should know that. I am content that Miss Bayger had nothing material to do with these suicides.'

'I didn't think there would be anything material. I was merely going to suggest that we should run a check on her. After all, she is an alien, travelling on an American passport.'

'Canadian, actually.'

'I see. Something else— '

'Two coffees,' Cheryl announced perkily. 'You sure you won't change your mind about afters, Mr Jolley?'

'Quite sure, thanks, Cheryl. I'm saving myself,' he told her, cheering up, 'for a large and rather special dinner tonight.'

'Oh, I might have known you were up to something. You'll have to watch him,' she told Marion again, giggling.

'So we can assume the case is closed then?'

'"We"? I'm not aware I ever put you on the case, Sergeant.'

'I was under the impression we worked together. I thought I was directly responsible to you and therefore automatically on your cases.'

'True. But when I tell you, when I ask you, not off your own bat and behind my back.'

'I did not go behind your back. I took a perfectly reasonable course of action and have reported the outcome in full to you and to no one else.'

'Next time, ask first.'

'Very well. But it will help me if I see rather more of you.'

'I shall make a note of that.'

'Thank you. *Are* you going to close the case?'

'Since I've discovered the author of that letter, yes.'

For the first time, Marion Glade looked nonplussed. Jolley felt better because he had, after all, outsmarted her.

'Charges?' she asked, but without any hope in her voice.

'It's a little like the lad who worked at the turkey farm,' he said. 'Not a lot of damage done and it won't happen again.'

'So I might have saved myself a lot of trouble,' she said miserably, staring at her coffee.

'Therein lies one of the many advantages of asking me first,' Jolley said, smiling at her. 'Now finish your coffee and let's get back to work, Sergeant.'


'You can give me a lift in and then pick me up at half nine,' Eileen said, staring at herself critically in the hall mirror, adjusting the brim of a blue hat which complimented her darker blue dress.

'Better not, love,' Jolley said, straightening his tie. 'I can't guarantee I'll be through by half-past nine. Better take your own car.'

'Oh, what a pity. I was quite looking forward to making an impression on my first night.'

'You'll make an impression all right,' Jolley told her, sitting to ease on the grey casual shoes she had persuaded him to buy last Christmas and which he had hardly ever worn. 'Going to a pottery class in an Ascot hat.'

'It's a perfectly ordinary hat,' she contradicted him, 'and I meant make an impression by being collected by my handsome, incredibly well-dressed husband.' She bent over him, brushing at the shoulder of his best dove-grey suit. 'Where are you going, anyway?'

'Oh . . . I've got a couple of calls to make,' he said, standing up.

'I didn't know you had a big case on.'

'You don't know everything.'

'And mustn't ask. All right. Well, I'll see you later, then. Wish me luck.'

'You'll wow them,' he said, kissing her lightly on the offered lips.

'And so, I've no doubt, will you.'

She went through the kitchen and out by the back door. Jolley heaved a sigh, inspected his grey and white striped shirt collar in the mirror.

'Cy? Don't forget to lock up.'

His face looked guiltily back at him. 'Of course I'll lock up.'

He continued to stare at himself as he listened to the sound of her Metro starting and drawing away. She sounded the horn once before turning into the high street. Time, he thought, for a drink before leaving. He did not want to appear too eager. But he did not move. He felt like a kid again, a boy of twenty. There were butterflies in his stomach, an itchy restlessness that demanded he should be off and moving. It was ridiculous, of course. He should have that drink and make it last.

He poured it and stood holding it, staring out of the window into the high street. A fine, warm night, Indian summer. And that's what this is for you, he thought, taking a swig of his whisky and water. Fantasies and feelings aside, he was a middle-aged man and the butterflies could as easily be attributed to subterfuge and tension as to excited anticipation. He tried to persuade himself that he had not lied to Eileen, not as such. He didn't talk about his cases, she didn't ask. There had been no point in passing on Dolores Bayger's invitation since she was going to her class. Withholding information wasn't really lying.

'Bloody liar,' he said aloud, scowling.

In a sense this *was* business. He was on a case. The drink tasted unpleasant in his mouth and he put it down beside the record player. Why not just relax and enjoy it? He could ask her about the location of Corr-Beardsley's body but he almost knew he would not. In a sense the case really was closed now, and this was the final celebration, the tying up of loose ends. He would probably never see Dolores Bayger again after tonight.

He slammed and locked the back door, checked it out of habit. He had put his car in the garage to leave the narrow drive free for Eileen. He was certain of one thing. She had not seen the bouquet he had collected from Philip's late that afternoon and stowed in the boot, throwing an old rug over it as an extra precaution. How absurdly guilty he had felt doing that. As if a man should go empty-handed to dinner. He backed the car into the quiet high street and realised that he had not put the outside lights on. Damn it. He was not going back now. It would scarcely be dark anyway when Eileen got home and there was a case to be made that the light only advertised their absence. The whole of Clifton Kings would know they had gone out, separately and both dressed up to the nines.

Even so he avoided Oversleigh, taking the long way round. Not because he did not want to be seen but because he had time to spare, wanted to arrive a few minutes late. He went via Brindsleigh, driving down into the village and turning sharp left at the pub. The back road as it was always known, followed the course of the river, more or less, and debouched on to a good B road half a mile from the Chuters turn-off. It was just on eight when he entered Chuters Lane. The trees made it seem already dark. There were a few people drinking on the village green, outside The Clouded Yellow, the lights of which glowed invitingly. Heads turned, of course, to follow his slow passage past the pub. He parked opposite her gate, drawing well up on to the verge. Just about where Corr-Beardsley must have done for himself, he thought, as he switched off the engine. The verge was bounded by a ditch and a well-kept hedge. Beyond that lay a small patch of allotments where estate tenants had once grown additional vegetables. Getting out of the car and deliberately peering over the hedge, Jolley saw that few bothered to cultivate now. The well-tended plots were easily outnumbered by those given over to weeds. A few neglected raspberry canes had rampaged, wild and uncared for. He walked around the front of the car, looking eagerly across at the house. Unlike the pub it was dark and somnolent-looking, but door and windows stood open, inviting. The air felt heavy, humid, was very still. He opened the boot and tossed aside the rug. The bouquet lay in its cellophane sheath, a fancy bow of blue fake ribbon around the long stems of delicately tinted chrysanthemums and he did not know what other flowers. He felt self-conscious to the point of foolishness carrying the bouquet. It was too large and ostentatious, would undoubtedly set tongues wagging.

'I thought I heard a car.' She appeared in the doorway, out of shadow. Her eyes dropped from his to the bouquet which, stiffly, he pushed towards her. 'Oh, you shouldn't have. Thank you.' She took the flowers and held them against her chest, looking at him, not smiling. Framed by her glossy black hair, her face looked pale yet seemed to glow in the semi-dark. 'Come in,' she said, turning, leading the way.

Her dress, which Jolley had not had time to take in, was virtually backless, flared out over her hips in silky folds. The expanse of bare back advertised the fact that she could not possibly be wearing a bra. He summoned the policeman in him, tried to fix exactly the colour of the dress but gave up in the sepia, softening dark.

She turned to face him as he entered the long room, the skirt swirling about her legs. 'Fix yourself a drink, would you, while I put these in water? I won't be a moment.' As she went towards the door she paused for a moment to turn up the volume on the record player.

Jolley smelled her scent and heard Callas launch into her hymn to the chaste moon. He experienced an unbearable tension, his restlessness having turned to a sort of heavy, leaden listlessness. The lace curtains obscured the windows, making the room almost dark. He went towards a tall lamp and clumsily, rattling the shade, searched for the switch. Its soft light glinted suddenly on a tray of glasses, bottles and decanters set on a low table behind the large settee. He needed a drink. His hand was slightly unsteady when he poured and he made it a stiff one. He did not understand why he almost wished he had not come.

'Chrysanthemums,' she said, coming back into the room. 'I love their scent and yet it's so sad, so autumnal. Don't you think?' She brushed past him, the flowers in a tall vase of clear glass which she placed beneath the back window. Jolley watched her tweak and fuss at them or rather watched the subtle play of shadow and light on her bare back. She had strong, prominent shoulder-blades. He cleared his throat. 'They're gorgeous. Thank you. Now have you got a drink?' He showed her the glass he held. 'Good. And Callas is to your taste, of course.' She smiled. The dress was cut straight across the line of her throat, clung to her bosom.

'Very much so. May I get you a drink?'

'Oh . . . please. A gin and tonic. No lemon.'

He put down his glass and began to mix her drink. He heard her move, sit down behind him.

'My wife . . .' he said, or began to say, his throat clogging, requiring to be cleared again. 'My wife sends

109

her apologies. I had completely forgotten that she had a long-standing arrangement herself for tonight. With my daughter.' The lie flowed easily off his tongue, extempore. She was seated on the little settle, her legs crossed. He carried her drink to her. 'She hopes you like the flowers.' Once you begin, he thought, avoiding her look, it is very difficult to stop.

'Please tell her that I do, very much. Cheers.'

Her eyes shone at him as she raised the glass and drank. 'Won't you sit down? You seem . . . nervous.'

Jolley, reminded by his recent lies that honesty is supposed to be the best policy, looking around for a chair, took the one on which she had sat at their first meeting.

'I am nervous,' he admitted. 'It's a very long time since I dined alone with a beautiful woman.'

'Oh, I don't believe that. I hear your wife is very attractive.'

'How did you come to hear that, I wonder?'

'Oh, I've been checking up on you. After all, you are a policeman. That gives you an advantage. I have to protect myself.'

'So you've been playing detective.'

'A little.'

'And what have you discovered?'

'Oh, nothing . . . revelatory. That you like avocado mousse, for example, but not plain avocados.'

'And how did you discover that?'

'The chef at the King's Palfrey in Seddington. I understand you also like steak and kidney and mushroom pie, but that is way beyond my capabilities. And then, of course, I know your taste in music . . . '

'*Some* of my taste in music,' he corrected her. 'You've been very thorough. What colour is that dress?'

'This?' She looked startled, looked down at the skirt, smoothed her hand along it. 'Green,' she said brightly, looking up at him, raising her glass.

'Er . . . ' He realised then that she must be colour-blind, badly so. That explained her surprise at his question, the slight defiance he heard echoing in her tone. The dress was an unusual, dark but definite red. 'It's very becoming,' he said.

'Thank you. But why?'

'My wife will want to know what you are wearing, everything about you.'

'Not quite everything, I hope. But you may tell her that my dress is green silk jersey and a thousand years old.' She laughed and he joined in. 'Why don't you put another record on while I go check on the food?'

He loved this little imperfection in her, was deeply touched by it. How on earth did she manage to drive, he wondered? Did she drive? He had never seen a car . . . He put the record away, looked through her collection. It was uncannily similar to his own and suddenly he did not want music, wanted her company, voice uninterrupted. He stood up and went to the door, turned in the direction of the kitchen which was brightly lit.

'Can I do anything?'

There was no reply. Through the partially open door the kitchen looked empty. He felt almost afraid for a moment, then thought she must have stepped outside, into the yard. Turning in the narrow hallway, he almost collided with her. For a second, startled, they simply stared at each other. Jolley wanted to reach out, touch her.

'I was just wondering— '

'I was checking the table . . . ' She indicated a door beside her which led, evidently, into the dining-room.

'I'm sorry.'

'We'd better eat the mousse now or the chicken will be spoiled. Excuse me.' He stood aside awkwardly to let her pass. 'I won't be long.'

Candlelight gleamed on a long black table, on modern silver and white napkins. There was no other light in the room so that beyond and all about the table deep shadows pressed. She had set just the two places, intimately together at one end of the table. Only two places, he thought, his blood quickening and then realised that she

111

must have removed the third, that that was what she meant by 'checking the table'. But he could see no sign of extra crockery, a third chair. Perhaps, after all, she had expected only him. He smiled at her as she came quietly back into the room.

The meal passed in a haze of pleasure. Jolley was scarcely aware of what they talked about, only that talking to her was easy, light, inconsequential. The wine was good and perfectly chilled, the mousse smooth and creamy, followed by lemon chicken, asparagus tips and green salad in a delicate dressing. He thought that Eileen would have approved and frowned at himself. Several times their hands touched and his fingers burned with the sensation of her skin lightly on his. She laughed, throwing back her head. She made him laugh. And apart from glances at his food, he could not take his eyes off her. She seemed aware of his gaze but not in a coy way, as though she was used to it, welcomed it. The summer pudding was the best he had ever eaten, the ideal combination of sharp and sweet, oozing blood-red juice, liberally topped with cream. He was replete, relaxed and, he was almost ready to admit to himself, deeply in love.

'Coffee? Cognac?'

'Both sound wonderful. Later.'

'These chairs are not very comfortable.'

'I am very comfortable. Very full. Very comfortable.'

'I'm glad.'

'We can sit for a minute.'

'Sure.'

He watched her fold a napkin, place it beside her plate with a little pat. He smiled suddenly thinking how nice it would be . . .

'Why do you smile?'

'Contentment. And a touch of guilt.'

'Oh, I don't like guilt. Don't let's talk of guilt.'

'I meant only that I ought to help clear the table, perhaps even wash up.'

'Is that all? Well, there's no need. You can put your

112

conscience to bed. I'll clear away in the morning and I have a very efficient dishwasher.'

'You are a woman who thinks of everything.'

'Ah . . . I hope so. I hope so very much indeed.'

'Where are you going?'

'Coffee.'

'Must you?'

'Yes, I must. It's already late and you've forgotten that you have to earn your dinner.'

'Do I? How?'

'You really have forgotten. I said I'd show you some of my work.'

'So you did.'

'Do you mind?'

'I'd like it very much. A person's work always tells you a great deal about them.'

'Don't be a policeman tonight, please. I just want you to . . . say what you think.'

'I told you I'm no expert.'

'I don't take pictures for experts. I just want to show them another world.'

Looking up into her dark, intense eyes, Jolley said, 'You do. You really do.'

'Flattery will get you everywhere. You haven't even seen them yet. You go fix yourself a drink and I'll make the coffee. Go on now.'

'Yes, madam. And thank you for a wonderful dinner.'

In the sitting-room he put on more lights, poured two generous brandies, sat on the big sofa at the far end of the room. All his nervousness had gone. He felt at home, very much at home. This room welcomed him, drew him in. He strained his ears to hear her moving in the kitchen but she moved silently, gracefully. He smelled fresh coffee. He took a little sip of brandy, holding it in his mouth, savouring its warmth. She would come back into the room in a minute . . . They would look at her pictures and talk . . . Perhaps they would play another record . . .

113

'I get ridiculously nervous showing my work. I never know how people are going to react ... '

He had not heard her return, sat up, twisted around. She stood behind the sofa, the drinks table, a heavy, black ring-binder clutched in both hands, held against her thighs as though its weight dragged on her slim wrists. She looked like a shy, awkward but very excited little girl. He wanted to reassure her, tell her not to worry, come, sit down ... Before he could say anything, she held the folder out towards him, like an offering.

'Here. You look while I get the coffee. Please ... ' Her tone, her eyes beseeched him. He put his glass down and reached across the back of the sofa, took the heavy folder from her. 'I'll just fix the lamps.' He held its considerable weight on his knees while she adjusted the lamp behind him, tilting its shade a little so that the light was concentrated on him, the folder. 'All right. I won't be a minute ... ' Her nervousness, he realised, excited him. Like the colour blindness, this was a kind of flaw, a change in her who seemed always so confident, so capable. And yet she could be like a little girl, hesitant and vulnerable but slightly demanding, amazingly uncertain of her own worth. That nervousness made him powerful, aware that she could be damaged, that beneath her poise was a softness, something not quite formed, fresh ... He opened the folder.

Each large black and white photograph was contained in a plastic envelope. He was reminded, fleetingly, of Lethbridge's reports, but only because his mind needed a moment to get over the shock. To be precise, each envelope contained two prints, back to back. He turned several at once, instinctively seeking a change of subject-matter. There appeared to be none. He went back to the beginning, turning each plastic page slowly, easing each set of holes around the ring-binder with careful fingers. They were all photographs of men. Nude men.

Some years ago, Jolley had been reluctantly involved in a pornography case, had learned the niceties of definition and distinction between the pornographic and the erotic. These pictures were not pornographic. He supposed they were erotic. How could he tell? Some were cropped, showed a mere portion of the body, a torso, a thigh with a clenched fist resting on it. The detail was precise, sharp and clear, the lighting, as far as he was competent to judge, expert. They were very good photographs, very professional. He supposed they were erotic but they struck him as ugly. He did not want to look at them. A woman, he realised in such and such a pose, the head thrown back so, the lips parted, the body taut and exposed . . . *That* he would perceive as erotic, but these pictures had a cold and chilling air. So much naked flesh, depersonalised, spread out . . . Suddenly he found the male body ugly, though he had never thought so before. And these were obviously healthy, honed, fit bodies, young bodies. They were beautiful but in an aseptic way. The manner of their depiction was ugly.

Again he turned several pages at once, barely glancing at the apparently endless, scarcely changing parade of flesh. Dead flesh, he thought. That was the trouble. Like specimens pinned by light and lens.

Then, at the very back of the folder, were six photographs of a face only, a terrible face. There was no mistaking a change in style, even to an amateur like him. The lighting, for example, was here bright, cold, flat, banishing shadows which before had softened and caressed the dead flesh. This merciless light showed the face more naked than any body could ever be. In some the eyes were actually rendered blind by light. It was a handsome face, long and bony, sculpted. Two wings of dark hair fell back from it. Stubble pock-marked it. Jolley shook his own head impatiently, perhaps a little in sorrow. All that was beside the point. This was a face, again depersonalised – almost a severed head, he thought wildly – photographed *in extremis*, a face made horrible and brittle by pain, nightmares, who knew what agonies? Impulsively he shut the book, the heavy leather covers closing with an unexpectedly loud thudding sound.

'You're shocked.'

He caught his breath sharply. How long had she been standing there, near the record player, looking across at him, studying him? Caught in his own pool of light he could only see her face as a white blur. The light faded half-way up her dark, red dress. The dress she claimed was green. She did not move, did not say anything more. Studying him in his light as she must have studied that face through her cold, implacable lens.

'No,' he said, sounding false and uncertain. 'No, not shocked. Surprised, yes— '

'What did you expect?' Her tone was sharp, interrogatory.

'I . . . honestly don't know. Nothing as powerful as these, certainly.'

'You think they are powerful?'

'Very much so. Uncomfortably so.'

'Oh, that's good. Oh, thank you for that.'

She came forward then, almost ran, sat on the edge of the armchair opposite him, her face thrust forward, her chin resting on closed fists. Her eyes burned with expectation, desire. Embarrassed, Jolley felt for his drink on the floor, picked it up and sipped gratefully.

'I knew . . . I *felt* you were a man who would understand. Most men – they just don't get the point. They are shocked, threatened. They don't see that these are *political* pictures.'

Jolley swallowed his brandy. 'Powerfully so,' he repeated.

'If they were of women . . . But of course you see that. You see what I'm trying to do.'

'Definitely. If they were women . . . your . . . models . . . they would be entirely different.' Jolley floundered.

'And because they are not women, you can see how women are debased and dehumanised by such poses. If you can see that then I have succeeded.' She threw herself back in the chair, lounged in it, her hands on the arms. 'I can't tell you what that means to me. For a woman to attempt, even to attempt to put herself into a man's shoes, to see through his eyes . . . Well, it took some doing,

116

can tell you. I had to learn how to see. I had to unlearn a whole cultural programme, years of conditioning, my own inhibitions, the men's inhibitions . . . You can imagine.'

Jolley nodded, felt suddenly naked himself, and awkward. 'The faces at the end— ' he began.

'Oh, those are much later.' She bounced up out of her chair, her step light and girlish. 'Coffee? That's part of a whole new sequence. Something I'm still working on. I'm not sure where it will lead. The idea is still only partly formed . . . '

'They are very disturbing,' Jolley said, thinking that that was an understatement if ever he had made one.

'Cream? Sugar?'

'No. Just black, please.'

'Disturbing. Yes, I guess. I want to concentrate on the eyes. Maybe just the eyes, eventually. I don't know. Windows on the soul, you know? Or is that a cliché?' She handed him a cup of coffee, almost absently. She went on talking, her voice rising, almost hysterically, laughter threatening. 'Can you imagine the effect my nudes had when I exhibited them?'

'It must have been . . . very effective. You exhibited them?'

'Sure. In the States. It was a great success and *very* controversial. It attracted a lot of attention . . . '

'I'm sure.'

She sat again, opposite him, her cup balanced on her knees, a flush of colour on either pale cheek, her eyes glittering. 'I was going to prepare a second exhibition pretty quickly, but that's when things got really difficult with my husband and, well, then . . . It's taken me a while to get back into it. But now, with the faces and the ravens, I feel! . . . I feel I'm really getting back into it and that feels good. It really does feel good.' She shook her head as she said this, as though she could not quite believe in her own good fortune. She was basically talking to herself, he thought, and drank his coffee down quickly, in one gulp. 'A little bit of you is shocked,' she said, her voice becoming low and serious again.

'Not in the way you think,' he said, equally serious. 'That face, in particular, disturbs me. Such a sense of pain there.'

'Yes.'

'I can't think how you managed it.'

'Oh . . . it's just another way of seeing.' She sounded guarded. 'Once you're behind the camera you're . . . '

'Immune?'

'Sort of. I guess.'

'I mean that I don't understand how you could bear to look on such pain and press the trigger or whatever it is one does.'

She laughed at this, flicking back her hair. Jolley realised how unfortunate his choice of word was. That face could have been staring at the barrel of a gun. But that wasn't it. The gun was inside, waiting to go off.

'It's just a trick,' she was saying. 'Professionalism. I'm not a cold or uncaring person . . . '

'I didn't mean— '

'You must see some terrible things yourself, much worse things. How do you manage?'

'I honestly don't know. You're right. One does.' But I am not, he thought, deliberately looking. I don't just stand and gloat dispassionately. He jibbed at this thought. By what right did he assume she gloated?

'In a way those pictures stopped me going mad.'

'Oh?' Jolley was surprised, could more easily imagine that taking them would produce the opposite effect.

'They enabled me to . . . detach myself from a totally destructive situation.'

'I don't follow you.'

'They are photographs of my husband.'

He felt ashamed then. He had misjudged her, formed an opinion on a scrap of evidence. Now, as this shocking but entirely comprehensible piece of information lent perspective, he understood why the pictures had so moved

118

him. He looked at her tenderly, contrite. The pain in those photographs was as much hers as the man's. That's what made them so powerful.

'I'm sorry,' he said.

'Whatever for? You're absolutely— '

'I almost misjudged you.'

'Did you? Oh, well, I guess I'm used to that.'

'Even so— '

'The important thing is, dear Cyril, that little word "almost".' She leaned towards him, held out her hand across the space between them. Jolley took it, held it in his. 'Don't say anything,' she said, almost in a whisper. 'We understand each other too well, you and I.' She increased the pressure on his hand for a moment and then slowly, with a kind of regret, drew hers away. 'I'm being a terrible hostess,' she said.

Jolley lifted the heavy folder from his knees and placed it on the cushion beside him. 'I really ought to be going,' he said, and finished his brandy quickly.

'So soon?'

'It's already late for me,' he said, glancing at his watch and standing up. She slumped back in her chair again. He was aware of looming over her. Her legs parted slightly. Her arms moved, lifted. 'I'm a working man. I must make an early start. And you've got all that washing-up to do.'

'I told you, I have a machine . . . ' She let her arms fall, levered herself up from the deep chair and, with the barest of glances at him, walked into the centre of the room.

'It's been a lovely evening.' He did not want to go, made himself walk past her when all he wanted to do was touch her. He thought of those photographs, a stain on the evening, and opened the door into the hall.

'Thank you for the flowers . . . and the talk . . . and, above all, thank you for understanding my pictures.' She leaned towards him with a slowness that was deliberate and studied. Her face swam out of focus as she lifted her lips to his and kissed him. Jolley managed, somehow, to stand like a statue when every instinct prompted him to seize her, crush her against him, run his hands across her naked back, bury his face in her hair . . . Her eyes were laughing at him. 'And so good-night, Mr Policeman Cyril.'

Outside, Jolley stood stock still on the path, his head reeling. The darkness was total. If Chuters had street lighting, it was obviously switched off at midnight. The brandy on top of the wine made the blood pound in his temples. Slowly, her lingering scent faded from his nostrils. He took several deep breaths and recognised the sweetness of honeysuckle. He looked around for its source but could only make out the boldest shapes and those dimly. There was no moon and the air had an airless, occlusive quality. He began to walk tentatively to the gate. The honeysuckle smell seemed to follow him. It must be of the late Dutch variety Eileen was always talking of buying. He could not remember the Latin name. He got the gate open, scraped one foot unsteadily on the slight rise of the road. He was in no fit state to drive. Leaning on the gate he looked up at the sky. Moon and stars were hidden by a blanket of cloud. No breeze, no breath, he thought, and pulled the gate shut behind him. He looked across at the dark bulk of his car but began to walk away from it, towards the dead end of Chuters, the wood.

He could have been with her now. No use lying to yourself, he thought, ambling rather than walking, grateful for the darkness which offered no distractions. Even if he went back now, he would find a welcome. Some things were just known, felt. She had put out the right signals and he, he supposed, had behaved like the callow boy he had felt himself to be earlier. God knew it wasn't moral strength or even moral scruples that had kept his arms still by his side, that had numbed his lips when she kissed him. In such situations notions of right and wrong and consequences seemed like so much air, became insubstantial, a subject for another time. He wasn't ready, wasn't sure. She confused him. It was, he thought, stopping suddenly, those damned pictures.

He looked up but could make out nothing but a line of greater darkness where the trees began. Trees to his left as well, encroaching. He would go a little further, to the edge of that darkness, just to clear his head.

He understood about the pictures. They sprang from an intellectual need to make a point, a valid point, he was prepared to admit. But the face was something else again. A good-looking bloke, her husband, or had been. Was that it? He stopped again, in surprise this time. The knowledge that that ravaged face belonged to her husband had inhibited him? Not thoughts of Eileen, his children, marriage, his career but her husband? He shook his head and turned around. Shaking his head was not a good idea, made things swim. Deep breaths, he told himself, a steady pace. She must have been under the most incredible strain when she took those pictures. Yes, but they were still cruel, unforgiving. She had had to be a little mad herself to save herself from madness. Or just uncaring. God knew that war correspondents, photo-journalists, were daily taking shots that made those look quite harmless. But not of their husbands. Not with that cold, clinical detachment. Come at it how he may, those photographs had done something to him, had given her a perspective that he did not like, could not handle. But for them he would probably be in her bed now, in ecstasy, lost. Instead of which he was pounding a country road, puzzling his head with something that was none of his business, that had happened long ago and which, probably, he would not understand anyway. Who was he to judge her work, her motives? How could a few pictures detract from his feelings for her as a woman?

The skin on the back of Jolley's neck suddenly began to prickle. Training, instinct made him keep walking, maintain the steady rhythm of his pace. He had the uncanny feeling that he was being observed, watched. Well, of course, he thought with relief. This was Chuters. The busybodies would be looking on in force. Except that there was no house near and no one abroad. He looked to his right, to the trees. Any one of them could have held a watcher in its shadow. He scoured the tree-line for a sign of movement, the tell-tale paleness of a face, watching. Fancy offered him many sightings which immediately revealed themselves as chimeras. Imagining things. A guilty conscience playing tricks upon him. He kept walking, looking around now, watching the outline of her house come closer, take on ever greater solidity. And the sensation of being watched, dogged by coldly curious eyes increased. He stopped suddenly then spun around, challenging whatever was there. There was nothing. Nothing to be seen or heard.

Time you were home and in bed, he told himself. You're too old for this kind of lark. You've lost your bottle, Cy, old man. He smiled then, but sadly, like a man who stares defeat in the face.

Her house was without lights, closed up. It was too poignant to think of her up there somewhere, behind one of those black windows, lying . . . He had made his decision when she had kissed him. Or perhaps he had read too much into that kiss? No. He had held back. What was it Eileen had said about him being a terrible flirt? Perhaps that was all he was good for, then. A burned-out case, dressed in flirtatious gallantry.

He felt for his car keys, walked decidedly across the road, thinking that he would have to watch out for that ditch in the dark. He didn't want to go home with a twisted ankle. A man could stand only so much ignominy in one night. He put his hand on the cool metal of the bonnet, peering down at the verge, looking for the edge of the ditch. He sensed something behind him, something approaching, coming at him. He swung around, confused and very frightened. He heard it then, a distinct, lazy flapping sound. He put up his arm, ducked his face aside. He never did see it, not really, not well enough to describe it, but he felt a movement in the air, a breath of wind, and heard the sound. He flung his arm out and would have sworn that, for a second, he felt feathers. Then he stepped back, lost his balance and fell heavily on his backside into the ditch.

The ditch was surprisingly deep. The impact of his

considerable weight hitting the ground jarred and hurt his spine. His head was half in the hedge and his legs were sticking up comically. The whole thing would have made him laugh if he had not been the butt of the joke, if he had not known that birds don't fly at night, except for owls, and he would stake a year's salary that it had been no owl. Somehow he knew it was a raven and that was impossible. He lifted his head, knowing that it would be a laborious and undignified business getting himself out of the ditch. It would take a bit of thought how best to do it. Thank God at least it was dry.

He saw it then, a definite movement near the side of the house. No more than that, just movement in the darkness. Something moving away, back deeper into the trees. His face reddened at the thought that he had been seen in this ludicrous position. And then he thought it must have been a trick of his own imagining. Self-punishment, the psychiatrists called it. Punishment for the deed not done, for wanting . . . He heaved himself over, using his elbows to propel himself into a semi-kneeling position, backside now aloft and no doubt deserving a damned good kicking. Some twig or branch in the hedge scraped his right cheek painfully. He swore, not quite under his breath, and straightened himself up. The suit would have to go to the cleaners. No doubt Eileen would have plenty to say about that. He managed to reach out and grasp the handle of the car's door. Slowly, he pulled himself up, leaned panting against the car. He felt something moist and warm running down his cheek and put his hand up to feel the trickle of blood. He swore again and then grimaced at the flash of pain in his lower back as he straightened up.

'What a bloody farce,' he said out loud, fishing in his pocket for his keys.

He did not care if someone was watching, lurking in the trees. He had had enough. Holding a clean handkerchief to his face, he got the keys out and into the lock, fumbling, pulled the door open. The interior light flashed on, a blessing. He sat, wincing with pain, one leg still outside the car, propping the door open. He grabbed the mirror and twisted it to inspect his face. It was only a superficial scratch, probably caused by a briar. The flesh on either side of the scratch was puffy, the blood already beading into a crust. He realigned the mirror and dropped the handkerchief into his lap. He would live, though his back gave him gyp with every movement. He closed the door and started the car, trying to ignore the stab of pain when he depressed the pedal. His lights flooded the road ahead, spread to the tree-line. Empty, innocent, nothing. But just to make sure he drove up to the end of the road, his eyes skinned and checking left and right as well as ahead. He made an awkward three-point turn and drove back past her pitch-dark house. It must have been an owl, he thought, but whoever had heard of a black owl that mistook an overweight man for a scuttling mouse?

Then he managed to smile and that made the scratch on his cheek smart.

# Five

The knowledge that he would never see Dolores Bayger again was like a leaden weight in his chest. It coloured all his days and much of his erotically charged and restless nights. Would never see her again alone, by appointment, as he had seen her last, just over a week ago. The possibility that he would see her again, by chance, was a perpetual but forlorn hope which caused him to stop now, on the curb outside the cleaners in West Street, looking left and right, up and down.

The Indian summer had passed as had something equally uncertain, infinitely more precious, and as he stood there a sudden wind caught at the plastic bag which covered his dove-grey suit and made it rustle. He walked into the road which did not contain her and opened the car door, tossed the suit on to the back seat, got in. He sat glaring at the rear-view mirror. There was a woman struggling against the distinctly autumnal wind. She was tall and she had black hair but she bore no true resemblance to Dolores Bayger. She was heavier, less graceful, older. As she drew closer, he saw that her hair was unnaturally black with dye, not jet and glossy as a raven's wing.

He started the car, fastened his seatbelt with more ease than he could remember. It was true then that he had lost weight. It was probably equally true that he was like a bear with a perpetually sore head. Eileen had made both comments, with a tight-lipped, worried look.

He overtook the woman as he drove away. Her lack of resemblance to Dolores Bayger made him angry. It had been a long, empty week. He had attended a conference in the county town on drug detection and had hung around the less salubrious local pubs putting his newly acquired knowledge into supposed practice. It had helped to fill the time, especially the impossible evenings. He had interfered in other investigations which required no help from him. He had nursed his pain and his regrets through almost eight long days and the ache and disappointment had not lessened. He had often filled the time by composing endless notes to her in his head. One had begun to be a reality, inscribed on paper only to be torn up and flushed down the lavatory. An adolescent action, he had thought at the time. More like that of a guilty, middle-aged man, he now admitted.

At any other time, in any other mood he would have welcomed and been intrigued by this sudden invitation to lunch with his daughter. Now he viewed it as another burden, an unwanted distraction from the satisfaction of picking his self-inflicted wound. The scratch on his face had healed up. His suit was as good as new. In time he would be restored to himself again and the name Dolores Bayger would cause his heart to lurch only a little. He knew all this. He even believed it, but like the intermittent pain in his coccyx, only souvenir of that night, he knew that it would not be so yet.

Leaving the town, he realised that he was not even curious to know why Audra wanted to see him so suddenly. Worse, he did not even want to see her and that made him feel sick with self-disgust. He loved her, after all. Of course he did. He loved his children equally and if he got on better with James, or had until he learned about James's homosexuality, it was only because they were father and son, had the unspoken communality of male creatures in a female world. Eileen said that was bosh. His coolness towards, his distance from Audra was, according to Eileen the oracle, entirely due to the fact that they were too much alike. Audra, Eileen always maintained, was her father's child and she could get the best of him when she wanted. What she would want today would be a cosy family chat neither of them really enjoyed. One of her long-time-no-see-and-I've-missed-you-how-*are*-you-really meetings in which she would tell him, once the niceties were out of the way, how fabulously well her husband was doing and was Jolley really still so upset about James? What Eileen called Audra trying to have a good relationship with him and to which he always replied that he had a perfectly good relationship with her and the best thing about children was that they grew up and left home and got immersed in their own lives and, by implication, should leave their long-suffering father alone.

He should have told her no, he was too busy. She would have accepted that. But by accepting her invitation he had provided himself with a bona fide excuse not to have to spend his lunch time with Marion Glade or Eileen or alone. Under other circumstances, of course, he might have spent it with Dolores Bayger. He put the radio on, occupied himself for several minutes identifying the music pouring from the speakers as Shostakovitch's Seventh, and felt pleased with himself. At least there was still music.

He had decided that he would not see Dolores Bayger again when he faced the fact that he had been drunk. There had been no watcher in the woods, no night-flying raven. There had been a deserved and undignified tumble into a ditch, leading to more lies by implication to his wife. He had let her believe there had been 'a bit of trouble', that he had been out on a case. At the same time he had known that if he did not put an end to this madness soon, there would be no more cases. He was putting his job in jeopardy as well as everything else he held dear. Of course he could just take off with Dolores Bayger somewhere, leave the lot of it, start again . . .

The symphony ended, or rather one of its movements, and Jolley, unable to tell which, switched the radio off. Like a man waking suddenly, he saw that he was already approaching Audra's village. There was another thing, driving without due care and attention . . . Trusting to luck that if a dangerous situation developed he would snap out of his wool-gathering and take the right action. But he had no idea how much of a danger he represented, driving as he so often did now on a sort of automatic pilot. He slowed for a bend, changed gear smoothly as the gradient increased. Perhaps Audra would be able to hold his attention, keep the endless thoughts at bay. But even if she did, he thought, his heart sinking again, they would be waiting for him, like a presence, in the car, whenever he might be alone.

Strictly speaking, Audra and Peter did not live in the village, but in a field atop the hill, from which it was possible to look down into the village. Today, as he turned into the long gravel drive, only the top of the church spire stood above the trees. There were tints of autumn in these trees and their leafy tops moved and bent in the wind. Audra's barn loomed ahead. He thought as he always thought that Audra and Peter did not really live anywhere. A barn in a field, albeit expensively converted and landscaped respectively. But that's what it was. And it was transient. They were already talking of selling, moving on. Perhaps another conversion, perhaps this time his architect son-in-law would design and build his own house. But, as far as Jolley was concerned, they didn't live anywhere.

As he revved the engine before switching it off, Audra appeared in the doorway. She wore jeans and a checked shirt in pastel colours. She did not come to greet him but waited in the doorway, watching him. Jolley realised that he should have brought something, some little token gift, but it was too late now. He doubted that she would mind. He always left that sort of thing to her mother anyway, so it would scarcely be expected of him. Except, of course, for the bouquet he had taken to Dolores Bayger. For a moment Jolley rested against the car, his face hidden from his daughter, willing himself to forget, put it all out of his mind.

'Come on, it's chilly out here,' Audra shouted and he turned, smiling broadly, and went towards her. She offered him each cheek in turn to kiss, holding his upper arms lightly in her hands. Audra had been dying her hair for years, convinced that she had inherited the gene that turned her mother's and her grandmother's hair white by the time they were thirty. Today it was the colour of a ripe conker and cut very short. The effect was to make her face look much larger. Jolley could never see the resemblance between them, though everyone else commented on it. He wondered if Audra could see it and if she minded. 'Come on in,' she said. 'Don't you think it's cold?'

He did not bother to reply but followed her into the house. It did not have rooms but areas and designated spaces. Despite the fact that a small fortune had been spent on furnishing it, it always looked under-furnished to Jolley. Eileen said this was nonsense, there was plenty of furniture. Maybe so, Jolley thought, but each piece, having made its statement, disappeared into the space about it. He paused for a second, looked at a great grey vase-thing which stood on the blond floor, its shape melting into the light from the enormous church-like window behind it. He was slightly relieved to see that Audra was standing, looking at him, in the eating/cooking area. At least the chairs were reasonably comfortable there.

'I won't offer you a drink,' she said, 'seeing you're on duty and driving. Apple juice?'

'Thanks.'

He pulled a straight white chair from beneath the stiff white refectory table and sat. Audra was silhouetted against the light of another window. A lamp hung too low over the table, obscuring the view straight ahead. Its shape, he realised, studying it, echoed that of the vase and – at this he felt really pleased with himself – that of a large white dish on the table which, for some unaccountable reason, contained a collection of what he was sure were cobble-stones.

'How are you getting on with your new deputy? Marion something, isn't that her name?' She gave him a tall glass of apple juice on a round white coaster and stood near him, arms folded, scrutinising him.

'Oh, fine. Glade,' he added, picking up the glass and watching the coaster melt into the table. 'Sergeant Glade.'

'I think that was really brave of you, Daddy. Taking on a woman, I mean. I'm very proud of you.' She turned away without seeing the wince of embarrassment her words caused him. He particularly wished she would not call him 'Daddy'.

'There was nothing brave about it, I can assure you. It was a case of Hobson's choice and whether it'll work out . . . Well, it's early days yet.'

'Of course it will. So, how have you been? It's ages since I saw you.'

'Fine. Plodding along.'

'Mummy says you really enjoyed your holiday. Lots of lovely music, I gather.'

'Yes. That seems a long time ago now.'

'I know. Holidays fade so quickly, don't they?'

He tried to remember when and where she and Peter had been that year and could not. 'How's Peter?' he asked instead, dutifully.

'Oh, he's fine. Very busy. They've got such a lot of work on and he's been approached to do some freelance.'

'Oh?'

'Yes. It's all very hush–hush at the moment. Well, it's not even agreed but he's very excited. If it works out it could be the first step to setting up on his own.'

'I'll keep my fingers crossed, then.'

She began to set the table. 'It's only quiche, I'm afraid, and salad.'

'That's fine.'

'Mummy's really enjoying her pottery classes.'

Was she? This was news to him. But then he had not asked. 'How's the choir going?' he asked, remembering by association.

'All right, I think. I enjoy it anyway. But it's difficult to judge progress. Mr Horne keeps splitting us up into groups and making us go over whole sections phrase by phrase.'

'It'll come together,' he said because he could not remember what the choir was singing and did not like to ask. The microwave made a 'pinging' noise and Audra went to it, removed the quiche in a white dish with white oven gloves. Jolley thought about their impracticality until she said:

'Help yourself, then. Don't say you've lost your appetite.'

'No.' He tried to laugh. The quiche was already cut. The white salad bowl stood near him. He helped himself without interest. Audra sat to his right, put a small helping on her own plate. 'Well, this is very nice,' Jolley said, trying to sound hearty.

'You haven't touched it yet.'

'I meant being here, the two of us.'

'Oh.'

They ate in silence. Jolley pronounced the meal good. Audra made some automatic remark about it not being up to Mummy's standard, said for the umpteenth time that she was not very interested in cooking, food *per se*. Peter, of course, was a wonderful cook and always catered for their dinner parties.

'Perhaps we put you off,' Jolley said, for something to say, 'your mother being such a good cook and me so greedy.'

'I think you've lost weight.'

'Please tell that to your mother.'

'She told me, actually.'

Jolley felt instinctively that they were getting close to it, the reason for his being here, almost asked point-blank but then let it ride. He repeated that the food was very good.

'Mother thinks there's another woman,' Audra said flatly, staring at the low lamp in front of her.

Jolley thought: In her directness she resembles me. Then: What a bloody cheek! And finally that it was a bad sign when Audra referred to either of them as 'Mother' or 'Father'.

131

'Is there?'

He made himself meet her eyes. They were cold and inquisitorial and very troubled.

'Whatever put that idea into her head?'

'Oh . . . a woman always knows.'

'You've had experience?'

'Certainly not! Peter is . . . completely devoted to me. He would never—'

'I'm sorry,' he said quickly. 'That was just a nervous reaction. I didn't mean—'

'I should think not.' She picked up her plate and carried it to the counter by the window, scraped its contents into the waste disposal unit. Jolley pushed his own plate away. 'It's almost as ridiculous as the idea that you . . . But mother believes it. Is it true?'

'Isn't that something I should be discussing with your mother, not you?'

'She says you don't discuss anything. She says she hardly sees you.'

'Did she put you up to this?'

'No. I'm concerned. I'm worried about her. I thought it was my duty to ask you.'

'Thank you for your concern.'

'You're not going to tell me, are you? Peter said you wouldn't.' The idea that she had discussed this with Peter made him angry. How dare she? By what right? He was her father, for God's sake. 'Don't you want that?' He shook his head and she took his plate away. 'No wonder you're losing weight.'

'Questions like yours have a habit of taking the edge off a man's appetite.'

She ignored this. 'Do you want some raspberries and cream?'

'No thanks.'

'Cheese?'

'No.'

'Don't shout at me.'

'I'm not shouting.'

132

'It *is* my business. I'm not interfering.' He knew instinctively that Peter had told her this. Full marks to Peter, he thought. 'I just can't bear to stand by and let you throw everything away.'

'I think you've got things a bit out of proportion, Audra.'

'It's my life as well as yours and mother's. It's my background, my childhood. Everything I am you're damaging, throwing away. I'm not going to stand by and let you do that without a fight.' Jolley stood up. 'Where are you going?'

'Back to the station before I lose my temper. I don't want to fight with you, Audra, but if I stay here . . . ' He gestured helplessly.

'Mother's very unhappy, very frightened . . . '

'I'll talk to her.'

'Are you going to give this other woman up? That's what we all need to know.'

'Audra, mind your own business.'

He turned and walked away from the table. The house seemed larger than ever. Reaching the front door was like going on a two-mile hike. He had a childish urge to smash the grey urn-like vase as he passed it.

'Daddy . . . '

He opened the door, took a deep breath.

'Not now, Audra. I'm sorry . . . '

He walked out, kept his eyes fixed on the car. Behind him, he heard the door slam. Now, he thought, she would burst into tears. He ought to go back and comfort her and he would be damned if he was going to.

Jolley sat in his car and stared at, but did not see, a field. Already he regretted having left Audra like that but regret see-sawed with anger. He did not know with whom he was most angry: Audra, Eileen or himself. What kind of woman went running to her daughter with her suspicions? What kind of daughter charged her father with infidelity? What kind of man provided the ingredients for such a situation? And just walked away from it when it blew up in his face?

Anger deflated like a balloon. He unclenched his fists and let his breath out in a long sigh. It would have been so easy to lie to Audra, less so to her mother. But still possible. It wouldn't even be a lie, not really, not in their terms. Nothing had happened. That was all they were concerned about. He had already given her up and was suffering because of it. What lie, he demanded of the silence? It would have been a lie because Dolores Bayger was still in his blood and his mind and his heart. She was still palpably there, for all his good intentions and sincere resolutions. 'Another woman'! It was that phrase that had done it. As if she could ever be 'another woman'. The phrase cheapened her and what he felt for her. She was the only woman.

He knew then, with a clarity that hurt, that they had all told the truth: Mrs Keene, Mrs Brimble, Marion Glade. Those three men had felt as he did now, had probably sat or walked alone, feeling as he did, that without her there was no point or savour to life, that after her, the woman, there could be no other woman. What damage had that done to Belle Smith and Mary Brimble, Corr-Beardsley's rejected girlfriend and confidante sister? What would it do to Audra, Eileen, his whole world?

He felt ashamed of his own weakness. It was this that had stopped him answering Audra frankly, which probably would prevent him telling Eileen how it was. He knew – or dared to presume that he knew – that Eileen would understand if he told her. She, like all those other women, would understand the effect of a woman like Dolores Bayger. She would not be happy about it. He did not think that she would forgive him, not right away, but she would understand. That would help her and she would then want to help him. And that he could not bear.

Maybe Mrs Keene was right and she would have been burned for a witch. He could believe in spells now that he identified with three dead men and could see the pain he was causing to his womenfolk. It would not embarrass him greatly to admit that he was entranced. Should be burned as a witch, he thought, and knew that one thing was absolutely certain: he would never light the fire beneath her. And he was not about to go to a premature grave either. He did not identify that closely with her other three lovers. Was that the crucial difference? Had he been saved by his inability to move, his failure to seize his chance?

He did not know and did not want to know. That way another kind of despair lay. He started the car, braced himself. There was work to be done, reparations to be made. A small part of his conscience was clear and that, perhaps, would see him through.

'Inspector?'

Jolley had not been in his office five minutes, had only just begun to go through his messages, had not begun at all to think what he would say to Eileen.

'Not now, Sergeant,' he told her dismissively.

'I'm sorry but this won't wait.'

'I said . . . ' She looked rooted to the spot. Her eyes were no longer clear and sharp, essentially mild, but blazing. 'All right. What is it?'

'May I sit down?' He nodded without enthusiasm. 'It's about my job, about the fact that I am under-employed and largely ignored by you.'

'Unfortunately, Sergeant Glade, I cannot arrange for people to commit crimes just to keep you occupied. I warned you that you would find Oversleigh a pretty sleepy place . . . '

'Why won't you talk to me, involve me? I know what's on the books. What I lack, what you are depriving me of, is direction. You are not being fair to me.'

Jolley looked at her, was wondering whether to dismiss her or invite her to resign when the telephone rang. It was his direct line and he picked it up eagerly. 'Detective-Inspector Jolley.'

Marion Glade studied the wall. Perhaps this interruption would take the wind out of her sails, give them both a chance to calm down.

'I haven't heard from you. I haven't seen you. Can I see you? I must. It's urgent. Please, Cyril.'

He felt himself melt at her voice, but something about its hushed rapidity, its hint of suppressed panic, alarmed him as well.

'I'm sorry about that. Yes, of course . . . '

'I don't want you to come to the house. Can we meet somewhere? Believe me I wouldn't ask— '

'You can ask. It's all right. Yes.'

'Thank you. It really is important.'

'Something's wrong?'

'I can't talk now. When can I see you?'

'Now, if you like.'

'Do you know the country park at Brisestock? Just off the new motorway link? Can you be there in half an hour?'

'Yes.'

'Thank you.'

The line went dead. He did not know the place, had heard about it. He looked at his watch. Could he make it in half an hour? He stood up quickly, anxious to get to her, be with her. He saw Marion Glade staring at him with a strangely knowing, almost pitying expression. 'I'm sorry, Sergeant . . . I can't talk to you now. I have to go out . . . '

'So I see,' she said and stood up.

'I'm sorry. Tomorrow— '

'It's all right. I understand.'

He thought perhaps she did.


They had built a new dual carriageway to link the motorway which ran like an arrow through the heart of the county with that which touched its western edge. There had been a lot of opposition from the residents of Brisestock and neighbouring villages, particularly about the loss of good farmland and natural beauty. The planners had won, of course, but had promised to create a new country park to heal the inevitable scars of construction. Jolley remembered reading recently that the park was now open, though incomplete, that a royal personage would open it formally in the spring, by which time the park would be complete. He had to use the new road for about a mile to reach the park. Why had she chosen it? How would she get there? Above all, what was wrong, what made her so anxious? The park was clearly signed and he swung on to the rising access road with five minutes to spare.

There was one other car in the car-park and it was empty. The car-park was on top of a false hill overlooking the park itself. It looked raw and unfinished. The place had been landscaped but only partly planted. In creating the road the developers had left no hedges, few trees. The place was like a model relief map of what would be. Narrowing his eyes, he tried to imagine the caterpillar tracks and wheel ruts softened by grass, the mounds of raw earth made beautiful by trees and bushes. He failed. It reminded him of nothing so much as a deserted excavation site which, he supposed, in a sense it was.

He got out of the car and felt the new force of wind. Audra had been right. It was getting colder. The wind blew especially strongly in this exposed, raised spot, and brought threatening, dark clouds with it. He wished he had brought his old raincoat. A rough path led down into the park and, near by and more invitingly, a flight of rough-hewn steps with new wooden risers to contain the earth. To avoid the worst of the wind, Jolley started down the steps, then hesitated, thinking that she would look for him in the car-park. He should have waited in the car. But he went on, partly to escape the wind and partly because he was too excited to stay still. He would not go far. She would be able to see him from the car-park, he her. Ahead of him ran a shallow stream, the only old and natural-looking feature in the park. It was crossed by a pretty, new, rustic bridge. He went towards it and his heart quickened when he saw a sign of life, a woman crossing the bridge towards him. She was followed by two dogs, was short and thin and elderly.

'Good afternoon. Looks like rain,' she said. Jolley nodded and patted one of the dogs, elderly like his mistress, while the other ran sniffing and lively ahead of her. He leaned against the side of the bridge and watched as the woman climbed the steps, calling to the dogs. Where the hell was Dolores? Suppose something had happened to her? Being colour-blind, she might have jumped a red light. If she was as agitated as she sounded, she might have driven carelessly, been in an accident. No one would think to tell him. No one knew where he was. He pushed away from the bridge, began to retrace his steps when he heard a sound and, looking along the bottom of the hill, saw her coming towards him. She raised one arm, waved. He began to run towards her.

He embraced her without thinking or speaking, hugging her gratefully to him. She wore some long, hooded, woollen garment that tickled his cheek as he pressed his head against hers. When he released her, she looked startled, as though she had expected some cooler, more formal greeting.

'Thank you for coming,' she said, searching his face with troubled eyes.

'Shall we go to the car, get out of this wind?'

'No.' She shook her head slightly, causing the hood to slip. She raised a hand to pull it forward again. He saw that she was not wearing make-up and that, perhaps as a consequence, she looked older. There was no mistaking the deep lines of worry etched on her face. 'Let's walk,' she said, tucking her arm through his. 'I don't mind the wind. In fact I rather like it.'

Awkwardly, he matched his stride to hers. She wore long, highly polished boots which disappeared beneath the mauve cardigan. Her arm felt warm and soft on his. He waited, almost holding his breath, for each brush of her hip as they walked.

'I didn't know where else to call you,' she said, sounding tired. 'I hope I didn't drag you away from anything important.'

'No. Nothing.'

'I also didn't know who else to turn to. Apart from anything else, I realised how very lonely I am here. And you probably know how very frightened one can get when one is lonely.'

He could not speak, only nod. If he had spoken it would have been with a promise to end her loneliness, make her life safe and good . . .

'I'm wasting time, aren't I? You're a busy man . . . ' She pulled her arm from his – he felt it as a bereavement – to cross the narrow bridge. The path wound into some trees, disturbed, forlorn-looking things that had somehow and perhaps not entirely happily escaped the bulldozers. He caught up with her, gripped her elbow.

'What is it?'

She stopped and turned to face him. 'You know, it already seems less . . . serious, less frightening, now that I'm with you. Suddenly I'm afraid that you'll laugh at me, tell me not to be an hysterical woman . . . '

'No . . . '

'The thing is,' she said, holding his eyes with hers, 'Jay-Jay's been released. I heard a couple of days ago. I thought I'd hear from you. I waited. I didn't want to bother you, my dear, and then . . . then I became so afraid . . . ' She moved away again, dragged her arm from his, walked on into the trees.

'Dolores,' he shouted, using his policeman's voice. She stopped. Her shoulders seemed to slump. He went to her but did not touch her. 'You must tell me— '

'There's so much I haven't told you,' she wailed, keeping her face averted.

'I'm a policeman. I can help you. Whatever it is . . . You *know* I'll help you, but you have to tell me.' She nodded once, moved deeper into the little stand of trees. Jolley felt the first spots of rain, a sudden chilling gust of wind. She leaned against a tree and faced him. 'Who is Jay-Jay?'

'My husband. John James Wilding. I always called him Jay-Jay.'

'He's been released from the hospital you told me about?' Again she nodded, but without enthusiasm. 'I would have thought you would be glad.' He was afraid she would be glad, was excited that she was not.

'There's so much I haven't told you,' she repeated, shivering as the rain began in earnest.

'You can tell me in the car,' Jolley said firmly. 'Come on.' He put his arm around her, hugging her close against his body. She seemed almost afraid of the rain, held her hood in place with both hands. Jolley urged her to run, preceded her across the bridge, pulling her after him. On the other side he embraced her again, hurrying her along. The steps were wide enough for them to climb side by side. Jolley held her protectively, afraid she might slip on the damp earthen treads. At the top, Jolley unlocked the car and held the door for her. The other car had gone, presumably driven by the woman with the dogs.

Dolores sat quite still, her shoulders hunched, her hood obscuring most of her face. After a moment, Jolley reached for her hand.

'You're cold,' he said. 'Shall I drive around? I'm afraid the heater—'

'No. Please. I'm all right. Not really cold.' As though to prove it she pushed the hood back from her head.

Jolley wanted to stroke her hair. He cleared his throat, shifted to a more comfortable position in his seat. 'Why aren't you glad your husband's been released?'

'Because I'm afraid.'

'Of him?'

'Yes.'

'Why, exactly?'

'Because it wasn't quite as I told you. What I told you was true,' she added quickly, looking at him to see if he believed her. He nodded. 'But not the whole truth. Over the years, Jay-Jay has come to blame me for his condition, his depression, for not allowing him to kill himself, I guess. I have become a cause as well as part of his madness. Sometimes he believes I am its sole cause and that he

140

will only get better if I am . . . not there. The reason I left him in the hospital, the *real* reason I came here, was because he became violent towards me.' She said this as though she were ashamed of the fact, lowered her head and whispered the words to her hands, clasped tightly in her lap. 'He has . . . threatened my life many times. I not only left him in the hospital but I left *him*, the marriage. I was advised to do it. I could no longer help him. I guess I would have done it anyway.'

'But you still feel guilty?'

'Maybe.'

'Understandably. However, if he's been released, surely that implies a cure, an improvement at least . . . ?'

'Oh, you don't know Jay-Jay. He's cunning. When in control, lucid – and he often is in control . . . It's a cyclical thing, I think I told you . . . When he's on a high he can be very persuasive. But deep down nothing changes.'

'His doctors would be aware of that. Have you spoken to them?' She shook her head sharply. 'I think you should.'

'No. I can't. I can't do anything that might lead him to me.'

'Then how did you know he was out?'

'A friend. A discreet friend . . . '

'I think you're worrying unnecessarily.'

'There's more. I didn't tell you because . . . because you're a cop. He's a drug-user, an addict. When he's hopped up he . . . He's the violent kind.'

'My dear,' Jolley said gently, 'unless they've dried him out they would never release him.'

'And the first thing he'd do when he hit the streets would be to make contact, get some dope. It's happened before. It's *all* happened before. You think I don't know the pattern?'

'Of course. But there's an ocean between you. You don't *know* that this time his condition is not improved. Does he know where you are?' She shook her head fiercely. From a pocket beneath her cardigan she took a handkerchief, dabbed at her nose. 'Then I don't think you're in any danger.' She twisted the handkerchief between her fingers.

'I guess not. When you put it like that, so rationally, calmly . . . I was just so afraid.'

'I know. I can see that.'

'But there's nothing to be done. Oh, I knew that all along . . .'

'I didn't say that. There's a lot I can and will do.'

She turned wide, hopeful eyes on him. 'What?'

'I can find out if he leaves the States, if he comes here. If he comes here – to this country, I mean – we can keep an eye on him. To put it at its worst, you will have plenty of warning. You have my word on that.'

'Are you sure? Oh, Cyril . . . Would you really do that for me?'

'Of course.'

'But that's . . . wonderful. How can I ever thank you?'

Jolley did not answer that. The sky had brightened suddenly. He put on the windscreen wipers to clear the glass. It had almost stopped raining. 'I'll get on to it straight away,' he said. 'As soon as I get back.'

'Thank you. You must think me very foolish.'

'Not at all.' He knew that he sounded stiff and formal and sensed that this hurt her.

'I really didn't expect anything from you,' she said, her voice taking on some of its old confidence. 'I wanted to tell you . . . yes, because I'm scared, but also so that, if anything should happen to me, you would not think the worst.'

Jolley switched off the wipers. Their sound was suddenly irritating. He looked at her, puzzled. She was staring straight ahead, apparently quite calm now. 'I'm sorry, I don't understand you.'

'Well, you can just imagine – who better? – what would be said if anything happened to me . . .'

'Nothing *is* going to happen to you.'

'But that's what I thought. That's why I called you. Not because I thought you could do anything, not because I expected . . . I just wanted to explain it to you, so you wouldn't believe what they said, if . . . ' She turned soft, pleading eyes on him.

'You mean gossip? As with Smith and Corr-Beardsley?'

'Exactly. And don't forget David Brimble.'

'Well, you need have no worries on that score. And I want you to promise me— '

'I really must go . . . ' She put one hand on the door handle, the other up to twitch her hood into place. Impulsively, Jolley took this hand in his, squeezed it.

'Promise me you'll put all thought of . . . anything happening to you right out of your mind?'

She looked at him. A soft smile slowly bloomed on her face. 'All right. If you'll promise not to forget what I've said. Just in case. Please? As a good-luck charm.'

'I promise. But nothing will.'

'I feel so much better now. But I really must go.'

'Where's your car?' He hung on to the hand she tried to pull away from him. She opened the door a crack, letting cold air in. 'Let me drive you . . . '

'No. It's . . . over there.' She gestured vaguely to the other side of the park.

'Then let me take you— '

'No.' She said it sharply, as though impatient or afraid. 'Oh, it's very kind and don't think I don't appreciate it— '

'That's settled then.' He let go of her, reached for the ignition. She pushed the door wide, put one foot to the ground.

'You must understand something, Cyril. You've given me courage. I have to test it for myself. I have to be alone. I'm going to be alone now, from now on, aren't I? We both know I'm not going to see you again. Not personally, anyway. Not like this. I have to get used to that. I have to use the courage you've given me.'

He let his hand drop on to his knee. She got slowly out of the car. Something inside him screamed that he should stop her, tell her that he would be there, could see her, often and soon. She put her head into the car, the hood framing it, her scent strong.

'We both understand, Cyril. I know you'll look out for me. I shall trust in that.'

'If I hear anything, I'll come to see you.'

'I know. And I do thank you. But I shall be all right now. Now that you know and as long as you remember your promise.'

'Nothing is going to happen to you.'

'Dear Cyril . . . I shall always thank you and think of you.' She backed away, stood up. He leaned across the seat, seeking her face.

'Dolores— '

'I must go. You must go . . . Don't make it more difficult.'

'One question. The last, all right?'

'What?' She sounded weary. Her eyes were already looking away, across the park. An essential part of her, he thought, had already gone.

'Corr-Beardsley was in love with you. The other two as well, probably. Tell me honestly, did you sleep with them?' He saw her chin come up, the hood slip a little from her glossy black hair. A watery sun broke through the clouds, spilled a pale light across the car-park, reflected in puddles. She turned her head and looked down at him. Her face was cold and closed.

'What if I did, Cyril? What the hell if I did? I didn't with you, Cyril, and that's all that matters.'

She slammed the door with a force that made the car rock. Jolley became aware of a nagging pain at the base of his spine. He sat up. She was already at the brow of the hill. He watched her disappear down the steps. He wanted to shout to her, take the question back. He whispered her name. Some questions cannot be taken back. Who had asked the question, the policeman or Cy Jolley? As she said, what the hell did it matter now? He crossed his arms on the steering-wheel and put his head down on to them. It was over now. He had put a bitter end to it with

144

a single question. It was over and some time it would stop hurting like this. One day he might even be able to forgive himself.

That night Eileen came into the sitting-room and did something she had never done before. She walked purposefully to the record player and touched the reject button. Jolley, slumped in his chair, looked up.

'There was no need to go on at Audra like that.'

'By the same token,' Jolley replied, pushing himself up, his back hurting, 'there was no need to go talking to her.'

'I was afraid,' Eileen said. 'For the first time since I can remember, I can't talk to you.'

'You're the second woman today to tell me she's afraid.'

'I don't expect *she* had any difficulty talking to you.'

'No . . . '

'I don't want to hear any more.'

'Yes you do. You want to hear that it's over. It is.'

'Just like that? You expect me to believe . . . ?'

'I don't know what you'll believe. I don't expect anything. I'm just telling you, so you'll know. I'd like to put your mind at rest.'

'It's a bit late for that.'

'Even so. It's over. And while we're on the subject, nothing happened, nothing that you need be concerned about.'

'Oh, thanks very much.'

'I didn't sleep with her, Eileen. I'm not going to pretend I didn't want to . . . But the fact remains.'

'I'm supposed to take comfort from that, am I?'

'I don't know. I'm just telling you so you can . . . put Audra straight, know where you stand.'

'It's over, you say, this . . . this thing where nothing happened.'

'That's right.'

'It's not over. I've only got to look at you . . . '

'It's not out of my system, no. But I won't be seeing her

145

again. There won't be anything for you to worry about.'

'Except you won't be here. You'll look at me and you won't see me or you'll see someone . . . someone you don't love. Whenever I talk to you, you'll be thinking of her . . . ' Jolley stood up, too quickly for comfort. He put his hand to the small of his back. 'Where are you going?'

'Nowhere. Just into the garden, to stretch my legs.' He walked into the hallway, towards the back door.

'You won't discuss it with me, then?'

'Not now, love, no. I haven't got any more to say right now, sorry.'

Eileen watched him go, biting her lip. She walked into the hallway as he opened the back door and shouted after him, 'You want to take that back of yours to the doctor, before it gets any worse.'

Jolley stood looking at his car, parked in the driveway. He began to walk towards it.

# Six

She was waiting in his office when he got in the next morning. Her blonde hair was scraped back into some kind of pigtail, the fancy plaiting on her skull having an incongruous West Indian look. She wore a pink sweater over the denim skirt, against the colder weather.

'Look, I'm sorry about yesterday,' he said, moving to his desk. 'If you've come to hand in your resignation, please don't. I've got some work for you to do. Urgent.'

'Right,' she said, and smiled. In any other mood he would have taken time to enjoy that smile, encourage it. It was fresh and open and it did wonders for her already pretty face. She pulled up a chair without asking, produced a notepad and biro from her bag.

'I want you to get on to immigration. I want a complete check, airports, sea ports, the lot. I want to know if a man called John James Wilding comes through— '

'But, sir— '

'I'm giving you something to do, Sergeant. As you requested. Now please have the courtesy to listen and get it down and then go off and do it, right?' She flushed a little, her head bent over the notebook. She nodded. 'About forty, at a guess. I'll try and let you have more details later. He'll be coming from America. American or Canadian passport. Back-date that for a week, say. If he's here, I want to know. And if he turns up in the next few days, I want to know. Have you got that?'

'Yes, sir.' She closed the notebook, clipped the pen to it.

'Well, get on with it then.'

'Just one thing, sir, if I may.'

Jolley sighed and rolled his eyes, pushed himself back in his swivel chair, wincing at the stab of pain in his back. 'All right. But make it quick.'

'John James Wilding's already here. He has been here for nearly two years.'

Jolley's blood froze. Then he thought he must be hearing things, that Marion Glade was completely mad. 'Come again?' he said, leaning towards her.

'I . . . er . . . took the liberty of checking, sir, after our chat the other day, at the Coffee Cavern. I know you didn't think it was necessary but— '

'To hell with that. Are you telling me the truth, girl?'

'Yes. Of course.'

'Then tell me. Quick.'

'I did an immigration check on Dolores Bayger, sir. It wasn't as easy as I thought. In fact, I drew a blank at first and then I had the idea that she might be travelling under her married name. I asked them to check again and the info came through yesterday. She was travelling under her married name and her husband, John James Wilding, came with her.'

'No. No, they've made a mistake. She was travelling alone. She must have been.'

'No, sir. The records are quite specific. John James Wilding and Dolores Bayger Wilding. Travelling together. He on a US passport, she on a Canadian one.'

Jolley put his head in his hands. She had lied to him. Why would she lie to him? Why now? Why say that she was scared Wilding would come after her . . . He stood up, sending the chair skidding across the floor. 'You've got the documentation?'

'Yes, sir. Next door.'

'Get it and meet me downstairs. And make it quick.'

'Yes, sir.' The smile shone again before she ran out of the door. Jolley snatched down his raincoat and followed her.

There was indeed, he thought, so much Dolores Bayger had not told him. This time, for the very last time, she would tell him everything.

★

In the car, he made Marion repeat the whole story. She added, 'I'm sorry I went behind your back . . . '

'Don't rub it in, Sergeant.'

'I didn't mean to.'

'The point is, you've done well. Thank God you ran that check.'

'I can't pretend I'm not relieved you see it that way.'

'Just make sure you don't ever do it again.'

'Are you going to tell me why it's so important?' she asked quickly, changing the subject. Jolley noted that she had not promised.

'Because Mrs Bayger has been lying to me and I want to know why.'

'Ah . . . So we're going to Chuters, then.'

'We are. And I'm going to get to the bottom of this once and for all.'

Turning into Chuters Lane he found the road blocked by a single-decker coach. Jolley swore and backed the car.

'The weekly bus service to Oversleigh,' he told Marion as he acknowledged the driver. Half a dozen curious faces were pressed to the windows, peering into the car. Marion smiled and waved to them. 'That,' said Jolley, putting the car into gear and easing it back into the lane, 'will give 'em something more to talk about. You'll be marked as my fancy woman before they reach the roundabout.'

Marion laughed but said nothing. They drove past the green and the pub, pulled up outside 'The Stables'. Marion undid her seatbelt.

'No,' Jolley said, touching her arm. 'Look, I'm not cutting you out, but I want to do this alone, OK?'

She pursed her lips, looked at him quizzically. 'OK,' she said at last. 'I'll wait here.'

'Thanks. I may need you later. I'll give you a shout.' He got out of the car and straightened his shoulders.

Marion Glade wound her window down and watched him go up the path, knock at the door. When it became obvious that no one was going to answer, Jolley turned

149

and signalled to her, pointing to the side of the house. She nodded and resigned herself to wait.

The gate was open just as it had been that other time. Jolley pushed through it. He would winkle her out of her studio or wherever she was. He could handle most things but not a deliberate, blatant attempt to mislead him or pull the wool over his eyes. At the back of his mind he could hear her laughing at him because he did not even know what she was doing. Weeks of lies, he now assumed. Jolley did not like being lied to.

The back door was ajar, just as it had been before. He went to it, pushed it open, called her name. The silence did not deter him. He felt instinctively that she was hiding from him. Somehow it seemed typical that she must know of his anger, feel his wrath. He went in to the kitchen, crossed it to a door he had noticed before but never opened. It gave on to a utility room, empty of human life. Turning back he saw the knife, isolated on the white table. His practised eye immediately placed it as the largest of a set which hung on a magnetised rack above the work surface. He checked the empty space, looked back at the knife. It was dirty. Its shiny metal blade was stained. He leaned over it, careful to touch nothing, not even the edge of the table with his jacket. Blood lost its distinctive colour in drying but it dries a special shade of brown that an experienced eye can easily recognise. A smear on the white table recalled to his mind butchers' shops, an image of Eileen slicing liver with just such a sharp knife, the blood staining the white marble slab she used for the purpose.

He hurried into the hall, calling her name, her full name to declare that he was a policeman not a social caller, that he was not playing games. The dining-room was empty, smelled musty from being shut up. It had, unsurprisingly, been cleaned and tidied since he last saw it. The stubs of candles in the candelabra caused him a brief, disquieting pang. The living-room, too, was tidy. Fresh flowers stood in a vase on the table, a record sleeve lay on the settle, but the stereo was turned off, the record still on the turntable.

He called again, nervously now, from the foot of the stairs. Only in imagination had he mounted these stairs, dark and mysterious. He felt like an intruder, hesitated. It was still relatively early. Suppose she was sleeping? She was, after all, a woman of leisure, dependent on no one . . . Jolley went up the stairs very quietly. The bathroom door stood open opposite the stairwell. Two other doors facing each other, a mirror image of downstairs. He went to the one on his right, tapped, then knocked loudly.

'Dolores Bayger.'

He lifted the latch and pushed the door open. Her scent pervaded this room, drifted out, invited him. She must be in the studio or out, he told himself. But he went into her room.

The bed stood opposite the front window. Another window faced him, set in the side wall of the house. Both were curtained with lace, nothing more substantial. Both windows were closed. The room was over-perfumed, too warm. He saw himself in triplicate mirrors atop a dressing table loaded with bottles and jars. He made himself look at the bed.

She lay on her back, one arm flung up, the hand clenched. The hair on the right side of her face was slightly fanned across the pillow. Her throat had been cut neatly, almost expertly. Blood had soaked into the bed around her shoulders, dried on her breast, stained the ivory satin on her nightgown. She looked like a ghastly, bleached photograph of herself. The stains reminded him of batik prints. He closed his eyes, squeezed them very tight. There were times when he wished he did not see in this clinical way, wished that he could not tell, at a glance, that the cut was precise, quasi-scientific, professional. Or that the ability to see and note such things in a split second would protect him from feeling this terrible loss, this pain, the release of grief which felt like some unstaunchable, inward bleeding.

He heard his own breathing, rasping, too rapid, opened his eyes again. A flicker of movement made him look from her to the side window. A cold, beady eye met his. A black beak tapped at the glass. Two ravens perched on the windowsill, one looking in, the other away. With a roar like that of a gored bull, Jolley hurled himself across the room, smashed both fists into the leaded glass. It seemed to him that the birds hesitated, marked insolent time for a moment before flapping lazily away, not at all alarmed. With a moan, aware that the sides of his fists hurt, he let his forehead rest against the cold glass and closed his watering eyes.

He heard her rapid step on the stairs, her voice calling to him. He straightened up, pulled a clean handkerchief from his pocket and held it to his face. Marion Glade opened the door across the landing with a crash, came into this room, stopped on sight of him.

'Inspector Jolley?' He cleared his throat. 'Oh my God!' He turned around slowly, blinking. 'I heard a noise . . . '

'Me, I'm afraid. Damned ravens at the window. I've got a thing about them. Sorry.'

Looking at the bed, she said, 'I'm sorry. Really, I am. I— '

'Get on the phone, will you, Sergeant?' Jolley cut her off. 'Fingerprints, photographs, police surgeon, the lot. And as many personnel as they can spare.'

'Right.' She began to leave.

'I'm pretty sure the murder weapon's in the kitchen, on the table.'

'I saw it.'

'Make sure it stays there, untouched until forensic have done with it. You keep your eye on it. There's a phone in the kitchen, I believe.'

'What about you? Will you be all right?'

'Perfectly all right. Now get on to it, there's a good girl. I want this bastard . . . ' He bit his bottom lip. She nodded and went, closing the door gently behind her.

And when I get him, Jolley promised himself, I'll pulverise the bastard. I'll personally do him over. I'll make him wish . . . He stared at the bed, his mind going blank. His lip hurt. He let his breath out, rubbed his bruised, slightly throbbing hands. He had always taken refuge in work. He wanted to cover her and knew that he must not. There was a matching satin peignoir on the chair near the long built-in wardrobe. His fingers itched to spread it over her, but he did not touch it. Sooner or later this room would have to be searched. Better him than some clumsy, callow constable. No time like the present. He had always taken refuge in work. Now, when he most needed it, he was reluctant to find anything.

He wrenched open the top drawer of the dressing-table, making the tripartite mirror shake, his fractured image tremble. More cosmetics, tissues, a woman's paraphernalia. Her scent stronger than ever. Underwear in the drawer below, silks and satins that burned his fingers, which he felt blindly, not daring to look until his fingers touched something hard and cold underneath. He tossed garments aside, feeling like a rapist, and uncovered a gun. A neat, pretty toy-like thing, with a blunt barrel and a mother-of-pearl butt. The sort of weapon you saw in American television movies – a lady's gun. He pulled it out, using his handkerchief, checked that it was loaded. He emptied the chamber into his left hand, put the bullets in one pocket, the gun in the other.

A drawer full of sweaters and blouses. He could not think about the gun yet. What was he looking for, anyway? A diary, personal papers, anything, nothing. Anything to keep his mind off her body. Because a search had to be made.

He opened the wardrobe. A light came on automatically. Her scent again, slightly stale, almost unpleasant. The back of the doors – there were two sets – held long, dazzling mirrors. What a lot of clothes she had. All expensive, soft, all giving off new waves of her perfume as he scraped the hangers aside, looking for – what? A shelf ran the length of the wardrobe, at head height. A jumble of shoes. She was not tidy. More sweaters. He pushed aside a long, velvet cloak, the backless red dress of poignant memory. A small

black box was fixed to the wall behind. A burglar alarm, he
supposed, or something to do with the central heating. He
felt too hot. If a burglar alarm, why was it not set, ringing?
He closed that set of doors, opened the others. The long
boots she had worn yesterday, still caked with Brisestock
mud. More clothes, trousers and skirts. On the shelf above,
the ring-binder of photographs she had shown him. He
pulled it out, placed it on the floor. He did not know how
he was going to handle the photographs, could too easily
imagine the comments and jokes they would give rise to at
the station. Work that out later, he told himself, searching
the shelf with his fingers. A flat, black book. He flipped
through it. A cuttings book. He placed it on top of the
binder. The drawer of the nightstand contained nothing
exceptional. Some homeopathic pills, a broken watch, a
nail-file. A funny, flat little metal ornament on a golden
chain. He lifted it out, held it dangling before his eyes.
He wanted it. A keepsake. Deliberately switching off his
mind, he dropped it into the breast pocket of his jacket.

He picked up the black book, trembling slightly, and
carried it to the front window. Only minutes before the
team would arrive, start picking apart her house, her life.
At least only his fingers and eyes had explored this most
personal room. Perhaps that would comfort her a little as
it did him, though he felt that he had intruded, soiled it in
some way. He opened the book to distract him. Yellowing
newspaper cuttings had been pasted into it. Some of them
contained photographs of Dolores, hair scraped back, a
turtle-neck sweater with a bold necklace around it. What a
necklace she wore now, he thought, beaded with her own
life-blood. Other articles were illustrated with some of the
photographs, the nudes. The headlines told enough of the
story. *Tables Turned by Feminist Photographer. Shocking Show
by Woman Photographer Raises Controversy. Ban These Saucy
Pics, Say Daughters of America*. And so on and so on. With
what relish and confidence she had collected them all,
the considered critiques rubbing shoulders with the cries
of public outrage. *Psychiatrist Discusses Controversial Photo*

*Show*. Another photograph of Dolores Bayger stared out at him. Defiantly smiling, she was posed against one of her own pictures, a chubby male backside peeping over her shoulder. Her hair loose, her eyes challenging. She wore white or some pastel colour. Jolley began to read to avoid her eyes.

'Psychiatrist Duane Kallman studied the Bayger-Wilding Show at the New Eye Gallery and pronounced: "This is the work of a woman who hates men. A deeply disturbed and resentful personality is discernible in every plate. No matter how Bayger-Wilding may dress it up as an attempt to show men how they abuse women in glamor photography and girlie-mags, these photographs constitute a calculated act of revenge which borders on the sick."' Dr Kallman went on to say that the show was fascinating. '"I would love to know what trauma, what damage caused this obviously talented woman to see and imagine in this chilling way . . . "'

Jolley closed the book as a siren split the silence, grew inexorably louder, closer. Lifting one corner of the lace curtain, he saw the first car arrive. He let the curtain drop and, studiously keeping his eyes on the floor, picked up the heavy binder and carried it, together with the cuttings book, out on to the landing. He closed the door behind him. In a few minutes she would be pinned in their flash-light, dead flesh.

The house seemed to shudder with noise. Footsteps on the stairs and in the upper rooms. The unavoidable noise of a systematic search, of men and women going about their business. Voices raised or muffled in semi-private colloquy. Jolley sat in the living-room, a quiet centre around which these noises washed and revolved. Another man might have found them intrusive, disrespectful. To him they were balm, proof that the structured search for her murderer was on. He watched PC Johnson search her record collection approvingly. The lad handled each album with care, was scrupulously thorough. No one would know he had been through it when he had finished. He glanced at the door, his attention attracted by raised voices.

'Shall I go and see, sir?' Johnson offered, looking at the door himself.

'No.' Jolley had already heard Marion Glade's voice cutting across the altercation. Moments later he saw her imperfectly through the lace curtains, apparently escorting a man off the premises.

'She obviously liked music,' Johnson said, pausing for a moment.

'Yes, she did.'

'Like you, eh, sir?'

'Yes, yes indeed.'

Marion came in, closing the door behind her. 'Can I just check a few things with you, sir?'

Jolley nodded. 'What was all that about?' He jerked his head towards the front door.

'Oh, some chap from the estate wanting to know why we let his ravens out. Apparently there's a cage of them out the back and somebody's cut the wire or something, set them free.'

'Any connection, do you think?'

She shrugged. 'Explains the ones you saw upstairs, presumably. The funny part was, when I disclaimed all responsibility, he said would we let him know if we spotted any and could we lend him some men to help catch them.' Jolley managed a watery smile. 'Apparently they're precious, or something. Anyway . . . ' She sat down on the arm of the sofa and flipped open her notebook. 'The side gate was open when you went to it, is that right, sir?'

'Yes. And the back door.'

'Then that's presumably how he got in. Or her. There's no sign of a forced entry, no damage. But the front door wasn't locked, either.'

She had told him that she always locked up, was very security conscious.

'She might have let the murderer in,' Jolley said in a flat voice. 'Someone she knew, had no cause to fear.

And then he made his way out through the kitchen, the side gate— '

'But she was killed in bed, sir, and with no sign of a struggle.'

*Did you sleep with them? Did you?*

'The police surgeon's with her now,' Marion went on. 'I've asked for an ambulance.'

'Fine.'

'I'll get some people on house-to-house, OK?'

'Please. I'm sure they'll find the neighbours very helpful.'

Before Marion could respond to this, to the bitterness in his voice, the door opened after a peremptory knock and a red-faced PC Roscoe came in.

'Oh, there you are, sir. These outbuildings at the back, old stables by the look of it. Got some fancy lock on the door we can't crack. Permission to break it down, sir?'

'No.' Jolley almost shouted, making Johnson jump, pause in his work and stare at him in surprise. Her privacy. Her neurotic privacy about her work. 'No, that won't be necessary,' he made himself say more calmly. 'That's her studio, photographic studio. I'll deal with it myself later. It isn't important.'

'If you say so, sir.' Roscoe sounded disappointed, unconvinced. 'You seem to know a lot about her,' he added.

'Inspector Jolley had questioned Miss Bayger about another matter, Constable,' Marion said quickly. 'Have you finished out the back, apart from the studio?'

'Yeah.'

'Good, then you can help me organise a house-to-house.' She led him briskly out of the room.

'You all right, sir?' Johnson asked quietly, replacing the last record in its rack. Zemlinsky. She kept her records alphabetically, Jolley knew. The Lyric Symphony. He had the same record . . . 'Sir?'

'Yes, yes, thank you, Johnson. Wool-gathering . . . '

'Only you don't look too good, sir.'

'Just get on with your job, Johnson, there's a good lad.' He got up and went to look out of the back window.

It faced on to a narrow strip of dark garden, which ended in the yard. He looked at the old stables. He did not want Roscoe or any of them gallumphing in there. It had been her *sanctum sanctorum*, more private, he thought with a bitter irony, than her bedroom. Besides, he wanted to be the first to see what other photographs she had in there. The imagination flinched from the possibilities. He would do it himself, later, when he felt stronger.

'Mr Arnolph would like a word, sir,' Marion said, holding the door open to let the police surgeon through.

'Thanks.'

Arnolph looked, as always, rumpled, as though he had slept in his clothes. The man attracted creases, ties that slipped. Even his round glasses – a recent acquisition – had a habit of sliding perilously down his snub nose. Jolley shook his moist hand without enthusiasm.

'Well,' he said with a heavy sigh, 'you saw for yourself, Mr Jolley. I understand you found the body.' Jolley inclined his head, admitting it. 'Throat cut. Enormous blood loss. Not a frenzied attack by any means. A single, strong cut. Someone who knew what he was doing, by the looks of it.'

'A doctor, you mean, or a surgeon?'

Arnolph looked offended. Jolley reminded himself that the man had no sense of humour whatsoever.

'Not necessarily,' he said huffily. 'A butcher. Anyone with a knowledge of anatomy. Of course, it might have been a stroke of luck . . . ' Arnolph did not see the pun, paused only because Jolley winced. He shook his head not understanding, and continued. 'If she was deeply asleep, not alarmed. Usually these things are more messy, more hit and miss because the victim puts up a struggle. Understandably,' he added. 'This lady appears to have been . . . taken unawares. Most likely deeply asleep. Perhaps she took something . . . '

'Perhaps she knew the killer and had no cause for alarm.'

'Well, possibly. But once she saw the knife . . . Anyway, the contents of the stomach will show if she took something, barbiturates, possibly. And might establish the

158

time of death which, I suppose, is all you're interested in, as usual.'

'It always helps,' Jolley said, not rising to the taunt.

'I'd guess between twelve and four on present evidence but I'll try to be more precise. Anything else I should know?'

'We've got the weapon. Big kitchen knife.'

'Mm. That'd do the job, if sharp enough.'

'Apparently it was.'

'Right. Well, I'll let you have my report as soon as possible.'

'I'll appreciate that.'

'I'll be off, then. You feel all right? You look a bit green around the gills . . . '

'I don't have your professional sang-froid,' Jolley said, relishing the phrase, 'about cuts.'

'Oh. Bit of a shock, eh? Funny, I always thought you chaps were hardened to it. Well, I'll be in touch.'

A cold and calculated murder, then. Not an act of frenzied passion. But then he had known that. So much had been apparent when he saw her. He just didn't want to admit it, that's all. Outside, he heard Arnolph telling his Sergeant she could arrange to have the body removed. Johnson was turning over the cushions on the settee, his work almost done.

'Anything?' Jolley asked.

'Nothing unusual. A few bills, bank statements, all the usual stuff in the desk over there. I've made a pile.'

'No diary, address book?'

'Not that I've come across.'

'What about a passport?'

'No sign of one. Perhaps in her bag.'

'All right, Johnson, thank you.'

Johnson continued with his methodical search while Jolley paced up and down, his mind refusing to fit the pieces together. Marion came in again.

'They'll be taking the body away in a few minutes, sir. And I've checked through her handbags. She carried a few pounds on her. There doesn't appear to have been any other money in the house. Make-up, keys, just the usual stuff.'

'Passport?'

'No.'

'And I don't think we can consider robbery as a motive, do you?'

'No, sir. And Mr Arnolph told me he doesn't suspect a sexual motive, either.'

Why hadn't he thought of that, asked? Because it would have been unbearable to say the necessary words.

'No. Fine. I didn't think . . . ' He faced the end of the room, his eyes averted from the windows. He recognised the sounds from above, the sounds of a stretcher being manoeuvred down the stairs.

'Revenge, then? Or hatred?' Marion suggested.

'Is hatred a motive?'

'I don't know, sir. A reason, certainly— '

'That's it, sir,' Johnson interrupted. 'Just those few documents which might be of interest.'

'Get them packed up and labelled, Constable. And well done.'

'Thank you, sir.' Johnson picked up the documents and went out.

'Why don't you sit down?' Marion said.

'You're not going to fuss over me, Sergeant, are you?'

'Absolutely not, sir. I was just suggesting that we mark time until the body's been moved. Then I reckon we can leave the men to finish up here.'

'I agree. Make sure they lock up when they've finished and I want the keys. Better leave a man outside for a few hours. How's the house-to-house going?'

'Roscoe's gone to fetch some help from Oversleigh. A couple of the men here can help when they've finished. It shouldn't take long.'

'Then we might as well clear out,' Jolley said, suddenly wanting to be out of her house, this atmosphere of death and order.

'In a minute or two, sir,' Marion said, glancing at the window. 'I'll just go and make a last check.'

'Very well. I think perhaps I will sit down after all.'

He sat on the settee, leaning forward, looking at familiar chrysanthemums in the copper bowl before the fireplace.

Marion drove. This was agreed without words or looks, as though their relationship had been accepted and was beginning to settle into a familiar pattern. Jolley fastened his seat-belt and waited while she got in, tossed her bag on to the back seat where he had already placed the book and the binder of photographs.

'All set?' she asked.

'Yes. Thank you for stepping in when Roscoe asked about the studio. I appreciate that.'

'That's OK. I didn't think it was the right time for you to be answering a lot of questions.' She backed the car to the village green, a little too quickly for Jolley's comfort, but with undoubted competence. As they drove past The Clouded Yellow and around the green to the lane, he noticed Roscoe talking to the landlord, WPC Anson coming out of one cottage gateway and going into another.

'The house-to-house is well under way,' he remarked.

'Yes. Maybe that'll give us a picture of her movements yesterday and last night. I assume you agree that's a priority?'

'Definitely. And I can help you there, Sergeant. I saw her yesterday afternoon.' If Marion was surprised she concealed the fact cleverly. 'At Brisestock Country Park. She left me about four fifteen.'

'She was driving?'

'I . . . think so. I didn't see her car. She just walked off in the opposite direction. I assumed— '

'I don't think she did. There's no garage at the house, no car outside that belonged to her. We didn't find a driving licence or a tax certificate.'

'She was colour-blind,' Jolley said.

'So?'

'I wondered how she managed. She was shy about it, pretended she wasn't.'

'They memorise the sequence of lights, or so I've heard. It doesn't prevent you driving . . . '

'But if she didn't drive— '

'How did she get to Brisestock?'

'Quite.'

'She could have got a lift . . . '

'Or a taxi.'

'I'll check as soon as we get back.' Jolley grunted and relapsed into silence.

Turning on to the main road, Marion accelerated. 'You know what this means, don't you?'

'No, what?'

'For the time being, you're the last person known to have seen her alive.'

'I don't think that's very funny, Sergeant.'

'It wasn't meant to be. A simple statement of fact, sir.'

'I think it's time you called me Cy, Sergeant. This formality is becoming boring.'

'OK, I will.' She glanced at him, a broad grin on her face.

The gun and its six small bullets were spread out on Jolley's desk. He stared at them. Was it because she was scared of Wilding that she had it, or was it just part of the domestic furniture of American women? How did she get it into the country? Did she have a licence for it? Certainly not one issued from this station. Did she plan to use it if Wilding came looking for her?

'Bingo,' Marion said, coming into the room. 'I've ordered some tea . . . What's that?' She leaned over the desk, her eyes glittering with excitement.

'Dolores Bayger's gun.'

'Why isn't it with the rest of her stuff?'

'Because I just put it into my pocket and forgot about it.' He swept the six bullets together, opened the bottom drawer of his desk. 'I know I shouldn't have, but I wasn't thinking too clearly.' He picked up the gun, still in his handkerchief. 'And since it obviously isn't the murder weapon, there's no harm done.'

'Aren't you going to turn it in?'

'Later.' He put the gun in the drawer and slammed it shut.

'Did she have a licence?'

'Not from us. I've told Johnson to check through her papers. Now, what have you got?'

She looked doubtfully at the drawer before answering. 'I've got a call out for Mr Traxel, the taxi driver . . . '

'I know,' Jolley said.

'His wife says he drove Dolores Bayger yesterday. He's out on a job right now. I've told her to get him round here just as soon as he shows.'

'Good. I might soon be off your list of suspects.'

'Possibly. Now, what have we got?'

'I'd better tell you about yesterday afternoon.'

'Look, it's none of my business . . . ' Marion said quickly, ducking her head.

'Oh yes it is. You're a policewoman. You're on this case. I wish, if you want to play it that way, to make a statement.'

'Don't be silly . . . '

'Then listen. And note.' He waited. Marion took out her notebook. 'Write it down.'

'You're sure about this?'

'Absolutely. Ready? Miss Bayger rang me about three. You were in the room. Would you say three?'

'A bit before. It was two minutes past three when you went out. I checked,' she admitted, not looking at him.

'I drove straight to Brisestock Country Park. She'd asked me to meet her there. She sounded distressed and said or indicated – I really can't remember – that it was urgent. I got there at three thirty, perhaps a bit before. She was not in the car-park. I went down into the park, such as it is. I passed an elderly woman walking two dogs. She spoke to me, something about the weather. I don't remember. Short woman, about five two or three. Blue anorak. Trousers.

163

Two labradors. One rather elderly, the other younger, very frisky. She drove a black car, four doors. Can't remember anything else. I met Miss Bayger at the bottom of the car-park. We walked across a little bridge and into a stand of trees. It was very windy and it started to rain. Because of the rain, I persuaded her to come back to my car. She told me that her husband had been released from hospital. That's a mental hospital somewhere in America. She had told me on a previous occasion that he was there. She was alarmed. She said that he had threatened her before, there had been violence and she was afraid that he would come after her. She said, and I quote, "If anything should happen to me . . . " She said it a couple of times. If anything should happen to her, she wanted me to know about her fear and not to believe any gossip I might hear. I didn't take it all very seriously. I did my best to reassure her. I promised I would find out if her husband entered or had entered this country. I was going to put you on to that first thing this morning when you told me you'd already checked and he was possibly already here. After that, Miss Bayger left my car. I asked her where her car was and she said, "Over there", pointing to the other side of the park. She walked away into the park and I came straight back here, arriving at about five? You can check with the desk. I never saw her again until this morning.'

'What did she mean about something happening to her?'

'Your guess is every bit as good as mine, now. She said she was telling me because she didn't want me to think the worst. I'm not sure what she meant by that.'

'A lover?' Marion suggested.

'Possibly a lover.'

'She was afraid for her life. That's what you're saying.'

'That's what it looks like. She seemed less anxious after we talked. I thought she was over-reacting. What else could I think? She told me she'd only just heard about her husband's release. I had no reason to think he wasn't in America. Frankly, it seemed to me a long shot that he would seek her out.'

'Tell me about the husband,' Marion said.

He did, searching his memory, piecing the fragments together.

Marion listened attentively, made the occasional note. When he had finished, she said, 'So why did she tell you all this but pretend that he was in America.'

'Perhaps he is. He could have returned to the States. All we can do is check the airlines. Did he fly in?'

Marion nodded. 'They did,' she corrected him. 'But if he wasn't in America and wasn't in hospital . . . No, it just doesn't make sense. Unless she was lying to throw suspicion on to him because she feared something from someone else.'

'But why go to all that trouble to throw me off the scent of a possible murderer, if that's what she feared?'

'Beats me,' Marion conceded. 'The whole thing is pointless if she was really scared.'

'I'm sure she was.'

'Maybe she believed he was in America— '

'Or maybe he was in hospital here and she heard— '

'Then why bother to lie about it? What difference does the country make?'

Jolley shook his head. The telephone rang and he answered it. The desk wanted to know if Marion was with him. Mr Traxel was downstairs asking for her.

'Send him up,' Jolley said. To Marion, he went on: 'Traxel. I'll see him. You see how the house-to-house is going and see what you can do about the airlines. It's a long shot but all we've got. And get back here as soon as you can.'

'Right. And look, I just want to say, that I appreciate some of this must be painful— '

'You just do it, Marion, that's all I ask.'

'Yes . . . Cy.'

Despite his name and now somewhat faded Teutonic blondness, Uwe Traxel was, in speech and manner, as English as Jolley himself. Traxel's father had married an

Oversleigh girl and started a taxi service in the town shortly after the Second World War. Uwe Traxel had inherited the business when his father died. Mrs Traxel had retired to Bournemouth or Hastings or somewhere like that, to be with an unmarried sister, Jolley vaguely remembered. He and Uwe were almost contemporaries, had been at school together. For some reason Jolley had never probed, he did not like Traxel, never had. But he greeted him cordially, invited him to sit.

'What's it all about then?' Traxel asked, rubbing his hands together as though in anticipation of some juicy scandal.

'I believe you drove Dolores Bayger yesterday. The woman who lived . . . at "The Stables", Chuters.'

'Yes. Well, I did and I didn't.'

'What's that supposed to mean?'

'She had a car booked for the morning, into Passington. I had another job on so Stan did it. Stan Michaels, young lad who works for me part-time. He took her into Passington at nine thirty and dropped her off. Then she rang and asked for another car about one. It wasn't logged because I took the call myself. I picked her up at one thirty and drove her to Brisestock. She said to pick her up about half four outside the antique shop, which I did. She was a bit late. I drove her home and dropped her off just after five, something like that.'

'You're sure about your times?'

'Give or take a minute, yes. What's all this about?'

'We're trying to establish her movements yesterday.'

'Why? What's she done?'

'Why would she do anything?'

'I don't know. Only asking.'

'Now, you say your man took her into Passington.'

'Right.'

'How did she get back?'

'Walked for all I know. Or took the bus to Oversleigh and then legged it, but usually she picked up a cab in Passington to bring her back. Probably that's what she did.'

'How do you know all this?'

'Because she was a regular customer. She's got an account. Soon after she come here I took her into Passington and I asked did she want picking up, like. And she said no, because she didn't know how long she'd be and she'd get a town cab to bring her back. And I know she used to do that because she sometimes chats to me about the other drivers, things they've said and that. So probably that's what she did yesterday. Why don't you ask her?'

'And then she called you again. About one p.m. you say?'

'Right.'

'And you took her to Brisestock at one thirty and she asked you to pick her up . . . '

'At half-past four, yes.'

'Why didn't she get a local taxi?'

'Probably because there ain't no local taxi service in Brisestock.'

'And what did she do in Brisestock for more than two hours?'

'Search me. You're supposed to be the detective, not me. I dropped her off and she went into the antique shop. She often did. This wasn't the first time. If you ask me, probably she was having it off with the bloke what runs it. Myers, his name is.'

'But I didn't ask you, did I? And why should you assume any such thing?'

'Because that's what they all said about her, wasn't it? And she was very friendly with him. That I do know. And she used to go over there 'bout once a month. All right?'

'And what about when you picked her up?'

'What about it? She comes along, a bit late, like I said, gets in the car and I drove her back to Chuters.'

'She "came along"?'

'Down the high street, yes.'

'Did she have any shopping with her?' Traxel shook his head. 'You're sure she didn't come out of the antique shop?'

'Positive.'

'And this was a regular trip, right?'

'More or less, yeah. 'Bout once a month. Not a permanent booking or nothing, but regular. Always booked the same day, though she normally give me more notice than what she did yesterday.'

'And you drive her to other places.'

'Yeah.'

'Where?'

'Anderton. I don't know. I can check. Most of it's logged.'

'I'd like to see your log book, please.'

'All right.'

'How did she seem yesterday?'

'A bit off. Normally, she was quite chatty, you know, and always dolled up to the nines. Yesterday, she wasn't. No make-up. She looked a bit done in, if you must know, and she didn't have much to say for herself.'

'You didn't think that was odd?'

'We all has our off days, don't we? It was nothing to do with me. Oh yes, I remember . . . She said it was a spur of the minute decision, deciding to go to Brisestock, she meant. She apologised for not giving me more notice. I thought she was sort of explaining about not being dressed up and that.'

'Why would she do that?'

'I don't know. Vanity. You know how women are.'

'Did she say anything else?'

'Not to speak of. Just when to pick her up and "thank you" and that sort of thing.'

'All right. Thanks very much. I'll get someone along to have a look at your logbook. I imagine you need it?'

'Just started a new one as it happens. You're welcome to the old one until the tax man comes around.'

'Thanks, I appreciate it.'

'Is that it, then? You're not going to tell me what she's done?'

'Miss Bayger is dead.'

Traxel's jaw dropped and then he pursed his lips and whistled incredulously. 'Well, I'll tell you one thing, mate. She was good and alive when I dropped her around five last evening.'

'You'll swear to that? In court if necessary?'

'You bet. I've got a business to think of. I don't want any . . . anything attaching to me.'

'Of course not. Well, we'll be in touch.'

'Here, when you said dead . . . '

'I meant murdered, yes.'

'Bloody hell.'

'Indeed.'

'Are you certain she wasn't ringing from a call box?' Marion said. 'You didn't hear any pips, money in the slot?'

'Definitely not. Besides, she said she didn't want me to go there. I remember that clearly. I naturally assumed she meant the house, Chuters.'

'Then Traxel must be lying . . . '

'Or she was.'

'She could have rung you from somewhere else, another private phone.'

'The antique shop. Traxel says she and the owner – Myers – were on good terms.'

'We'd better talk to Myers,' she said.

'I will. You get someone to check Traxel's logs. Check his whole story. Then get the results of the house-to-house together. I'll be back as soon as I can.'

'Hadn't you better ring him first?' she said, reaching for the local directory. 'Just to make sure he's in.'

'You think of everything,' Jolley told her, taking the directory from her. Dolores must have been very sure of him, he thought, running his fingers down the list of Myerses, if she took a taxi an hour and a half before she rang him. Unless something happened in Brisestock to frighten her into making the call. 'I think,' he said, picking up the receiver, 'we're on to something here.'

Marion crossed her fingers and held them up for him to see.

Joseph Myers was tall, thirty-seven and dressed a little too fashionably for his age. He was also very nervous.

His office opened off the shop, at the back. The office window overlooked an overgrown orchard of old apple trees.

'Can I give you a drink, Inspector? I was just going to have one.' He took a bottle of Scotch from a drawer in his beautifully preserved roll-top desk.

'No, thank you. I'm on duty.'

'Of course. How silly of me. You don't mind if I do?'

'Not at all. You live here, Mr Myers?'

'In the flat upstairs, yes. It's a bit small but big enough for one.'

'You're not married?'

'Divorced. Two years ago.' He drank the whisky neat, with the air of a man who needed it. 'Irretrievable break-down. And I'm certain the maintenance is up to date . . . ' He bent fussily over the desk, looking in pigeon-holes, presumably for a bank statement.

'I'm sure it is,' Jolley said reassuringly.

'Well, if I've handled anything bent, it's without my knowledge. I'm scrupulous about— '

'It's about Dolores Bayger. She is a customer of yours, I believe.'

He froze over the desk. When he looked at Jolley his face showed surprise and confusion. His breathing was rapid. 'Bayger . . . '

'A regular customer, I understand. Came here, on aver-age, once a month . . . '

'As often as that? Really? I wouldn't have said . . . Not regularly anyway.'

'You do know her, then?'

'Ye-es . . . ' He still sounded uncertain.

'She was here yesterday afternoon.'

'That's right. Yes. So she was.'

'Did she buy anything?'

'Oh no, no . . . ' he said quickly and took a gulp from his glass.

'She did buy from you, though?'

He seemed to wince at this, took another drink and then put the glass down. Still without answering, he crossed the room to where his jacket hung, took out a packet of cigarettes and lit one with an old-fashioned gold lighter. 'She has done, yes.'

'You would have receipts, a record?'

'Oh yes.'

'Can you recall anything— '

'Some glasses. Crystal. Nineteen-thirties. But all my paperwork is with my accountant right now. We're rather late with the tax returns this year.'

'But you could supply me with records?'

'Oh yes. Certainly. I could, yes.'

'Mr Myers, I have information which leads me to believe Miss Bayger was a regular customer of yours and yet you seem vague . . . '

'She didn't buy very much. Of course I know who you mean . . . '

'She just came to browse?'

'Yes. That's it. To browse. Mostly.'

'What was your relationship with her, Mr Myers?'

'My relationship? We didn't . . . I wouldn't say we had a relationship. She was a customer, as you say . . . A customer, yes.'

'Who called about once a month . . . '

'Well, if you say so but it really didn't seem so often to me. She bought a few pieces from me. Some glasses, some copper, I think. It's so difficult to remember . . . Mostly she used to call in when she was passing, to have a look round . . . She appreciated fine things, I think . . . '

'When she was passing to where?'

The man looked positively startled at this, blinked several times rapidly. 'Well, I . . . er . . . I couldn't really say.'

'She just looked around?'

'Yes. She'd ask if I'd got anything new in. That sort of thing . . . '

'You weren't by any chance her lover?'

'Good God – no! I mean . . . well, no . . . '

'That's all right, Mr Myers. I apologise. But you do seem very vague about her.'

'Well, only because I . . . I mean I don't really know her. Don't know her at all, really. She was just a customer. That's all.'

'Yesterday,' Jolley said patiently. 'You do remember her coming here yesterday?'

'Oh yes.'

'Can you tell me about her visit?'

'Well . . . yes . . . She came in. I was on the phone but I saw her through the door – that door there, into the shop, I mean. I always leave it open when I'm in the office in case someone comes in. Anyway, I saw her and she waved and I waved back. When I'd finished my call I went into the shop and we passed the time of day. She was interested in that blue bowl . . . I'll show you . . . ' He started towards the door.

'There's no need, Mr Myers. I'll take your word for it.'

'Oh. Right. Fine. Thank you very much.'

'Sit down, Mr Myers, would you?'

He sat in an old swivel chair which, Jolley guessed, matched the desk in period if not quite in style. 'I told her the bowl was nothing special. She asked if I'd got anything new in. I hadn't, much. Trade hasn't been too good just lately, well, not for most of this year, really. I haven't bought in much stock. No room, you see and, well, cash-flow problems. But I showed her what I had and then she went off.'

'Did she ask to use your telephone?'

'Oh no. Why?'

'Could she have used your telephone, without you knowing?'

'Well . . . yes . . . no . . . I don't know.'

172

'Did you,' Jolley said, speaking slowly, trying not to show his impatience, 'leave her alone at any time?'

He tilted his head back, obviously thinking, or, Jolley thought, considering what it would be wise to tell.

'Yes, as a matter of fact, now you come to mention it, I did. I've got a few pieces of Coalport upstairs. They're quite lovely and I've had them in the flat. I went up to get them.'

'And where was Miss Bayger when you went upstairs?'

'Why, in here. I asked her to sit down, right there, where you're sitting and I went ... ' His eyes followed Jolley's to the telephone on the corner of the desk. They were both within easy reach of it. 'I see what you mean,' he said, sounding relieved.

'How long were you gone?'

'Oh, a few minutes ... I ... er ... I ... er ... went to the bathroom while I was upstairs. I hadn't had a chance ... The phone, as I told you ... Frankly, I was bursting. So I took the opportunity to ... And then I got the Coalport and brought it down.'

'So she could have made a phone call?'

'Yes. I suppose she could.'

'And when you came down?'

'I showed her the pieces and she admired them but I could tell she wasn't really interested. And she left at once.'

'And you haven't seen her since?'

'Well, yes, actually I did. I saw her later on, through the shop window, getting into Traxel's taxi. I waved but she didn't notice me.'

'Thank you very much, Mr Myers. That's very helpful.'

'Has she made a complaint? Is that it? Something I sold her ... ?'

'No, Mr Myers. Do you think she should?'

'Oh no. Only, well, you must know what this business is like. I am *very* careful. I only buy from accredited dealers or direct from the owners but, well, sometimes, well, you can't be one hundred per cent sure ... I don't take risks, Inspector. I can't afford to. But then one never can be sure one hasn't handled something that isn't, well, perhaps . . . '

'One hundred per cent,' Jolley finished for him. 'I understand. And I can assure you that if anything suspect should be traced back to you, you will be the first to know. Now, Mr Myers, what did you do after you saw Miss Bayger getting into the taxi?'

'What did I do? Oh, well, I . . . um . . . I suppose I . . . just pottered around the shop.'

'Did you have any more customers?'

'No.'

'What time did you close?'

'Half-past five.'

'And then?'

'I went upstairs.'

'I want to know exactly what you did last night, Mr Myers. You just take it slowly and tell me, in your own words, and I'll listen. All right?'

Dumbly, Myers nodded, and finished his drink.

'I suppose he must be dealing in dodgy goods,' Marion said when Jolley had finished telling her about his interview. 'We'd better keep an eye on him.'

'Save that for a rainy day. He's jumpy all right but I'm sure he wasn't . . . intimate with Miss Bayger and he could just be the nervous type. Any more coffee in that pot?' Marion pushed the pot towards him and he helped himself. It was earth-tasting canteen coffee but it staved off, or seemed to, the weariness that threatened them both. 'What have we got then, Sergeant?'

'Traxel's statement checks out. Three locals in Chuters saw Miss Bayger getting out of the taxi and going into her house. They would appear to be the last to see her alive, always excepting her killer. People remember seeing lights in the house later on. If they can be trusted it would appear she went to bed around ten p.m..

'Oh, I am sure the good people of Chuters timed

her with a stopwatch and logged every move much more efficiently even than our friend Traxel.'

'You're bitter,' Marion said, leaning her cheek on her hand and looking at him. During the long day her make-up had faded or worn off, leaving her looking younger and more vulnerable. 'Anyway, it was the ten o'clock news on ITV which fixed it for them.'

'And that's it?'

Marion nodded.

'Well, then, suspects.'

'The husband, obviously.'

'Leave him for a moment.'

'Belle Smith, the Brimbles, Mrs Keene.'

'Ah . . . Here I have news, if I can only find the damned thing.' He searched in the mess of papers spread over his desk until he found some notes of his own, scrawled on various scraps of paper. Marion looked disapproving at this haphazard method. 'Belle Smith and her mother were at the Bingo in Nusford until ten. Corroboration that they were out from a neighbour – can't read my own writing – who kept an eye on the boys. PC Withers is even now trying to get corroboration from the Bingo Hall and the woman who gave them a lift there and back.'

'How long for them to get home?'

'Fifteen minutes?'

'Bayger wasn't killed until much later.'

'Belle Smith and Mrs Keene have no transport. How could they get to Chuters and back?'

'Even so, we should check.'

'Even so . . . The Brimbles are on holiday. Left on Monday, due back Sunday. WPC Anson is checking that they are indeed in a caravan at Clacton with Mrs Brimbles's married sister.'

'Rule out the Brimbles?'

'I am inclined to do so, but . . . even so . . . let us not be hasty.'

Marion made a note on her own pad. 'Myers?'

'Myers says he had a drink at the Cock in Brisestock at about seven, dined with some people called Pelliser from eight until midnight and returned to his bed. All being checked. And I don't think he could kill a mouse,' Jolley added.

'And I don't see that he had any motive.'

'While I don't think it's a woman's crime – referring back to Mesdames Smith and Keene. Which rules out everyone else but Mr Brimble.'

'And Wilding.'

'Brimble, if he was on the spot, didn't share his wife's dislike of Miss Bayger. I think he's a man who would settle for a quiet life. I don't even think he saw Miss Bayger as a factor in the cause of his son's death.'

'But men have done some pretty funny things to satisfy a nagging woman and get that quiet life,' Marion pointed out.

'Now who sounds bitter?'

'Cynical, possibly. I reckon we can rule out Corr-Beardsley's sister and girlfriend, if only on geographical grounds and your theory about it not being a woman's crime. Which would leave us with Wilding and A.N. Other.'

'Oh? Who's he?'

'You didn't rule out the possibility of a lover, earlier.'

'No. Indeed I did not. At the same time, we've no reason to believe there was a lover.'

'True. So, Wilding.'

'We've got to find him. If he is in this country and he did do it, then now's the time he'll want to get out. Which means we've got to make sure he doesn't. To which end, I must show you something.' Marion raised her eyebrows, looked interested. From the bottom drawer of his desk, Jolley lifted the folder of photographs, opened it to the back, the last six pictures. 'I warn you, it's not very pleasant.' He turned the volume around and handed it to her across the cluttered desk. She stared at the face, at each image in turn. He saw her lips tighten, the colour fade slowly from

176

her cheeks. 'That,' Jolley said drily, 'according to Dolores Bayger and to the best of my knowledge is John James Wilding.'

'You're joking,' she said, but without conviction. Jolley shook his head slowly. 'But these are— '

'I did warn you . . . '

'Who could take these?'

'Dolores Bayger.'

'God in heaven!' She looked back through the folder.

'Come,' Jolley called in answer to a knock on the door. Marion flipped back through the folder as WPC Russell handed Jolley the keys to 'The Stables'. He slipped them into his pocket.

'Sergeant Hadfield says do you want another man on the house only PC Dyer's due for relief? He can send Doulton if you want.'

'No,' Jolley answered. 'Not Doulton. It won't be necessary. Tell him to bring Dyer in.'

'Right you are, sir.'

'Thanks, Penny.'

Marion glanced up at him. He saw that she had found the nudes. She inspected several of the plates closely, a smile spreading across her face. After a moment, she laughed.

'You find those amusing, Sergeant?' Jolley said, trying to conceal his embarrassment.

'Yes, I do. Don't you?' She looked across at him. 'No, sorry, I can see you don't. Well . . . ' She turned grimly back to the pictures of the tortured face. 'I suppose you're going to say we'd better circulate these.'

'I'm afraid so. I'd rather not but I don't think we have any choice. Wilding may be here, under our noses somewhere. If we're going to stop him getting out the immigration boys will need every help they can get. But we'll have to get on to America as well.'

Marion cracked open the ring-binder and extracted the six photographs. She put these aside, closed the folder and handed it back to him. Jolley took it and put it back in the drawer.

'Have you still got that gun in there?' she asked sharply.

'Yes.' He closed the drawer.

'Hadn't you better turn it in?'

'I will later. First things first.'

'Just don't forget. OK,' she said, hurrying on as she saw his thunderous frown, 'Airlines, ports, ferries, passport control, all police stations?'

'Everybody gets a copy of those photos.'

'Do we have any other description of him?'

'None. And we don't know when those were taken. The last two years?'

'Any idea where in America he was supposed to be?'

'In a mental hospital from which he has recently been released. But the hospital could be anywhere in that vast country.'

'If it exists at all.' She leaned back in her chair, pushing her hands into her tightly plaited hair. 'This is going to take time.'

'Somebody just might remember him. We might strike lucky.' Jolley did not even sound as though he believed it.

'What about local mental hospitals?'

'Good idea,' he agreed. 'And we'd better get on to the Drug Squad as well. She told me he was a user. If he is around, presumably he'll need to buy.'

Marion picked up one of the photographs, peered at it. 'Nice bloke,' she said. 'Violent, unstable, depressive, suicidal and a junkie ... You're sure she took these?' There was disbelief in her voice and something stronger. Jolley nodded. 'What kind of person was she, for God's sake?'

Jolley made no attempt to answer this. It was a rhetorical question anyway. But in his mind there were so many answers and each contradicted the other. 'I'll take America,' he said, reaching for the phone, pushing papers aside higgledy-piggledy. 'You start on the airlines, etcetera ... Do as much as you can tonight and then get off home. Get a good night's sleep. Then, first thing tomorrow, go to Passington and organise the photos, distribution ... We

can't handle it from here. You'd better ring the duty officer.'
She stood up, stretched, gathered up her bag, notepad and
the photographs.

'What time is it in America?'

'Earlier than here. Leave it to me. And get Johnson
to help you.'

'OK.'

'And then get off home.'

'What about you?'

'I'll go as soon as I've run out of answers from America.
I want you in Passington at crack of dawn. And as soon as
you've finished get back here pronto.'

'I'll say good-night, then.'

'Yes. Good-night.'

He lifted the receiver, sighing.

Jolley leaned back in his creaking chair, rubbed his eyes
with his knuckles. The station was never silent, not even
at this late hour, but there was a different kind of noise at
night. Like an engine, he thought, that had settled down,
was just ticking over. He heard a door squeak, rubber soles
approach down the corridor past his door. In the yard
below he heard a car start and drive away. He had done
all he could. Messages had been left, telexes sent, checks
started. He had received promises of help. Everyone had
said it would take time. He stared at the clutter on his desk,
wondering what he had missed. He was tired. This was just
the nag of anxiety. Leave it now, he told himself. It would
all be there in the morning and he would be able to view
it with fresh eyes. If he had missed anything, he'd spot it
then, not now when his brain ached . . . He stretched and
pressed his hands to his chest. Beneath his left hand he
felt something hard in his breast pocket. He remembered.
With forefinger and thumb he fished it out, held it up in
the light of his desk-lamp. A fine gold chain, a funny little
metal figure, like an amulet or charm. Pre-Columbian, he
thought, not knowing what he meant by that. It was just
something, some style he associated with America and this

little metal object had a primitive look to it. He closed his eyes and allowed himself to see Dolores Bayger as he had seen her that morning.

This time he did not use his professional eyes. The room, her bedroom seemed to form around him. She lay on her back, peacefully sleeping, one arm thrown up, the hair on the right side of her head fanned across the pillow. He winced at the stain on the front of her gown. Her scent. Safer ground this. The feel of her clothes on his skin, watery materials that slipped and flowed through his clumsy fingers. The dark red backless dress that she had called green sliding along the rail, its skirt swaying, giving off clouds of perfume. The boots she had worn yesterday, still muddied . . . He went back to that red dress, his left hand on the cold metal hanger. He slid it to the left . . . He saw it then. His whole body stiffened. His eyes opened, sharp and clear. He lifted the chain again, stared at the metal pendant. What a bloody fool he had been! It all fell into place. Images of her, in a white blouse and black slacks . . . How could he have missed it? No need to ask that. She had clouded his mind, blinded his eyes . . . He got up quickly, pushing the chair back. Hang on a minute, he told himself, think this through carefully. But he could not. Before the pieces had quite slotted into place, formed a coherent picture, he was out of the office and running towards the back stairs, cursing himself for his stupidity. At the swing door, he paused just long enough to put the chain and pendant into his pocket. The rush of adrenalin spurred him on. He knew, even if he did not know quite what it meant, that somehow it was all within his grasp.

# Seven

He stood alone in her bedroom again, the heavy torch dangling from his hand. He kept the light pointed at the floor, tried to remember the layout of the room, banged against a chair, barking his shin. He raised the torch. The bed had been stripped. He tried to ignore the stain on the mattress, leaned over and put on the bedside lamp, turning his back quickly on the bed. He switched the torch off and placed it on the nightstand.

Now that he was so close, he hesitated. He was glad that he had not kept a constable on duty at the house all night. Perhaps subconsciously he had known all along that he would need to get back into the house without having to explain to colleagues. Hand in his pocket, he fingered the gold chain, what he had mistaken for an ornament. He pulled it out and let it hang, looped over his finger. The curiously shaped, flat metal object gleamed in the light. It seemed ridiculous now that he could ever have mistaken it. He opened one of the wardrobe doors, his eyes searching for the red backless dress. Its full skirt crushed between a black and blue-figured dress caused him no pang now. The adrenalin which quickened his blood subdued emotion. He rattled the hangers in his sudden haste, pushing the dresses left and right. He stopped when he saw the small black box again, stared at it intently. He searched it with his fingers, delicately exploring its shape. There was a hairline crack, no more, to suggest that it opened, that half of it was a door or covering which could be removed. Then, low down on the right-hand side, he found a wider aperture, a slot. He stuck his head into the wardrobe, not remarking the heavy smell of familiar perfume, but could see nothing. He needed more light.

The irregular stain on the mattress made him catch his breath. He supposed forensic had not taken it away yet for lack of suitable transport and thought that if he were doing his job properly he would know their precise arrangements. He picked up the torch and went back to the wardrobe. He shone the beam on to the black box. The little slot did not look like a keyhole in any conventional sense but he was prepared to bet that the object on the chain would fit it. He swopped chain and torch, left hand to right. Gently now, he warned himself, holding the metal key steady. Don't put it in the wrong way and get it jammed or stuck. Tentatively, he slid the metal into the slot, met resistance. He pulled it out and turned it over. This time, his heartbeat accelerating, it slid home easily. You did not have to twist or turn it. As he pushed it home there was the faintest of clicks and the front portion of the box moved slightly towards him. He opened it fully, the key still in place, the chain swinging, catching the light.

Jolley was no handyman, lacked any aptitude for things mechanical. Even if he had possessed such skills, the device was too complicated for any but a professional to under-stand. Too complicated and yet, in another sense, obviously simple. A small clock with a scarlet second hand was set at midnight. The scarlet needle moved in regular, perfectly timed jerks. Below the clock-face were two rows of buttons with figures marked in white thereon. He brought his face close to the mechanism, directed the beam of the torch on it. Below the numbered buttons were two more, the letters above them slightly scratched with use by long fingernails. One was labelled *Set*, the other, *Over-ride*. That button, like the second hand was scarlet. He touched nothing, shone the torch instead on the inside of the covering. It contained only one instruction, in shiny silver lettering on a black plate. *Warning. Over-ride will only function after combination is keyed in. Misuse may damage the mechanism.* He withdrew, as though in response to the warning. He stared at it again, as though by force of will he could prise out its secret. Then, transferring the torch to his left hand, he looked at his watch.

He moved quickly, with a sense of cautious purpose. He put out the bedside light and used the torch to find his way to the door, which he closed behind him before he went down the stairs. The keys were in his pocket and he locked the front door from the inside, glancing again at his watch. The kitchen table had been moved aside, shrouded in plastic, labelled by forensic, awaiting removal. He crossed the kitchen quickly and unlocked the back door. He directed the beam of the torch around the stable yard, remembering the ravens. The rents in the wire of their cage showed clearly. No dark malevolent eye or black shining feathers glared back at him. He closed and locked the back door, went quickly to the tall side gate and checked that it was bolted. Satisfied, he swung the light over to the stable block, let it settle on the heavy black door. He walked slowly towards it, his footsteps sounding loud in the silence. Nothing for it now but to wait, he thought. And if it was a wait in vain? He shook his head. It would not be. He was certain of that. Whatever lay on the other side of that door, he could not lose. If the worst came to the worst . . .

He stood, facing the door, ready. He switched off the torch after one more glance at his watch. The minutes passed with numbing slowness. Nothing happened. The possibility that he was wrong about the black box grew closer to a certainty. He put the torch on again, nervously. His watch showed a few seconds past midnight. But was his watch right? When had he last set it? His mind was blank. He knew it gained slightly. Usually, he checked and corrected it by the 8 a.m. news on the radio. The second hand swept around, upwards. At a minute past midnight by his watch, he heard a slight whirring noise and then the smooth, almost silent click of sliding metal. The door remained still and steadfast, but he had been right. An electronic time-switch. He stepped up to the door, holding the torch at hip level. With his right hand, he pushed the door. It was heavy but well maintained. It opened smoothly inward. The beam of his torch cut through darkness. There was a stale, musty smell of warm air over-used. Jolley stepped over the threshold, paused, swung the light about, seeing little, the gleam of metal. He took a few steps deeper into the room and instantly sensed rather than saw something moving rapidly towards him, coming at him out of the dark. He put up his hand, hearing the whistle of something moving through the air. An image of a raven came to him, a raven flying at him, intent on black mischief. Then something exploded on the back of his neck. Pain, liquid, yellow, like flames, rose up from the back of his neck and engulfed him. He pitched forward, staggered. The second blow, almost gentle in comparison, struck him across the shoulders and the floor, hard and cold, rose up to claim him.

Marion Glade's back ached from long hours of sitting. Her eyes were hot and gritty from staring at the green glimmer of the VDU. Using her feet, she propelled the chair which had become a subtle form of torture, away from the computer to the desk on her left. Gliding up to it, she bent over her carefully prepared list and, taking a red felt-tipped pen, worked carefully through it, making a broad tick beside each task done.

'Finished,' she announced, standing up, her hands pressed to the small of her back. Sergeant Bayfield of Passington Police HQ grinned at her. He was in his shirtsleeves and used green elastic bands to hold his cuffs back.

'Pretty good going,' he complimented her. 'You look like you could use a coffee.'

'Oh, those are the most beautiful words I've heard in hours.'

'I'll take you down to the canteen,' he offered, glancing around the room to see that all was in order.

'Thanks.' Marion collected her jacket, bag and pad.

'It'll have to be quick, though. I've got to get back to Oversleigh.'

The swing doors opened with a squeak and a clatter. A tall, dark man with chiselled features glanced around the room, his eyes coming to rest on Marion.

'Sergeant Glade?'

'Yes.' She returned his stare. He came over, hand out.

'Dave Hughes. I used to— '

'I know. Pleased to meet you.' She grasped his hand, shook it.

'I was just going to take Miss Glade down to the canteen,' Bayfield said.

'I'll do it,' Hughes said. 'I wanted a word anyway.'

'Thanks for all your help, Sergeant,' Marion said, shaking hands with Bayfield. 'I appreciate it. And so will Inspector Jolley.'

'My pleasure. See you around. And good luck.'

'Thanks.' She smiled and turned to Hughes. 'Right. Lead me to coffee.' He grabbed the swing door and held it open for her.

'Tait wants to see you,' he said as soon as they were out in the corridor. 'What's going on?'

Marion shrugged. 'Search me. Have we got time for coffee first?'

'He'll organise one. He wants you now.'

'Well then . . . ' She set off down the corridor, towards the lifts.

'Hang on . . . ' Hughes caught up with her, touched her arm but she shrugged him off. 'How is Cy?'

'Fine.'

'Well, what's all this about then?'

'We've got a murder on our hands. I've just been organising a general alert for a suspect.'

'Word is,' Hughes said, 'that Jolley's somehow involved.'

'Well, of course he's involved. He's in charge . . . ' She looked impatiently at her watch. 'And he wants me back there. Now if I've got to see the Super— '

'I meant personally. What's going on?'

185

Marion stopped, turned towards Hughes. She decided she did not like him, resented being pumped.

'I don't know what you're talking about. And I don't think you should listen to gossip.'

'Listen . . . ' He glanced up and down the corridor, lowered his voice. 'I'm not interested in gossip. Jolley means a lot to me. He's the best. If something's up, I want to help.'

Marion regarded him suspiciously, then relaxed a little.

'OK. As far as I know there's nothing wrong. Just a case that requires us to move quickly. And you ought to know that when Jolley says quickly— '

' . . . He means quickly. Right. So why does Tait want to see you?'

'That I will find out when I see him. Now, excuse me— '

'He's got a bee in his bonnet about something and the word is— '

'I don't want to know what the word is,' Marion said, reaching to press the lift button. 'As far as I'm concerned, everything's going according to plan.'

'Don't you care for Jolley at all?' Hughes said, looking furious.

The silver lift doors slid silently open. Hughes immediately stuck out his arm, barring her way.

'Yes,' Marion told him. 'And the best way I can help him is to get on with my job. Let me pass, please.'

'So he's not involved?' Hughes persisted. The doors started to close and Hughes instinctively grabbed the edge of one, pushing it back. Seizing her chance, Marion ran into the lift and swung round to face him as the doors began to close again.

'And you say you know Jolley,' she said with heavy sarcasm. The doors shut fast and she punched the button angrily. The lift glided upwards.

But his words disturbed her. Police stations are, after all, only communities of people and where there are groups of people there is an insatiable curiosity about human behaviour. Gossip thrives and feeds on itself. She

186

squeezed her eyes shut against tiredness. She knew that she had not been alone in noticing Jolley's – she searched for a neutral word – attachment to Dolores Bayger. She had overheard Hadfield telling Roscoe and Doulton about the dead woman bringing a fancy package to the station for him, an obvious present. She had ignored the gossip for fear of fuelling it. And because she was new and as yet regarded with a certain amount of suspicion by her Oversleigh colleagues, no one had sought her opinion or tried to involve her directly. But she had not considered that it could have spread to Passington.

With a little lurch, the lift stopped and the doors parted. She stepped out into a carpeted corridor. And what if it had? What if they were saying Jolley had been attracted to Dolores Bayger? Did they think he was less than human? OK, so he may have made a bit of a fool of himself . . . Pausing before the Superintendent's door, pushing her loose hair tidily behind her ears, Marion Glade was surprised by the strength of her own feelings: feelings of loyalty towards Jolley and a kind of sorrow for his position. But she should not be surprised. She, after all, had seen his face in Dolores Bayger's bedroom. She had seen the mistiness in his eyes and the look of frozen grief that transformed him. Although she had not admitted it at the time, she had known then that he had loved the dead woman on the bloodstained bed. It wasn't a matter of routine attraction. It wasn't, as the gossips no doubt had it, a case of Jolley wanting a bit on the side . . . Her lip curled at the ugly phrase. It was something real and deep and dreadful for him and she had admired the way he was handling an impossible situation. A lot of idle talk was not going to detract from that. Not if she had anything to do with it.

She raised her fist and banged too loudly on the door, venting her anger. A muffled voice answered her and, feeling slightly foolish, she opened the door.

'No need to knock the door down, Sergeant,' Tait said, turning from the great window behind his desk so that he appeared as a featureless silhouette against the light, the elegant spire of Passington Cathedral rising behind him. 'I was expecting you. Indeed, I was looking forward to seeing you.'

'Sorry, sir.' Marion closed the door behind her and waited, looking at him.

There was a chair placed before his desk. After a moment, he invited Marion to sit in it. She did so with a feeling of being in the hot seat. Superintendent Tait did not sit but paced up and down the space between his desk and the big window. For some moments he did not speak. His pink brow, beneath the perfectly smooth, rigorously parted white hair, was furrowed but somehow he did not have the look of a truly worried man. He turned to Marion suddenly, a quite disarming smile transforming his face. 'And how are you getting on with Mr Jolley?'

'Very well indeed, sir, thank you.'

'And you've got all your little jobs done for him? I'm so glad we could be of assistance to you.'

Mentally, Marion bit her tongue at this calculated way of demeaning her morning's labours. 'Yes, thank you, sir. We are very grateful.'

'And do you like Oversleigh?'

'More and more as I get to know it.'

'Good. Good.' He turned away again, stood, rocking slightly, looking out of the window. His hands, folded loosely together behind him, fidgeted. Marion watched them. 'How do you *find* Mr Jolley?' he asked. Then, spinning round suddenly, he leaned towards her. 'You may speak perfectly frankly, Sergeant. This is strictly *entre nous*.'

Marion regarded his cold blue eyes for a second, then said, 'Very much as you predicted I would, sir. A first-rate policeman. Loads of experience. A bit of a character but very kind-hearted.' It was obvious from Tait's controlled expression that, for once, he did not enjoy being quoted. 'And a bit impatient, sir. Without wishing to be rude, he did tell me to get back to Oversleigh as soon as I was finished here.'

'Ah . . . ' Tait straightened up, turned back to the window, measured its length in slow, deliberate, thoughtful paces. 'First, tell me what is your opinion of this case, Sergeant. In a nutshell.'

'In a nutshell, sir, we need to find the woman's husband. My feelings are that we can eliminate him very quickly if, say, he turns out to be in America, or he is going to be our man. At the moment, we don't have anything else, sir.'

'Oh? And is this Mr Jolley's view as well?'

'To the best of my knowledge, sir.'

'You're quite . . . convinced of that, are you?'

'I'm sorry, sir, I don't— '

'I wondered if you might have formed some private view of the case which your . . . er . . . position would make it . . . awkward for you to share with Mr Jolley.'

'Absolutely not, sir.'

'And you're confident that Mr Jolley has shared all his thoughts with you?'

'To the best of my knowledge, sir,' Marion repeated. 'Of course, Mr Jolley is under no obligation to confide in me but I have no reason to think he's held anything back.'

'No, no, of course not.' Tait sighed heavily, looked distressed. 'I am extremely sorry, Sergeant. What must you think of me? I haven't offered you some coffee. I'm sure you must need some. I am much preoccupied this morning. You must— '

'No, thank you, sir. I really must be getting back . . . '

'But I insist . . . ' He lifted the white internal phone on his desk, ordered coffee. His smile returned pallidly as he replaced the receiver. 'Yes, a perplexed man, I assure you,' he went on, swinging his black leather chair round towards him and sitting in it with a show of relief. 'Not that that is any excuse for my neglect . . . '

'That's perfectly all right, sir.'

'Yes, a perplexed man. Even worried.' He swung the chair into the desk, leaned his forearms on it and poked his head forward in a gesture that reminded Marion of a turtle, fixing her with his eyes. 'May *I* confide in *you*, Sergeant?'

'Certainly, sir.'

'I mean can I *trust* you, Sergeant?'

'I hope so, sir.'

'So do I, Sergeant. So do I.' He continued to regard her, examining her face, until she began to feel thoroughly uncomfortable. A tap at the door, discreet and unobtrusive, broke the spell. 'Ah, coffee . . . '

Never, in Marion's experience, had coffee been supplied so quickly in a police station. Not only that but it came in a stainless steel pot, with hot milk and fine china cups. It was served by a young woman with a deference Marion could only think was the result of the Superintendent's personal training. When they were alone again, Marion said, 'You were saying, sir . . . ?'

'It's not that I don't trust you, of course . . . You must forgive me if I appeared to suggest anything like that . . . I am reluctant to put you in an ambivalent position, you see.'

'I'm not sure I do, sir.'

'*Vis-à-vis* Inspector Jolley,' he said. There was something about the way he came to the point that reminded Marion of a snake striking its prey.

'I wouldn't care for that myself, sir,' she responded.

'Of course you wouldn't. You are loyal. That is how it should be. However . . . Sometimes we have to rise above loyalty, we have to go beyond the inhibitions set up by our most laudable feelings in order to find the truth. Is the coffee to your taste?' Marion, startled by the irrelevancy, nodded. 'You know, of course, that Inspector Jolley had an assignation with the dead woman on the day she met her tragic end?'

Marion felt a flutter of relief. If that's all it was . . . 'Yes, sir. Mr Jolley told me himself. In fact, he insisted on giving me a full account of the meeting and ordered me to take it down. It will be included in the report, sir, just as soon as I can get it typed up.'

'Well, there you are you see. Jolley is a most conscientious officer . . . '

'Indeed he is, sir.'

'Which is what makes it so . . . painful to be forced to regard him with . . . suspicion. So painful,' he repeated, shaking his head sadly.

'Suspicion, sir?' So there was more, she thought. Just gossip, and she would tell him so.

'Alas, yes.'

'I'm absolutely sure— ' Marion began, flushing, but was silenced by Tait's upraised, forbidding hand.

'We take your loyalty as read, Sergeant Glade. Now, please, do try to see beyond it. Look at the facts.'

'I'm not aware of any facts— '

'First, Jolley admits meeting this woman shortly before her death . . . '

'Scarcely "shortly",' Marion corrected him.

'Secondly, later that same day he simply walked out of his house in mid-conversation with his wife, got into his car and drove away. He did not return until three a.m. and he offered Mrs Jolley no explanation for his absence. Now, perhaps you can enlighten me as to his whereabouts at the time of this woman's death. Perhaps Mr Jolley insisted on making a statement about that, too, which I shall have the pleasure of reading in the report . . . when, of course, you have time to type it up, Sergeant.'

'No, sir,' Marion said softly. 'I didn't know about that.'

'Quite. But you do see what it means?'

'I'm not sure that I do.' She felt cold suddenly, wanted to finish her coffee but was afraid to pick up the cup in case her hand shook. She did not want Tait to see how concerned she was.

'It means that, until we can establish what Mr Jolley was doing during those hours, we must consider that he had an opportunity— '

'No,' Marion burst out. 'Absolutely not.'

'Furthermore, we think he had a motive— '

191

'That's preposterous. Mr Jolley wouldn't . . . couldn't harm a hair of her head.'

'Oh? And why not?'

'That's not for me to say, sir. Because of the man he is. You know how . . . You know him better than me . . . '

'Much as one may deplore the fact, Sergeant, men do change. You should know that. Human creatures are capable of transformation. Of all the phrases in the English language, I believe the one about never hurting a fly to be particularly empty, the least deserving of credence by anyone who has observed his fellow men and women.'

Marion had been about to use that very phrase. For a moment, she was nonplussed. Tait leaned back in his chair, secure of his advantage. He regarded her through slightly lowered lids, reminding her again of a reptile, smooth and dangerous.

'In my opinion, sir,' she said, trying to make her voice neutral, 'you should take this up with Inspector Jolley, not me. I have no doubt he can explain himself . . . '

'And I agree with you. Of course. You are undoubtedly right. The trouble is, Inspector Jolley is not available to provide answers. Your superior officer, Sergeant, has apparently vanished into thin air.'

'Vanished?' Marion shook her head. Anything less like Jolley . . .

'Which is why you are here. When did you last see him, Sergeant?'

'Last night.' She told him exactly what had happened, how she had left Jolley about to ring America while she started contacting the airlines and preparing her list of duties for this morning's visit to Passington. 'I don't believe he's gone missing. There must be some perfectly reasonable explanation.'

'Indeed I hope so. But the facts are these. At some time last night, Inspector Jolley left Oversleigh Station without anyone seeing him. He left his office light on. He took his car, though nobody appears to have heard him do so.

192

And he did not return home. Nor has he reported in this morning. His wife – poor woman – rang the station to speak to him this morning and when she was told that he had not been seen she had the good sense to telephone me. It is from her that I learned of Jolley's mysterious absence on the night of the murder and deduced a possible motive. Which means that as far as I am able to ascertain, no one has seen him since you bade him good-night.'

'But that's impossible . . . '

'Apparently not. And the vulgar among us might conclude from all this that Inspector Jolley has – now what is that phrase? – ah, yes . . . that Jolley has "done a runner". Indeed, that is precisely what a lot of people do think, under the circumstances.'

'Mr Jolley wouldn't do that. More likely he's following up some lead, something that suddenly occurred to him . . . '

'My view exactly. My dearest wish. The point is, we do not *know* this for a fact. Therefore, how long do we give him to keep us in mystification? How do we, meanwhile, contain the situation?'

'Is it contained?' Marion asked, thinking of Hughes. His questions now made ominous sense. Gossip which began at the top was always more powerful than canteen chit-chat.

'As far as I am aware,' Tait said coldly. 'And now, Sergeant, it's up to you.'

'To me?'

'Naturally. Consider the position we are in. If I put someone else on to this case, our suspicions about Inspector Jolley will have to be voiced. I can see that you find that as repugnant as I do. I have decided to give him until tonight. Until then, you are in charge, directly responsible to me. I shall, of course, make discreet inquiries of my own as to his whereabouts, but until he puts in an appearance or until – shall we say eight tonight? – I shall rely upon you. I shall, of course, speak to you from time to time . . . Now, is there anything you want to tell me?'

'No, sir,' she said without hesitation. A man who thought Jolley capable of Dolores Bayger's murder would never understand his love for her. That, too, would be used against him, she thought miserably. 'Except to say, sir, on the record, that I disassociate myself entirely from these "suspicions".' She stood up, partly because it seemed the full force of Tait's anger was about to be unleashed upon her. His face was the colour of dark brick. A prominent vein appeared and throbbed in his left temple. His hands, normally so fluent, almost a second tongue, were unnaturally still. She waited for the storm to break or pass.

Slowly, he stood up and turned again towards the window. 'Then you had better find him, Sergeant Glade, hadn't you?'

'I'll do my best, sir,' she said, taking this as a dismissal. She forced herself to walk at a normal pace to the door. As she touched the handle, Tait spoke again, anger roughening his voice.

'And if you do you had better get a full and complete statement from him. Nothing – do you understand me? – nothing else will suffice.'

'Yes, sir.'

She wanted to slam the door behind her but did not dare. She closed it gently and ran for the waiting lift.

There was light at the end of a tunnel. Jolley could see it. A distinct cone of light that seemed to be held in place by the darkness. Like light in a modern painting, contained by thick black lines. Stylised, he thought. Then all sharp, clear lines dissolved. Something, shapes, moved in the light, fluttered, rose and fell. Jolley tried to lift his head, thinking thereby to clear his indistinct vision. Pain gripped his neck and spread steely, victorious fingers up the back of his skull. He cried out but the sound emerged as no more than a sharp exhalation of air. He tried to move his hands and could not. Something tore at the fine hairs on his wrists. The light swirled and spun, a Catherine wheel that exploded into darkness again.

194

★

On the drive back from Passington, Marion worried not
so much about what had become of Jolley as to whom
she could trust to help her. Sergeant Hadfield she dis-
missed at once. Too lax, too set in his ways and far too
much of a gossip. Sergeant Bentinck she hardly knew. He
seemed to hold himself aloof from her and now was not
the time, she thought, to try to break through his reserve.
The women she knew only on the most superficial level,
though Penny Russell was undoubtedly devoted to Jolley.
Roscoe was too macho, too headstrong and Doulton hope-
less. She considered Withers but again knew too little about
him, where he stood in the complicated network of police
station loyalties. Everything, she concluded, by which she
actually meant a gut reaction, instinct, pointed to Johnson.
Johnson had always been friendly but not pushy. Johnson
respected Jolley, she was sure of that, and thought he could
keep his own counsel. So she settled for Johnson. But what
for? Until she had decided on a course of action . . .

For want of a plan her mind turned inevitably to Tait's
suspicions. Instantly, anger rose in her, but she pushed it
down. She had to look at the facts, had to milk them for
what they had to yield, not dilute them with her own
convictions or bias. Jolley had met Dolores Bayger on
the Thursday afternoon. There was nothing suspicious in
that. Dolores Bayger had been killed late Thursday night
or Friday morning. Jolley had found the body. That was
something that Tait had not mentioned and now, suddenly, the Inspector's insistence on going into the house
alone seemed sinister to Marion. Could he possibly have
known what he was going to find? Did he need a few
moments to check that he had not made any mistakes,
left anything incriminating? But Marion remembered the
crash and the cry she had heard, the terrible sounds that
had set her running after him. She had seen his face. No
one who had seen that face could doubt the grief . . . But,
another cold, reptilian voice interrupted her, who is to say
that a murderer may not feel grief? What about Othello?

Does not he feel remorse? In *crimes passionels* were not grief and regret common factors? On the other hand, she believed that Jolley had simply wanted to question Bayger alone. Because of his special relationship with her, he had wanted to speak to her alone, to demand why she had lied to him. She had understood that at the time and still could understand it. She wanted to go on believing that had been his sole and only motive.

Then, on the night of her death, he had disappeared without explanation for several hours. That represented opportunity. Opportunity could not be denied. Now he had disappeared again, had been missing for what – eleven, twelve hours? This thought fell flat, a stone which disappeared beneath the water without a ripple of disturbance. It had the finality of a dead end. Marion felt her mind go blank. She drove for several minutes as though in a fixed trance, her body reacting, her mind hanging in limbo.

Three men, three other men connected with Dolores Bayger, had taken their own lives. This was a fact. Jolley had been missing for twelve hours. This was a fact. She would not let the thought form. She must not.

Tait's facts implied nothing more than opportunity. There was no motive, no matter what he implied and hinted. There was the opposite of motive: love. Unless, of course, Dolores Bayger alive and rejecting was a pain too great for Jolley to bear. Marion had seen evidence of his temper, had been aware of his preoccupation, his obsession with the dead woman. She had been in the room when Dolores Bayger had rung him from the antique shop and had seen the effect her voice had on him, had seen him melt and become strong and purposeful again.

'No,' she told herself aloud. This was speculation, interpretation at the best. She had to stick to the cold facts. She must not let herself think of those other three men, their cold and dismal fates. And she had to present a calm, unruffled front to her colleagues. She had a few scant hours to do something positive. She must not waste them in idle, frightening speculation. She must not give way to her own fears.

It seemed as though no one at Oversleigh Police Station, which Marion Glade entered a few minutes later, had anything to do. A group of men and women were clustered around the desk, drinking tea and talking with Sergeant Hadfield. They fell silent as soon as she came in. One or two picked up papers or folders, tried to look busy. How Jolley would have bawled them out, she thought, but tried to ignore them. It was Hadfield who broke the silence, acknowledged her.

'Have you seen Inspector Jolley, Sergeant?'

'No. I'm just back from Passington,' she said and managed to smile. Let them think what they wanted; she was going to give them nothing. 'I'm going up to his office now. Put his calls and any for me through there, please.' She ran up the stairs before Hadfield could say anything else. She heard the babble of their subdued but excited voices as she reached the first landing. There was nothing she could do about that. If she turned on them now, she might forfeit their support and she was only too aware that she might need a lot of support later. Johnson, she thought, hurrying on up the stairs, had not been among the crowd downstairs. Please God he wasn't in court or something. But that could wait. She burst into Jolley's office and looked at the desk. It was just as she had seen it last night, a mess. Only now the mess looked sad, vulnerable. She leaned across it and picked up the phone. Hastily consulting her notebook, she punched in his home number. Any trepidation she felt was quashed by the reminder that this was what a good policewoman did – start with the only lead you had.

Eileen answered after one ring. Marion had a picture of her sitting there, one hand hovering over the receiver, willing it to ring, bring her good news.

'Mrs Jolley?'

'Yes.'

'This is Marion Glade. We haven't met . . . '

'Have you got news?'

'No. Nothing I'm afraid.'

'I've heard nothing,' Eileen said, the life draining out of her voice. 'He hasn't phoned or turned up here.'

'I'm sorry. I only heard about it a little while ago, in Passington. I wondered if you'd mind answering a few questions?'

'I've told Teddy Tait all I know,' Eileen answered, sounding tired and impatient.

'I know. But it would help if you'd tell me. The Superintendent has put me in charge of the case until Mr Jolley returns. It might help me to— '

'I don't know. I don't know where he is.'

'I appreciate that, Mrs Jolley. But if you could just tell me . . . I understand he went out Thursday night?' Eileen sighed. For a panic-stricken moment, Marion sensed that she might put the phone down. 'Please, Mrs Jolley. I've got to find him.'

The silence at the other end of the phone had a muffled quality, then Eileen said, 'All right. He went out . . . We were having a conversation and he suddenly got up and walked out. I asked him where he was going and he said just into the garden to get a breath of air or stretch his legs. Something like that. I can't remember. A few minutes later I heard the car start. I ran out but it was too late. I just saw the car going down the high street.'

'What time was this?'

'About half-past ten, maybe eleven.'

'And when did he return?'

'Ten to three.' Eileen Jolley made a sound like a suppressed sob.

'Did he say anything to you?'

'No. He didn't speak and neither did I.'

'Where do you think he went, Mrs Jolley?'

The sound again. Marion waited, eased around the desk and sank into Jolley's chair.

'I don't know.'

'Surely you must have ... had some idea. After all, it wasn't like him, was it, to go out like that ... ?'

'No. But then he hasn't been himself for some time now.'

'I think I know what you mean, Mrs Jolley ... '

'How could you? You're new. You don't know him ... '

'I think I do, Mrs Jolley. Please trust me. I only want to help.' Eileen said nothing to this. She blew her nose, holding the receiver away from her so that the sound was distant, blurred. 'When did you last see him, Mrs Jolley?' Marion asked gently.

'Friday morning, at breakfast.'

'I was with him all day. He was at his desk last night when I left him.'

'And no one's seen him since,' Eileen declared, her voice cracking.

'I'll find him, Mrs Jolley. I swear to you I will.'

'Thank you.'

'When he came back at ten to three Friday morning, how did he seem?'

'I don't know. Calm, if that's what you mean. Dejected, I suppose. I thought he might be angry if he knew I was still awake so I didn't ... I didn't say anything. But he seemed all right.'

'And you've really no idea where he might have gone?'

'I thought ... ' Eileen's voice broke. She swallowed loudly. 'I thought he must have gone to her, to that woman.'

'Dolores Bayger,' Marion said and hated the name, wished she had never heard it, that she did not have to speak it now.

'Yes.' Eileen sobbed.

'Thank you, Mrs Jolley. I'm so sorry to have bothered you. I'll be in touch as soon— '

'I didn't know, not till this morning ... I had no idea she was dead ... I didn't know.'

'Please don't upset yourself, Mrs Jolley. I'll let you know— '

'Yes, yes.' Eileen said and put the receiver down.

199

*I thought he must have gone to her, to that woman.* Shaken, Marion found herself staring at the pediment of Jolley's desk with its three deep drawers. On impulse, she opened the bottom one. The binder of photographs lay on top, the mother-of-pearl grip of Dolores Bayger's gun obtruded from beneath it, gleaming. The intercom buzzed. Catching her breath, Marion answered it.

'Sergeant Hadfield here, Sergeant Glade.'

'Yes, Sergeant, what can I do for you?'

'We have a report, Sergeant, from a Miss Lancaster of 21 Chuters.'

'Yes, Sergeant?'

'Lady says she saw a light in "The Stables" late last night.'

'How late?' Marion snapped.

'The lady couldn't be precise, Sergeant. I told her that was impossible— '

'Very well, Sergeant. Thank you. I'll deal with it.'

Marion emptied the bottom drawer. Penny Russell had brought the keys in, given them to Jolley. She searched the desk thoroughly, patted the layers of paper on its top for something hard hidden beneath. The keys to 'The Stables' were not there.

*I thought he must have gone to her, to that woman.*

Marion picked up the pretty little gun, stood there, weighing it in her hand.

The world was red. The world was a tunnel of red with a light at the distant end of it. A cone of light. Jolley forced himself to focus on that. He tried, very carefully, to lift his head. It felt as though bone rubbed against bone, splintered. The back of his head felt like a drum, constantly beaten. A membrane stretched taut, throbbing, reverberating with each malicious blow. He imagined the timpanist's hand on the skin, deadening the noise, the pain. There was no such benign hand, only the constant blows that set his head oscillating like a drumskin, which made his vision blur and dissolve. Red seeped into the bright cone of yellow light, making it indistinct, watery. He told himself that he must not pass out again. He kept his head down, willed himself not to black out. Bile rose in his dry mouth. He swallowed compulsively against the desire to be sick. His swallowing matched the rhythm in his head. He opened his eyes again and watched the cone of light hold back the red, settle and become still. His heart thudded as he recognised arms in that light, bare arms, resting on a surface, a table. In the red, if he tried hard, he could make out the shape of a table, the pink gleam of white shoes beneath it. He made a noise, a combination of a burp and cry for help. The figure at the table moved. Jolley could not keep it in focus. His eyes could not adjust and he dare not lift his head for fear of hurting his neck again. My neck is broken, he thought. It was the only clear thought he had had and it remained in his mind. My neck is broken. The light ended, leaving only the red. Something moving in the red. Something coming towards him. A smell. Then his brain understood before his eyes could make out what was happening. He shut his eyes tight as something cold and wet hit his face, making him jerk his head back in shock and surprise.

The pain nearly made him lose consciousness. He cried out and blessed drops of water ran into his dry mouth. Head back, the pain momentarily forgotten, he stuck out his tongue, lapping water like a rabid dog as it ran down his face, soaked his shirt. Hungrily seeking the water, he heard the slap of feet against wood, steps receding, returning. He dare not move his head from its present position of locked pain and was too frightened to open his eyes. Water dribbled into his mouth, became a stream. He swallowed greedily, with difficulty. The stream became a torrent. He could not swallow fast enough. Water entered his nose. He was drowning. He began to cough and bring back the water. Coughing made him move his head forward, his neck screaming against needles of new pain, fire. The water dashed on to the top of his head and ran, dripped down his face, on to his shoulders. And he heard soft, amused laughter.

★

He must have passed out again, but only for a few minutes. Water still ran from his hair, seeped unpleasantly under his collar. He licked what water he could from his face, even caught water drips from the end of his nose. The water he had swallowed gurgled in his stomach and nausea threatened again, yet his throat remained dry, unquenched. He raised his eyes a little and saw that there was no light, only the red glow. At the same time he realised that he was not alone and this thought awoke memory, clarified recent events. Someone had thrown water in his face, poured water into his open mouth and doused his slumped head. But he was alone now. He could not turn his head, had no idea how large a space lay behind him. The dead quiet, the absence of that true light convinced him that he was alone. Alone in a red glow, a half-light that smudged the edges of things and made him think of blood. Whatever else, the water revived him. He had some semblance of memory. Take stock, he told himself. His head, though throbbing, was no longer a single, reverberating drum. He could think after a fashion. Make use of the time, he told himself. Think, damn it, think.

This burst of impatience made him try to move. He could not move his hands or feet. He remembered too well what happened if he tried to move his head. Within the compass of his eyes, then, what could he see? His feet on the floor, the toe-caps of his shoes, stained red by the light. The fuzzed, black outline of a table some distance from him. On it, the shadow of an anglepoise lamp, reflecting spots of concentrated red from its black metal. The lamp was the source of that light he had seen. He rolled his eyes left and could make out nothing but the wooden floor, stretching away to a point where red became shadow and darkness. To the right, then. A sink. Perhaps several sinks. White porcelain made pink. The gleam of taps.

He could not move his hands or legs. He was sitting. Consciousness of this fact brought an awareness of numbness in his buttocks, a whisper of familiar pain in his coccyx. It seemed friendly compared to that which gnawed at his neck. Forget the pain, he told himself, gritting his teeth. Push it away. Careful of his neck, he leaned forward. He had some freedom there. The chair to which he was apparently fastened bit into his bicep, defining the limits of his permitted movement. He tried to slide his feet forward but his calves were too tightly restrained. With what, he wanted to know, but could not see. He leaned back again, wriggling his hands. Fastened at the wrists and forearms. The movement caused a prickling sensation. He remembered then that he had known before, or recognised, the small hairs on his skin being pulled out. Some kind of sticking plaster, he deduced with a kind of triumph. His mother, tearing a plaster from his arm, assuring him that it hurt more if peeled away gently. Sticky tape. He was fastened with some kind of adhesive tape. He felt better knowing. But even this small effort seemed to exhaust him. The pain thrummed again. He worked his mouth to make more saliva. The pain began to claim him, not with the violence of former times, but almost seductively. He felt himself slipping away into the pain, giving himself up to it. His eyelids closed against the red light. He tried to shift his backside and started pins and needles. They provided a brief distraction from the pain. Then the pain became clamorous. Thinking, trying to remember what he had learned of his situation became a pain in itself. He drifted deep into swirling dark, his chin resting on his damp chest.

A noise woke him. Jolley felt his whole body jerk awake. His head felt clearer, clear enough for him to appreciate the difference between waking and regaining consciousness. He raised his head a fraction, careful of his protesting neck. The table-lamp was on. For the first time he noticed more light beyond the table. A door, open, with light beyond it against which, suddenly, his gaoler was silhouetted. The man – or what he assumed to be a man – came to the table. Jolley thought, I was right then. His hunch, his crazy guesswork had paid off. Any elation he felt was quickly cancelled by the myriad discomforts of his body, the numbness in his wrists and legs.

The man was doing something at the table, apparently oblivious of his prisoner. The light showed only his hands and forearms, part of his torso. Jolley remembered the electronic lock and the wild idea he had formed before that, that her studio, the *sanctum sanctorum* would provide a perfect hiding place. Remembering this, he identified the pervasive red light. This was some kind of dark-room, hence the sinks . . . Forgetting in his excitement, he raised his head quickly to verify this and grunted with the pain. But after the first shock, the pain was less. Not bearable but . . . And this, he thought, was because the bones in his neck had locked somehow. He could not raise his head, or no more than the fraction that stirred the monster pain which now growled and gnawed, making his eyes water.

Through the mist of his weeping vision, Jolley watched the man settle at the table, one arm stretched out in the light. He blinked rapidly. Any knowledge, anything he could observe and remember might provide him with an advantage. His vision cleared. The pain in his neck spread slightly to his head but was overridden by this idea that knowledge might mean survival. He forced himself to concentrate, to store what he saw.

The man was wearing a yellow shirt, short-sleeved. He was binding something black around his left arm. His head entered the light, his face obscured by a fall of long black hair. He was using his teeth to fasten the loose end of the black binding around his arm. The head disappeared into shadow again, but now Jolley's eyes had adjusted sufficiently to this glare of light for him to make out the indistinct shape of a face, very pale and featureless, in the shadow beyond the light. The other arm moved now on the table, neat, rapid gestures which Jolley could not interpret. But he did not need to. He already knew what was going to happen and who his strange companion was.

The light showed him the milky plastic syringe. The

needle, thin as a thread of cotton, existed for him only as a briefly flashing line of light. He winced as the needle met flesh, saw now the mottled discoloration on the arm. The man was incredibly still. Jolley listened to his own heartbeats thudding, setting off the drums in his head. The man pushed the plunger home so slowly that Jolley could make out no movement. At last, his head appeared again. This time Jolley caught the flash of white animal teeth as, with practised ease, he undid the knot of the black tourniquet. The syringe fell, rattling softly, on the table and the man leaned back into the darkness, his left arm crooked in a gesture that reminded Jolley of rampaging football supporters and angry drivers. He heard a long, sussurating sigh of satisfaction or, perhaps, despair.

Jolley moistened his dry lips, filled his mouth with saliva and swallowed. He spoke as loudly and with as much authority as he could muster. 'You are Jay-Jay Wilding.'

The man leaped up, his unseen chair crashing on to the floor. The noise startled Jolley less than the resonant loudness of his own voice. The man seemed frozen for a moment, then he came around the table, towards Jolley, blocking out the lamp's light. His left arm was still crooked and his right, crossing his chest, held it so. Jolley tried to raise his head, to look the man in the eyes, but his locked neck refused to budge, promised worse pain if forced. He desperately wanted to see that face. Slowly, the man bent towards him. Jolley strained to see his face but he saw only his lips, slightly pouting, and shut his eyes just before the man's projected spittle hit him. He gave up the struggle with his crushed neck and let his head slump forwards again as the man's spittle rolled greasily down his face.

PC Johnson got into the car beside Marion Glade and sat looking at her. He had the appearance of a man recently aroused from deep slumber. He had come out of the house still fastening his tunic, his hat tucked under his arm. He smelled a little too strongly of after-shave.

'I'm sorry to drag you out when you're off-duty,' Marion said, looking at her own hands, white-knuckled on the steering-wheel.

'That's OK. What is it? It must be something important.'

She told him the bare facts, concentrating on Jolley's disappearance, only touching on Tait's suspicions. When she had finished he whistled softly and shook his head.

'Can I trust you?' she asked, looking at him fully for the first time.

'How do you mean?'

'I think this is all a ghastly mistake. The Inspector was involved with Dolores Bayger. Quite how much I don't know. But he was very badly affected by her death.'

'I could see that for myself,' Johnson said. 'The way he just sat there while I was searching her sitting-room. I thought he was going to burst out crying or something. And that's not like him at all.'

'Then you know he couldn't have killed her.'

'No way.' He laughed, albeit a little nervously. 'Old Jolley's got a terrible bark but he can't bite. It's just not in him.'

'Right.' Marion put her head down, afraid that she would weep herself, with relief that her instinct about Johnson had been correct. 'I need someone to help me,' she said.

'To do what?'

'To find him. The only way to clear all this up is to find him.'

'OK. But how?'

'There's something else,' she said quickly. 'And before I tell you what, I want you to swear that if I'm wrong, you'll never breathe a word to anyone.'

'I can't promise about something I don't know.'

'There's more than enough gossip flying around as it is.'

'So what? Mr Jolley may have been smitten with the woman— '

'Forget all that. You saw him. You saw what I saw and now I think there's a chance . . . that he might have

206

done something to himself.' Johnson said nothing. He sat, looking through the windscreen, trying to absorb and weigh what she had said. 'I pray I'm wrong. And if I am, I don't want anyone to know that I ever thought it. He must never know. That's what I want you to promise.'

'Right.' He nodded his head firmly. 'You can count on me.'

'Thanks.'

'But— '

'And this whole operation is unofficial. You'd better understand that, too. Tait has put me in charge of the Bayger case until eight tonight and I think he'll turn a blind eye if we find Jolley. If we don't, we could be for the high jump. I'll take responsibility, of course, but— '

' . . . you're new and I ought to know better.'

'Precisely.'

'Well, I wasn't expecting promotion anyway. Yes, I'll help you. Though I hope to God you're wrong.'

'If I'm not,' Marion said, 'I can't face finding him myself . . . '

'I'll be there,' he said. 'Now, let's get going.'

Marion smiled and turned the key in the ignition, checked her rear-view mirror.

'Where do we start?' Johnson asked, as soon as they were moving.

'The only place I can think of. Dolores Bayger's house.' Johnson looked at her startled. 'I know, but I have reasons. Mrs Jolley put me on to it, really. She said she thought he must have gone there Thursday night, when he just went off without explanation. And somebody in Chuters says they saw a light in the house last night. If he wanted to do something to himself, where would be more fitting?'

'Right. I wish I didn't think so . . . Or he might have gone back there because he suddenly thought of something . . . I can't believe he'd— '

'Either way, I can't think of anywhere else to start, can you?'

'No.' Johnson shook his head. 'Sounds good to me.'

'Another thing, I think Jolley took the house keys with him when he left last night. I hope you can pick a lock?'

'Perhaps he left the door open . . . '

'Perhaps. Can you pick a lock?'

'Shouldn't be too difficult. I think I've got my boy scout penknife on me somewhere.'

'Good man,' Marion said and felt better for the first time in hours.


Wilding dragged the chair he had knocked over from the table and placed it squarely in front of Jolley. Jolley had no idea whether minutes or hours had passed. The spittle must have dried on his face, but then his face was wet with perspiration from the pain and fear he felt. Wilding walked away again, twisted the lamp upwards and around so that its painful glare fell on Jolley. Then he returned and sat down opposite him, arms folded across his narrow, yellow chest.

His face was recognisably the same as that in the terrible photographs Dolores had shown him, which, a lifetime ago, Marion Glade had extracted from the folder in order to have them copied and distributed. The same two wings of greasy-looking black hair rose from the broad forehead and fell in strings to his shoulders. There was even less flesh on the face now, though, and the weird red light accentuated its skull-like hollows. Only the eyes seemed to glitter with life. Jolley cleared his dry throat, preparing to speak again.

'And you're Mr Policeman . . . ' The voice was unexpectedly high and light, naturally nasal. It had a taunting smile in it. 'Mr Cop. Mr Fuzz. Mr Pig. Oh I like that,' Wilding crooned, rocking himself slightly in his chair. 'Mr Pig. Mr Pig-shit.'

With a speed that confounded Jolley's tired eyes, Wilding's right arm flashed out and struck him squarely on the side of the face, knocking it to his left. His neck cracked and he screamed. The scream was cut off by a

208

second blow, with the open palm of the hand this time, repeating the dreadful movement in his neck. Jolley heard himself beg, 'Don't.'

Wilding laughed, but he folded his arms again. Jolley kept his head still, lolling to the right, stinging cheek crushed against his damp shoulder, the pain raging down between his shoulder-blades now as well as up into his pulsing head.

'The last time I saw you, Mr Pig-shit, you were sitting on your fat butt in the ditch, with your little piggy trotters in the air.' Jolley remembered but could not speak. It had not been imagination, then. But the raven . . . He wanted to ask about the thing that had flown at him, out of the night . . . 'You don't look no better now, man. In fact you look worse.' Wilding leaned forward to bring his face close to Jolley's. His eyes gleamed with points of reflected red light, making them look mad. 'In fact you look like a man who's about to die . . . ' Wilding leaned back again, laughing softly.

He was silent for a long time, just staring at Jolley, unconsciously rubbing the bruises on his left arm, picking at dry scabs. His foot tapped occasionally as though marking time to some unheard tune.

'Can I . . . Can I . . . ' Jolley said, ' . . . Drink of water?'

'No,' Wilding spoke the word with lip-smacking satisfaction. The light timbre of his voice and the manner in which he sat and spoke, reminded Jolley of a mother, teasing a recalcitrant child. 'You cannot even have piss to drink, Mr Pig-shit. Your last hours are going to be very uncomfortable.'

Hours, Jolley thought, almost with gratitude. I have hours . . .

'What good . . . will killing me . . . do?' His voice was a dry rasp.

'It's what you deserve, man.'

'You killed Dolores,' he said. It was important, suddenly, that he should make Wilding admit it. A confession would pass the time, perhaps give him some slight hope.

'Oh no, man. Oh no. *You* killed her. The moment you came sniffing around that bitch with your runny little piggy snout, you marked her out. You killed her.'

'That's . . . nonsense,' Jolley said, avoiding the word 'crazy' out of instinctive fear of its possible effect on Wilding. 'You cut her throat.'

'You were one too many, man. She had to be stopped. But if you hadn't come . . . ' His voice tailed away wistfully. 'You killed her, Mr Pig. You're the one responsible.'

'Is that why you're going to kill me?'

'Maybe. Maybe not. You see, Mr Pig-shit, the nice thing about having you here is that I don't have to tell you anything. I don't have to talk to you. You see, Mr Pig-shit, I'm in the driver's seat now. Dolores, you, no one can touch me, man. Nobody can tell me nothing, and that feels good. That feels sweet, Mr Policeman.'

'What have you got to lose? You can tell me anything because you're going to kill me.'

'Confession's good for the soul, huh? I haven't got a soul, Mr Pig. She took my soul, years ago. And my pleasure will be to deny you anything you want.

'You must have loved Dolores very much,' Jolley said. He did not know why he said it, only that it was important to keep Wilding talking until whatever he had pumped into himself took hold or wore off. He wasn't sure which. At some time the door must open. He tried to look at the door but was defeated by his neck.

'Maybe I did, maybe I didn't.' Again he used that high, feminine sing-song. 'I love the birds. Oh, those are beautiful creatures, the ravens. I let 'em all out. I let 'em fly away. Made them free.'

'Not all,' Jolley said. 'There are many more . . . '

'What do you know, Mr Pig-shit? I say I let 'em all go. What I say goes. Right? Mr Cop? Mr Pig?'

'After you cut Dolores's throat,' Jolley persisted quietly. 'A sort of celebration, I suppose.'

Wilding leaned back in his chair, tilting the two back legs. He began to whistle. If he could only move his legs,

Jolley thought, he could kick the chair over, send Wilding sprawling on to the floor. But his legs would not move. He realised that he could no longer feel them, except as a cold, aching numbness. My God, he thought, panic seizing him. I am dying, bit by bit. The whistling hurt his head but he found himself listening to it and gradually made out a tune. The notes, clear and musical, slowly worked on him, calming him down.

'Your wife loved music,' he said, trying again to pierce the man's armour. 'It was something we had in common.'

The whistling spluttered, stopped. He started to laugh but stopped suddenly. 'She knew nothing,' he spat out. 'Is that what she told you? Oh, man, that bitch really took you for a ride . . . ' He laughed again, as though enjoying himself hugely.

'She was very knowledgeable,' Jolley insisted. 'She had a fine record collection— '

'She was tone deaf, shit-head. My records. Mine. All of 'em mine. She knew nothing.' He leaned forward, the chair banging against the wooden floor. Jolley felt excitement rather than fear, knew that he had caught the man's attention. He brought his face close to Jolley's again. 'You remember that pretty voice, huh? She spoke real pretty, right? But she couldn't sing a note in tune. She was tone deaf.'

'Colour-blind,' Jolley said.

'Yeah, that too. She'd wear a green dress and swear it was red and spout off her mouth about Mozart and Wagner and all the time she was reciting what she'd learned from me. She copied me, stole my words. She couldn't— '

'I don't believe you,' Jolley said. He did not want to believe it. That at least had survived. Her love of music had been something good, something he could hang on to.

'Don't you tell me, Mr Pig-shit.' Wilding stood up, loomed over him. 'I tell you she was a fake. She didn't know nothing about music. It was just something else she stole from me. She had to steal everything because she had nothing. And she was greedy. She sucked you dry, man. But the laugh was, she couldn't even hear a note of music.'

'I talked to her— '

Wilding's hand touched the top of Jolley's head, his strong fingers twined in his thick hair. 'Don't answer me back, Mr Pig-shit,' Wilding said with a new, cold calm. 'You listen when I tell you something. And look at me when I'm talking to you, bastard.'

'No,' Jolley shouted, but too late. The fingers tightened on his hair and yanked his head backwards. The cascade of pain forced a single, hollow scream out of Jolley's mouth. Wilding forced his head right back. The scream sounded outside Jolley, hurting his ears, fading into a remorse-fully tuneful whistling. The last thing he saw was Wilding's face, lips pursed, whistling, whistling, his breath brushing and bathing Jolley's pain-stretched skin.

Johnson pronounced the front door lock too complicated for him to pick. 'If he came here, what the hell did he want to lock himself in for?' he demanded, glaring at the door in frustration.

'If I'm right,' Marion reminded him dryly, 'he'd scarcely want to be interrupted.'

'Oh Christ,' said Johnson miserably. 'I might be able to kick it in,' he added.

'Try round the back. Back door locks are always easier, aren't they?'

They contemplated the high gate at the side of the house. Johnson, standing on tiptoe, could reach over it but not as far as the bolt.

'Could you climb it?' Marion asked.

'It's only wood. A couple of kicks— '

'I'd rather you climbed it. I don't want to advertise our presence any more than I have to.'

'Right, OK.'

'Can I give you a boost up or something?'

'No, it's OK. Stand back.'

Johnson took a run at the gate, leaped and pulled himself up easily. Under his weight the formidable wooden structure seemed less secure. He wobbled precariously, clinging to the top, trying to swing one leg over.

'Be careful,' Marion called but he only grunted in reply. She was left looking at his hands just grasping the top of the gate, then he dropped out of sight. Moments later, the bolt slid back and he stood grinning at her, slightly out of breath. 'Great,' said Marion, walking into the yard. She turned and bolted the gate behind her. 'Go and have a look at the back door,' she said. 'We're wasting time.'

She had never really inspected the yard before. Not that there was much to see. The vandalised ravens' cage looked forlorn in contrast to the stable block with its smart black woodwork. Mind you, she thought, it was a funny-looking place, an eyesore, some would have said, with all the windows and doorways blocked and painted black.

'Sergeant? I've got it.'

'Wonderful,' Marion said, running to join Johnson. He held the back door open for her with a flourish. 'Let's stick together,' she said, going inside. 'And take it room by room.'

'Right you are.'

The house smelled musty, almost airless. It was silent, very silent. As they moved from the utility room to the passageway to the dining-room, Marion felt her spirits sink. The house was too silent to contain a living person. But then, she reminded herself, she had not expected to find Jolley here alive. If he was here, he would be . . . She prayed that he had gone elsewhere.

'Nothing,' Johnson said after a quick look around the living-room he had so recently searched meticulously.

Marion led the way upstairs. They checked the spare room which was furnished as sparsely as a monk's cell. It was without hiding place, empty. Marion hesitated outside the door to Dolores Bayger's bedroom. Seeing this, Johnson squeezed in front of her, lifted the latch and walked in.

213

'Someone's been here,' he said at once.

'How do you know?' Marion followed him, stared, like him, at the open wardrobe doors.

'I helped take the body down. Those doors were all tight shut. Mr Jolley searched this room himself and left it immaculate.'

'Maybe somebody came back after you took the body down.'

'Sure. Several people. But I did the last check up here just before we all left and locked up. I closed the bedroom door myself. Someone's definitely been here.'

'Jolley?'

Johnson shrugged. He moved to the open wardrobe and peered in. 'Ah-ha,' he said.

'What?' Marion craned to see around him. He moved aside. She stared at the open black box, the gold chain hanging from its concealed key. 'What is it?' she asked, glancing at Johnson.

'Some kind of timing device. An electric lock, I reckon. Let's take a closer look.' Marion waited impatiently while Johnson made a thorough examination of the device. 'That's what it is right enough,' he said, sounding muffled. 'A timed lock.' He pulled his head out of the scented cupboard.

'But what for?'

'Search me.'

'Think, man, think.'

'A safe? Something you wouldn't want anyone to get into. Like a strong room. A place you wanted to be really secure. Somewhere you kept— '

'Her studio,' Marion said. 'The stable block out there,' she explained, gesturing to the yard. 'Jolley said it was very private, her *sanctum*. He didn't want anyone in there. How do we make it work? I want to get in there.'

'Until midnight you don't,' Johnson said firmly.

'Midnight? Who the hell takes photos at midnight?'

'You're right.' They exchanged a look of alarm. 'Hang on a sec,' Johnson's head disappeared again into the cupboard.

214

'We can open it . . . ' he said, re-emerging, 'if we can get the combination.'

'And how do we do that? Did you see anything in Bayger's papers? Any numbers that didn't make sense?'

'No. Nothing like that.'

'Well, then, how?'

Johnson frowned, concentrating on the problem while Marion watched him, almost hopping up and down with frustration.

'You could contact the manufacturer and you could ask them nicely to give you the combination. But I don't think they would.'

'Oh yes they would,' Marion said grimly. 'We're police officers, right?'

'Come on then. We need a telephone directory,' Johnson said, already halfway across the landing.

'Wait a minute,' Marion called, inspecting the black box again. 'Wouldn't she keep this box locked up?'

'Depends how secure she felt,' Johnson answered from the bottom of the stairs.

'If it was open before,' Marion said softly, to herself, 'when Jolley searched the room he would have noticed it . . . He'd have guessed, then— '

'Sergeant? I've got it,' Johnson yelled up the stairs. 'Do you want to ring 'em or shall I?'


Wilding was pressed against the door, listening, muttering to himself occasionally. Jolley saw him through a fog of pain. His whole body cried out. If he could just move he knew the pain would get easier. Then he thought, There isn't any more pain. All the pain in the world is concentrated in my body, my neck. This is it. There can't be any more. Wilding paced away from the door, went back to it nervously. Summoning all his strength, Jolley called, 'When does the door open?'

Wilding looked at him. His expression suggested that he had completely forgotten Jolley's existence. When a sort of recognition came into his dull eyes, he came towards Jolley.

'When she wants.' He pushed his hands into the pockets of his jeans, stood looking down at his captive with a vaguely interested expression. His manner, voice had changed. He seemed calm and yet remote, almost too relaxed. Jolley could not decide whether this was a good sign or a bad.

'She's dead,' Jolley reminded him.

'Oh, she's got one of those cute little electronic things in case she wants to go out or should oversleep. She's very considerate and she thinks of everything.'

'So how long before the door opens?'

'Oh . . . any time.'

'You're going to get away when the door opens, aren't you?'

'Oh . . . ' Wilding wriggled his shoulders like an embarrassed teenager. 'I got to find where she keeps the stuff.' He turned abruptly on his heel, walked to the table. From somewhere in the shadows near it, he picked up a black camera bag. Jolley recognised it as the one slung from her shoulder the day he had surprised her leaving this very building. Wilding turned it upside down, shook its contents out on to the table. A couple of individually packed, disposable syringes rolled on to the floor. Wilding pushed the rest and whatever else the bag contained around on the table, as though spreading out the pieces of a jigsaw puzzle. 'Hey, man, d'you know where she keeps the stuff?' he asked suddenly, over his shoulder.

'I might do,' Jolley said cautiously. Perhaps by pretending that he knew where the dope was he could do some kind of deal. Wilding, however, to his disappointment, seemed to lose interest in the subject. He ambled back towards Jolley.

'You want some, huh?' He sounded completely affable, mellow.

'I'd like a drink of water,' Jolley replied, hoping his need did not show too nakedly in his face.

'Water? Oh, sure.'

He watched, blinking, as Wilding disappeared towards

the sinks. He heard a tap running. Then Wilding stood in front of him, holding a plastic cup of water, brimming. He held it out to Jolley, seemed not to understand why he did not take it.

'Please?' Jolley said, a whine in his voice.

'Oh, sure. Here . . . ' Quite gently, he held the cup to Jolley's lips, angled it so that he could drink. 'Want some more?'

'Please,' Jolley gasped. He could drink a well dry. Water had never tasted so much like nectar.

Wilding drew him three cups in all, tended him as gently as a trained nurse.

'Thank you,' Jolley said at last.

'Only there really isn't very much there. I think she must have . . . I guess she . . . ' His voice tailed away. His eyes were drawn back to the table. He dropped the cup, as though unaware of it, on to the floor and went back to the table, bent over it again, sorting out the contents of the bag.

'Where does she get it from?' Jolley asked, his voice coming easier now.

'Some guy in Brisestock . . . ' Wilding answered automatically, going on with his counting, his arranging the contents of the bag into two distinct piles.

Jolley seized this piece of information, so easily and naturally given. Please God he would live long enough to nail Myers, he thought. Now he understood his nervousness, his vagueness about his relationship with Dolores Bayger. But this was a side issue. In his present, oddly detached mood, what wouldn't Wilding tell him? He tried to think, to formulate the right questions, but the effort seemed to arouse the pain in his head to new heights.

'How long have you been here, Jay-Jay?' he asked, the first thing that came into his head, to distract him from the threatening pain.

'Oh . . . shit, I don't know. I guess in her room, huh? In her room in the house, don't you think?'

'Possibly, yes.'

Wilding walked around the table, opened a door behind it, a door Jolley remembered being aware of hours or was it days ago? It was a rectangle filled with light into which Wilding walked. Living quarters, Jolley wondered? Had she kept him here . . . ? The idea seemed no less preposterous than the stories Dolores Bayger had spun for him. Wilding reappeared.

'It's just that I don't like to let supplies get too low, you know what I mean? I like to keep some stuff by me.' He took something casually from the table and walked back into that consuming light.

'Of course,' Jolley said, raising his voice as much as possible. Wilding was silent and invisible, then Jolley heard him cough. Perhaps he had gone to sleep, Jolley thought. Perhaps he would pass out. A cold panic seized him. Suppose Wilding overdosed . . . ? 'Are you all right?' he called. He heard the cough again. After a while, Wilding appeared in the door, a finger held beneath his nose. He stared in the general direction of Jolley but said nothing. 'I said— '

'Sure, man.' Wilding came further into the room, his stride loose and easy, almost relaxed, Jolley thought. 'How's it going with you, huh?'

'You . . . er . . . If you could just undo my hands . . . '

For a moment, Jolley really thought he was going to agree. Then a frown crossed his face. He walked round behind Jolley, reappeared at his side.

'No, man. No can do.'

'Yes you can. You're in the driver's seat, remember? You can do anything you— ' Jolley heard the note of hysteria creeping into his own voice.

'No, sir, no can do.'

It was as though they were changing roles, Jolley sounding mad and out of control, Wilding calm and patient.

'Why not?' Jolley asked hopelessly.

'Because you killed Dolores and I'm going to kill you.'

'No. I didn't— '

Wilding suddenly swung around, his whole body tensed like a cat about to spring. Jolley could sense the power in him, the nervous energy coiled into latent strength. He moved quickly, silently across the room to the door, pressed his ear against it. The mechanism, Jolley thought. He must be attuned to it. It must be time . . .

'You hear anything, man?' Wilding whispered.

'No,' Jolley said because it was the truth.

'Sh.' Again he listened at the door. Jolley began to pray, fast, incoherent words flapping on his tongue. Stealthily, Wilding moved back from the door, leaned into shadow, bending. When he straightened up he was holding a crow-bar, holding it easily, but tensely. He remained staring at the door, almost quivering with tension, his right arm drawn back, ready to use the crowbar.

It was not easy. The security firm who had supplied and fitted the electronic lock was not about to give private information to a voice on the phone. It required all Marion's powers of persuasion to make them listen to her at all. It used up all her patience. Even then she had to agree to a compromise. She had to go and collect the code in person, with identification. This involved a round journey of almost thirty miles. She left Johnson at the house, with strict instructions to watch, to call for help should anything happen. Her air of authority frayed by desperation helped her to wheedle the combination out of a reluctant managing director. Thank God he didn't think to ask about warrants, permission. All this, she thought, for a few meaningless figures scribbled on a piece of paper. Time was running out. She had to get back before eight, before Tait pulled out the plug or the rug from under her feet, whichever it was . . . Even so, she made herself stop off at the station in Oversleigh. If Tait had telephoned, she wanted to try, at least, to stall him, buy a little more time. He had not rung. Her relief was short-lived. Neither had Jolley, nor had he put in an appearance. She lied to Sergeant Bentinck, watching herself as though observing another person. She told him she needed two men to help her search Dolores Bayger's studio. She told him Jolley had ordered her to do this, that Tait had told her to carry out his orders. She saw in his eyes that he thought she was being officious, trying to solve the case and steal the glory behind Jolley's back. She did not care what he thought. She drove PCs Doulton and Wildsmith to Chuters and left them in the stable yard while she and Johnson went inside, upstairs with the scrap of paper.

'What do we do now?'

'Key in the numbers, press over-ride, re-set the clock and Bob's your uncle.'

'Do it.'

'Where are you going?'

'Down there, of course. I want to be first in.'

'I'll come— '

'I've got two capable blokes down there. I want you to get that bloody door open, OK?'

'Let's agree a time, at least,' Johnson said, giving in.

They checked their watches. Marion told him to give her five minutes.

Out in the yard, she stationed Doulton and Wildsmith on either side of the black door, close against the wall. She took up a position facing the door, some five or six feet away from it. Aware of the amazed look on the constables' faces, she took Dolores Bayger's gun out of her handbag, cocked it and took aim at the door, holding it in both hands, at arm's length.

'Miss— ' Doulton said, moving from his position, his face as white as the proverbial sheet.

'Shut up, Doulton and get back to your position,' she hissed, 'or I'll shoot your balls off.'

The door made a noise. Jolley heard it clearly. So did Wilding. His eyes went to a point above the door. Jolley, following his gaze, could just make out a little black box on the wall. That was the source of the noise.

But there was no precious, remembered click.

'It shouldn't do that,' Wilding said in a hushed, almost hurt voice.

'Must be time,' Jolley said.

'Shut up!' Wilding screamed the word, turned towards him, the crowbar raised menacingly. Jolley pressed his lips together. Slowly, Wilding turned to face the door again. He took one step closer to it, holding the crowbar across his body, the clawed end held loosely in his left hand.

*Click!*

Jolley recognised the sound. So did Wilding. For a split second the man looked at him suspiciously, as though he were in some way responsible. The door did not open. Jolley tried to count but could not force the numbers into sequence.

'Inspector Jolley?'

It was Doulton's voice and if anyone had ever told him that Doulton's voice would sound like music . . . Wilding raised the crowbar, waved his free hand frantically at Jolley. He bit his bottom lip, forced himself to be silent. Oh, Doulton, Doulton, I love you, he thought. Oh, please God, let Doulton be careful.

The door crashed open. Wilding swung the bar up above his head, let out a scream. A single shot tore into the room, the sound echoing and clamouring in the confined space, splitting Jolley's ears, making his head explode with a new and terminal pain.

# Eight

He was sitting up in bed in the little side ward with a plaster collar around his neck which forced his chin unnaturally high. A drip fed into the back of his left hand and he was shouting at the top of his voice. 'Get this bloody thing out of me! What's it supposed to be for anyway? I demand to see Scotney. Where is he? You have no right to detain me here against my will.'

Eileen stood in the doorway, unnoticed, watching him and the apparently unruffled back of Sister Crane who was checking the valves on his drip.

'I am a police officer . . . ' he yelled, attempting to throw back the tightly tucked-in bedclothes with his free hand.

'As the whole world must be aware,' Eileen said loudly, hurrying forward, her heels making a brisk staccato on the shining wooden floor. 'Be quiet, Cy, for heaven's sake.'

He stared at her, his mouth hanging open, or as open as the collar would permit. Close up, his face looked ravaged, sunken, newly lined. His eyes were bloodshot and ringed by a dark discoloration which Eileen thought, in a moment of sentimentality, made him look like a bewildered panda. Those eyes took on a sheepish look and a slight blush spread across his cheeks.

'I want to see the doctor,' he said, fighting the impulse to let his anger go, seize the comfort of Eileen's presence.

'And no doubt you will in the fullness of time. Now leave that alone, Cy,' she said, pulling his right hand from his left where his fingers were picking at the plaster which held the drip in place, 'and stop behaving like a two-year-old.' She leaned over to kiss his forehead and put her heavy bag down at the same time. He closed his eyes. The familiar scent and touch of her broke over him like waves of balm. He fumbled her hand into his, squeezed it. 'And don't you ever speak to Sister like that again.'

'Sorry, Nurse,' he mumbled, glad of the distraction. He had this terrible impulse to weep, to put his head down on Eileen's breast and sob out his relief and fear and bitter sorrow. Except that he couldn't put his bloody head anywhere, neither back nor forward, left nor right, without encountering the solid constriction of the collar.

'*Sister*,' Eileen hissed in his ear before straightening. 'This is Sister Crane who has taken marvellous care of you.'

'Glad to see you're feeling better, Inspector Jolley,' the tall, calm woman said and popped a thermometer into his mouth before he could speak. 'I won't be a moment,' she said to Eileen. 'Perhaps you'd like to give him some water when I've done, then I can leave you alone.'

Dumb, he could only listen to their plotting, watch the Sister make marks on his chart, Eileen start unpacking her bag.

'Temperature's almost back to normal anyway,' she said drily. 'You'll live.'

'I want to see Doctor Scotney,' he repeated, though with less bluster.

'Doctor will be round about six this evening,' Sister Crane answered him. 'I'll leave him to you, Mrs Jolley.' Her shoes squeaked her out of the room. Eileen held the end of an angled plastic straw to his lips. Its other end disappeared into a lidded beaker. He was suddenly thirsty and drank, even though he resented being ministered to in this way.

'Enough?'

'Take it away.'

'Don't you snarl at me, Cy. I should think after all that shouting . . . '

'Where am I? How long have I been . . . ?'

'In the cottage hospital, of course. You're lucky no one else needs this side room . . . ' she added, looking at the other, empty bed. 'And if you carry on like this they'll send you to Passington General and you won't like that, I can assure you.'

'What day is it?'

'Sunday. I've brought you some orange barley water. They said that would be all right . . . ' She began placing things on his locker, then suddenly looked at him with alarm. 'You've not lost your memory, have you?'

'Of course I haven't lost my memory.'

'Good. Now— '

'Will you shut up and answer my questions?'

'You're not in the police station now, Cy. You're a sick man.'

'I'm as right as rain. But I'll go mad if somebody doesn't tell me what is going on.'

Eileen sighed theatrically, set her bag aside and pulled up a chair. She sat in it meekly, her plump hands folded in her lap.

'Well?' he barked.

'Well, what? You're the one with all the questions.'

'What am I doing here?'

'Getting better, if you behave yourself.'

'There's nothing . . . ' He stopped as, trying to twist his head towards her, he felt the shadow of a remembered pain and pinched the flesh of his neck against the plaster collar. 'What's this for?' he asked more gently.

'You've got a damaged neck. Something to do with the upper vertebrae. You'll be in that thing for some time, but Doctor thinks it'll do the trick. You're lucky he didn't have to operate. You're lucky not to have a broken neck and be paralysed. Oh, Cy, you're lucky not to be dead.'

It was she who gave way to floods of tears, burying her face in the white cotton counterpane. This action pushed her straw hat askew and Jolley, unable to do more, lifted it from her head and touched her soft white hair.

'Steady on,' he said. 'I'm as fit as a fiddle – almost. There's no need to take on . . . '

'You don't know what it's been like. I've been out of my mind with worry.'

'I know. I'm sorry. I'm so sorry, Eileen.'

'Well, try to behave then,' she said, sitting up and taking a wodge of tissues from his locker to dab her face.

'I meant for *all* the pain I've caused you.'

'Don't let's talk about that now. I can't face that yet.'

'It's all over, Eileen.'

'Last time you said that you disappeared for hours and they all thought . . . Then you disappeared again . . . ' More tears overcame her. Jolley held her hand and waited while she snuffled into the ball of tissues.

'They all thought what?' he asked when she was calmer.

'I don't know. Did I say that? I don't know what I'm saying half the time.'

'You were always a dreadful liar, Eileen.'

'Anyway, that's police business and I'm not to discuss it with you. You're to rest and not worry about anything. Teddy Tait sends his best and says everything's under control . . . '

'They got Wilding?' he asked, squeezing her hands. She nodded dumbly. 'He wasn't shot?'

'No. What ideas you have. They'll tell you all about it when you're well enough.'

'My brain's not damaged. I'm well enough now.'

'That's for the doctor to say, not you. And I don't know anything more, so there's no point in badgering me.'

'Something's going on,' he said. 'Tait's got to you . . . '

'How many times have you told me police business isn't my business? All Teddy said was that you were to rest and get well. He's very concerned about you.'

'Ha! Then they must have it sewn up,' he said bitterly.

'Sometimes,' Eileen told him, 'you're a very unpleasant, selfish and cynical man. You make me ashamed of you.'

By turning his whole torso, Jolley could look away from her, out of the window. Her words smarted as much as his eyes. He saw tree-tops already turning autumn gold, a clear blue sky, the elegant spire of St Nicholas's rising into it.

'Is Doulton all right?'

'As far as I know. Why shouldn't he be?'

'I heard his voice, shouting to me just before . . . ' There his mind went blank, but the sound of that single shot still echoed in his ears. Its sound, he thought, had blasted him into oblivion. 'Fancy them letting Doulton have a gun,' he said softly to himself.

'I don't know anything about that,' Eileen said. 'All I know is they rescued you and brought you here. You were unconscious. They had to do X-rays and goodness knows what else. They kept you sedated. You've got to keep your neck still, you see, so it can heal. I thought it was touch and go, Cy.'

'Don't be so daft. And don't start crying again.'

'I'm not. It's just that— '

'I know, I know, love.'

'Do you?'

'Yes.'

She eased herself on to the edge of the bed and he was able to put his right arm around her. She held him tight, so tight that he thought she would suffocate him. He wanted to tell her that Dolores Bayger was dead and not just, not primarily in the physical sense. Where she had been – lodged in his heart, he supposed a poet might say – was now a raw shame, a sense of his own foolishness and carelessness.

'I am so very sorry,' he whispered. 'Forgive me?'

She pulled her wet face from his shoulder and looked at him, her eyes shining, her make-up ruined. 'Haven't you got any sensible questions to ask?'

'Yes. When can I come home?'

'When the doctor says so,' she answered, getting off the bed. 'And not a moment sooner,' she added, rummaging in her bag again. 'And it'll be a long time before you can go back to work. You're on official leave, by the way . . . '

'There's nothing wrong with my head.'

'There must be or you wouldn't have got yourself into this mess. Here, look what I've brought you . . . '

She dumped a heavy silver and white box on his bed. He glanced at it without interest. 'What is it?'

'A cassette player. With earphones. Well, I knew you wouldn't be satisfied with the radio and you can't go disturbing the other patients with all that opera. Do you think it'll plug in somewhere? I can't get any batteries until tomorrow . . . ' He watched her pull the little life-saving machine out of its box, hand him the featherlight earphones.

'That's brilliant, Eileen . . . ' he said, his throat closing painfully. Suddenly an enforced stay in hospital, with music at his fingertips, did not seem quite so bad.

'You must tell me what records you want me to tape. In the meantime, I've brought these from your shelves . . . ' She tipped half a dozen cassettes on to the bed. *Les Nuits d'Eté*, the Elgar Cello Concerto . . .

'You'll never operate the record player,' he said.

'Audra will.'

'I don't want her messing with my records . . . '

'There you go again. You're an ingrate. Well, you can just make do with these then.'

'Sorry. How is Audra?'

'She's been wonderful. I don't know what I'd have done . . .  Peter went into Passington specially yesterday, to get the cassette thing.'

'Very kind of him,' Jolley said. 'When is someone from the station coming to see me?'

'When they're good and ready and when the doctor says you're fit enough,' she said, removing the player and the cassettes from the bed. 'Audra will come and see you tonight.'

'That'll be nice,' he said. Unaccountably, he suddenly felt very tired. Eileen fussed with the pillows behind his shoulders. 'Head aches,' he said.

'Do you wonder? Try to sleep.'

'Mm.' He opened his eyes. 'Eileen?'

'Yes, dear.'

'Hang on a bit, will you? Don't go rushing off.'

'Of course not.' She sat down and took his right hand loosely in both of hers.

'Thanks,' he said.

The pain reminded him of many things he did not wish to examine. Not yet. He closed his eyes and breathed deeply. There was no pain in his neck, he realised and was, belatedly, grateful for the cumbersome collar. Wilding, he thought. Doulton with a gun . . . Somebody must have taken leave of their senses . . . And her lying there with her beautiful throat cut.

He woke with sensations reminiscent of a hangover. A cheerful little nurse fed him some tepid, watery soup and changed the bag on his drip. She took his pulse and his temperature, humming to herself tunelessly. When he asked, she told him he had slept through Doctor Scotney's round.

'Why on earth didn't somebody wake me?'

'Doctor said not to. Rest's what you need, Mr Jolley. The more sleep the better.'

'I want to know what's wrong with me.'

'I should've thought that was perfectly obvious. Now, do you want the bottle?'

'What bottle?'

'Do you want to go to the toilet, Mr Jolley?'

He scowled at her. 'No I do not. And when I do, I'm not using any . . . bottle.'

'Bed-rest,' she said firmly. 'Just let me know when you want it. I'm going to get a bowl now and then I'll give you a nice wash before your visitors come.'

He didn't want washing. He could wash himself. He wanted to see Scotney, wanted to bully him into letting him up. He wanted that bloody needle out of his hand. He hated needles, the thought of metal sticking into his flesh. It was unnatural, sickening . . . He thought of Wilding injecting himself. He had said she got the drugs from Joseph Myers in Brisestock . . .

'Now what do you think you're doing?' the nurse demanded in an exasperated tone as she watched him fumble with the bedclothes. She placed a bowl of water on the table which swung like a beam across his body and tugged the bedclothes straight and tight again.

'I've just remembered something very important. Is there a phone I can use?'

'No, there isn't. Now hold still . . . ' She bent over him intimately.

'This is official police business. I've got to have a phone— '

'It'll just have to wait,' she said, muffling his protest with a wet, soapy flannel. He tasted soap, felt diminished by her competent attentions. 'You're supposed to shut your eyes,' she said, 'or I'll get soap in them.' He closed his eyes and suffered her to wash him. 'There. That feels better, doesn't it?' She patted his face with a thin, coarse towel. Then she produced a comb. 'I'll be very gentle,' she said, when he flinched away. 'You've got a fine head of hair, Mr Jolley. Sorry. Did that hurt? Never mind, nearly done. There. Now you look as good as new.' Humming to herself, she went away with the bowl.

Eileen had said Audra would come. Heaving himself round he looked at the already darkening sky. If Myers knew they'd got Wilding surely he would do a bunk. He was already jumpy. Chances were they'd never find him. And who else was he supplying? Jolley stared at the metal stand which held his drip, wondered if he could manoeuvre it if he managed to get out of bed. If he wasn't such a coward, he would tear the needle out of his hand and . . . He lay back against his pillows. He'd get Audra to phone the station. Audra would bring him grapes. He'd bet a pound on it. She could bring him anything she liked as long as she would make that call. He closed his eyes, his head hurting again. The hangover feeling had intensified into a slow throbbing at the temples. Had Dolores Bayger been a junkie, too? He'd seen no signs of it. Had she really kept Wilding locked up in that place, dependent on a daily ration of oblivion or happiness or whatever it was? Just so that she could point her cold lens at him? He knew that he would go mad if he did not get an answer to these and a hundred other questions soon.

'Inspector Jolley?' He opened his eyes and saw Sister Crane standing over him, a minuscule plastic cup in her fingers. 'Just swallow these, if you please. Open wide.' He obeyed her without thinking. She popped two capsules into his mouth, stuck the angled straw between his teeth. She was not quite quick enough. He tasted something dark and bitter before the water washed the capsules down his throat. He coughed and that hurt his head. 'There we are. All comfortable? Your visitors will be along in a minute.'

'I must— ' he began.

'You might feel a bit drowsy, but don't worry about it. Rest is what you need.'


Audra brought him grapes. The white plastic supermarket bag could not conceal their green plumpness.

'Hello, Daddy,' she said, smiling, kissing him lightly on the temple. She smelled fresh, like the weather outside, he thought. 'I couldn't think what else to bring you,' she said, holding the bag open under his nose. 'Would you like one now?' He moved his head a little from side to side. It hurt. He hated grapes, especially green ones. Funny, he thought, we call them green now, but when I was a lad the done thing was to call them 'white'. Always puzzled me, that did. Like white horses being 'grey' and the red coats of the huntsmen at the Boxing Day Meet being 'pink'. His mother had been a stickler for the 'correct' word. 'Daddy?'

'Sorry. It's those pills,' he said. His mouth felt dry. He tried to roll over, reach the beaker.

'Why don't you ask?' Audra said crossly, bossy as Sister Crane. At least she had the sense to place the beaker in his right hand. 'Well, you gave us a scare, I must say. How do you feel now? Really feel, I mean.' She sat on the bed beside him.

'Fine. Where's your mother?'

'She'll be along in a minute.' Her face clouded and he felt immediately sorry that he had blurted this out. 'They don't want you to have too many visitors at once. That's why Peter didn't come. He wanted to, but Mummy and I thought it best that he stay away tonight. Perhaps tomorrow, if you're up to it. He sends his love, of course. You mustn't get too tired, you see.'

'I thought that was the whole point. I'm supposed to rest.'

'There's a difference, Daddy. Now, is the cassette player all right?'

'I haven't used it yet. Fell asleep. It's a nice thought, though. Thanks.'

'Peter went to Passington specially . . . '

'Yes, your mother said. Very good of him.'

'Now, what records shall I tape for you?'

'I haven't thought yet. I'll let you know.'

'It'll be no trouble. I can do them on our record player while I'm doing other things.'

Jolley had a vision of his precious records being carted about in the back of Audra's untidy car, subject to a strange stylus, mishandled.

'I'll let you know,' he said again. 'Just now I get a lot of headaches. I'm not really up to— '

'Poor Daddy,' she said and patted his hand. 'You have been in the wars.'

'Audra, will you do something for me?'

'Of course. If I can.'

'Oh, there you are. I looked for your car downstairs . . . ' Eileen arrived, slightly breathless at the side of the bed, kissed him quickly.

'I parked on the road. There are no restrictions this time of night and I thought it was silly to squeeze into that car-park. There's hardly room to turn . . . '

'How are you, dear?' Eileen asked.

'Tired,' Jolley answered honestly.

'Well, of course you are. We won't stay long.'

'Daddy was just asking me to do something for him.'

Two pairs of eyes focused on him, waiting, appre-
hensive. You'd think, he thought, I was going to ask
them to raise the bloody *Titanic* for me. Audra had his
eyes, small and dark brown. Eileen's eyes were wide and
blue and pretty.

'It's all right,' he said. 'Your mother can do it.' Eileen's
fierce frown told him he had said the wrong thing, the
tactless thing again. 'It's police business,' he told Audra.
'It's best your mother does it.'

'Very well.' She stood up, brushing at her straight black
skirt. 'It's lovely to see you looking so much better, Daddy.'
She kissed him again, perfunctorily. 'I'll wait downstairs,
Mummy. You'll come back and have supper with us, won't
you? Peter's preparing it.'

'Thanks,' Eileen said. 'I won't be long.'

'Thanks for coming, Audra,' Jolley said. 'I'll be better
next time.'

She smiled warmly. 'I hope so, Daddy. Take care, now.'

'Why are you so clumsy with that girl?' Eileen demanded
in a low voice as the door closed behind their daughter.

'I don't know. I don't even mean to be. Look, there's
something you must do for me— '

'Well you *should* know. And you should try a bit more— '

'I will. I promise. Listen, I want you to ring the station— '

'Cy, I told you. It's all out of your hands and you're
not to— '

'Wilding,' he said, raising his voice, 'told me something
important. Ring the station and tell – who's in charge,
anyway?'

'I don't know.'

'Well, find out. Or tell Hadfield. Tell somebody . . . '
He closed his eyes against a sudden spasm of pain.

Eileen took his hand. 'All right. Tell them what, dear?'

He took a deep breath, waited for the pain to recede.
What were those bloody pills for, anyway? Just to knock
him out? He sighed.

'Wilding told me she got his drugs from Joseph Myers,
the antique dealer in Brisestock. He was off guard. Maybe

232

he won't tell them. Tell them to bring Myers in. It's important . . . '

'All right.'

'You promise?'

'Yes, dear.'

'Now.'

'In a minute . . . '

'You'll forget.'

'I'll do it as soon as I go downstairs. There's a public phone in the lobby.'

'Perhaps you should call Tait . . . '

'If I can't get hold of anyone sensible at the station, I will. Now will you please stop worrying about it?'

'Please . . . Go and do it now and come back and tell me. Then I'll forget about it.'

Reluctantly, she let go of his hand. She knew that nothing else would satisfy him. 'All right,' she said, 'but then you've got to concentrate on getting better.'

'I will. I promise.'

He watched her go. She had left her handbag, as a sort of security, he supposed. Only she wouldn't have any change. He tried to raise himself, to call after her. She'd borrow some from Audra, of course. He tried to relax. Or perhaps she was carrying her purse in her pocket. She did that sometimes. She could always dial 999 . . .

He looked at the bag, lying near his feet. There was a pink and lilac scarf tied to its strap. He remembered her buying it that summer in Austria. She had dithered outside the shop window for what had seemed like hours, converting the exorbitant price, debating whether a dark green and crimson one of similar design would be more practical . . . Later, they'd caught a coach and gone to hear Gundula Janowitz . . .

When Eileen came back, the call made, he was fast asleep, breathing noisily through his mouth. She remained for some minutes watching him. She wanted to hold him, to lie down beside him and hold him fast. But she did nothing to disturb him, crept out of the ward as quietly as she could. For the first time in weeks, she began to feel safe again.

Jolley squinted at his X-rays, held up to the bright light of the morning window by his doctor, William Scotney. The grey and black images made little sense to Jolley, though the area of damage which the doctor repeatedly pointed out appeared to him disastrous in his present gloomy mood.

'However, it's not as bad as it looks,' Scotney concluded, handing the X-rays to Sister Crane. 'Thank you, Sister. There's a lot of bruising. Any idea what he hit you with?'

'A crowbar, I think. When can I get out of here?'

'In a few days . . . ' The doctor unhooked his chart and studied it with pursed lips. 'How are the headaches?'

'Bloody awful.'

'I think then, Sister . . . ' He and Sister Crane went into a huddle, whispering, their backs automatically turned to Jolley. He watched them with resentment. 'The thing is, old man, to get your whole system settled down. Rest. Quiet. No worries. The bad news is that you'll have to wear that collar for some time. Comfortable, is it?'

'No.'

'Good. I think we did a pretty good job on that. And when it comes off you'll have to wear a detachable foam rubber one for a bit. Absolutely no driving. The alternative, before you start complaining, could be permanent damage. You're lucky we didn't have to do surgery, as it is. Very risky in that area. Could be paralysed— '

'Thanks a lot.'

'Good man. Now, we'll take the drip out later today. That should cheer you up a bit, and Sister'll give you something more effective for the headaches. They'll go. Time's the best healer. And we'll keep an eye on your blood pressure.'

'What's the good news?'

Scotney stared at him, wrinkled his nose. 'You've lost weight. Should lose a bit more. A lot of the trouble is shock. Give the system time to recover naturally. That's the main thing. Right. I'll leave you in Sister's capable hands and look in on you again tomorrow. Take care now, Cy. Thank you so much, Sister . . . ' He watched them, heads bent together, walk to the door. 'Oh yes . . . There's one of your chaps here to see you,' Scotney said, suddenly remembering.

'About time, too,' Jolley said, breaking into a grin. 'Well, send him in.'

'You're not to get excited, now. Don't go getting yourself worked up.'

'All right. All right.' He lay back on his pillows, the collar forcing his chin up awkwardly. The long sleep had reduced his headache to quiet, distant discomfort. He had eaten some scrambled eggs, drunk two cups of tea. Life was almost bearable, especially now that they had deigned to send him some news . . .

PC Johnson stood just inside the door, staring at him hesitantly. His lower body was almost obscured by an enormous, ornate basket of chrysanthemums.

Jolley looked at him, blinking, carefully eased himself up on the pillows. 'You look like a bloody lemon standing there with that lot. Come in, man, come in.'

'Morning, sir. How are you?'

'What's that?'

'From the station, sir. We had a whip-round.'

'Put it down.' Johnson looked around for somewhere to stand the basket. 'Put it over there, by the other bed. Where I can see it,' he added, for form's sake. Johnson placed the basket on the locker beside the empty bed, fiddled with it. 'What are you doing, Johnson? Fancy yourself as a flower arranger, do you?'

'I thought you'd like to see the card, sir.' Johnson came to his bedside and handed him a small card which Jolley accepted with a graceless grunt. 'I didn't think flowers were very suitable, actually, but we couldn't think of anything else.'

'They're very nice. Tell everyone I'm very touched.'

He dropped the card on the bed-table. 'Now sit yourself down and tell me what's going on. Why has no one been to brief me? Did you get my message about Myers?'

'Yes, sir. Marion said to say a special thank you for that and she sends her love.'

'Marion?' Jolley frowned at him. 'Oh, I see. Marion, now, is it?'

'Sorry, sir. Slip of the tongue.'

'Is she running the show? What's happening?'

'No, sir. The Superintendent put Inspector Lethbridge in charge. Mar . . . Sergeant Glade's working with him and I'm assisting, sir.' He watched nervously as Jolley's face turned a shade of puce, then purple. 'My instructions are, sir, not to worry you with details. I've got to— '

'Lethbridge,' he breathed on a long, hissing breath. 'If he touches my files I'll— '

'The thing is, sir, this is by way of being an official visit . . . '

'They've taken me off the case. That's what you're telling me, isn't it?'

'You're on sick leave, sir. I don't see as they had much choice.'

'Sick leave? An excuse. Anything to ease me out . . . '

'Please, sir. I was told not to let you get worked up.'

'I am not worked up. I am furious.'

'Yes, sir.'

Jolley took several deep breaths, held them, exhaling slowly. His face gradually became pink. 'However,' he said at last, 'it's not your fault. Now, tell me what else is going on.'

'Can't, sir. Sorry. I've got to get a statement from you, if you feel up to it, and they said downstairs I wasn't to stop long.'

'You mean Lethbridge instructed you to keep me in the dark.'

'Not exactly, sir, no. I'm to tell you that they are still questioning Wilding and hope to charge him in the next twenty-four hours. Everything is in hand and you are not to worry yourself, sir. And everyone sends their best wishes for a speedy recovery.'

'Knowing full well that I'll never get better if nobody will tell me what is going on.'

'Doctor's orders, sir,' Johnson said quietly.

'And you know what the doctor can do with his orders, don't you, Johnson?'

'I can guess, sir.'

Jolley swivelled his eyes around the room, looking for something else on which to vent his anger and frustration. They came to rest on the basket of flowers. Great incurving chrysanthemums of purple, white and gold backed by smaller ones in lilac and bronze. Funeral flowers, he thought. A floral tribute to a dead man.

'What statement?' he demanded suddenly, glowering at Johnson.

'About what happened, sir. How you came to be imprisoned by Wilding and what happened while you were there.' He pulled out his notebook and an expensive-looking silver pen. 'Just for the record, sir,' he added, looking relieved.

'Why should I give you a statement when you won't tell me what's going on?'

'You're an important witness, sir. Inspector Lethbridge needs your statement for corroboration and with the possibility of bringing charges, sir. And I can't tell you what I don't know. Marion . . . sorry, Sergeant Glade— '

'I don't care what you call her. You can marry her for all I care . . . '

'It's not like that, sir. Nothing like that,' Johnson said, sounding shocked. 'It's just that we've been working together the last few days— '

'Yes, yes Constable. All right. Take no notice of me.'

'All I wanted to say, sir, was that Sergeant Glade said she'd be in to see you as soon as she could and she'll give you a full report then. That's off the record, sir.'

'Very good of her, I'm sure. Tell her I appreciate it. Off the record, of course!'

'Right you are. Now if we could— '

'Yes, yes, the statement. Right, ready?' Johnson inclined his head. 'Friday night. After I'd done everything I could, with Sergeant Glade's help, to put out a check on Wilding as the man we needed to eliminate from our inquiries, I remembered something. Earlier, when I searched . . . Bayger's bedroom, I noticed a small black box on the wall at the back of the wardrobe. At the time, I didn't think anything of it. Or I thought it was something to do with the central heating or a fuse box – am I making myself clear, Constable?'

'Perfectly, sir.'

'Anyway, I suddenly remembered it. And I remembered something else. We had not searched her studio, in the old stable block. You may remember I'd forbidden Roscoe to break in . . . '

'Right, sir, yes. I was there when you said you'd handle it yourself.'

'There was something else. Another piece of the jigsaw. While searching her room I'd found a gold chain with what I took to be a small metal ornament on it. I took it from the victim's nightstand and put it in my pocket. You had better note, Constable, that that is an admission of theft on my part. I had taken it as a keepsake. I know that I was wrong to have done so. However, looking at it again, I realised that it wasn't, as I had thought, a pendant, a piece of jewellery. I wasn't sure, but I thought it might be a key, a key to that black box. I was still in the dark as to what that would tell me, but I remembered that once I had seen Bayger leaving the studio. She had not locked it, but I knew she was very security conscious and very protective of her studio. I put two and two together. Oh, when I say she had not locked it I mean she did not turn a key or do any of the usual things one associates with locking a door. The idea of an electronic, timed automatic lock seemed a possibility.'

'So you went to check it?' Johnson suggested after a long pause, looking up at him.

'Yes. And I found that the key did fit the box and the box was some kind of timing device, set for midnight

. . . It was almost midnight by then so I went down and waited in the yard until the door opened of itself. And then, like a bloody fool, I marched in there and got whacked on the back of my neck by Wilding. When I came to . . . '

Jolley was surprised to discover how little he remembered. The time sequence in particular eluded him. As he recounted such details as he could recall, he found that he could not say in what precise order they had occurred. He heard himself repeating that he must have passed out but could not be sure how many times. Fragments of what Wilding had said remained in his mind but they seemed detached from any real context. It all sounded inadequate, vague, as though it had happened to someone else. Above all, the recollection of it was surprisingly unemotional. He knew that he had felt intense fear, but he could not re-experience it. He began to understand what Scotney meant about shock. Shock darkened the mind, made recollection hazy and selective, created a kind of detachment. His head began to ache.

'I'm sure there's more, but that's all I can tell you right now. My head's still a bit woozy,' he confessed.

'That's fine, sir.'

'Then I heard Doulton shout my name. Wilding indicated that I shouldn't answer. I didn't know what to do for the best. Either way it seemed I would put Doulton in danger. Then someone kicked the door open and I heard a shot. To be honest, I thought I'd been shot. But that, apparently, was an illusion. I must have passed out . . . '

'You were unconscious when we came in, sir. It looked like you must have tipped your chair over, sir, and banged your head on the floor.'

'I don't remember any of that. Just the sound of that shot. Then everything's black and I woke up with this damn thing around my neck and a needle in my hand.'

'That gives us a pretty good picture, sir, thank you.'

'Then in return perhaps you will answer me just one question? What idiot issued a gun to Doulton?'

Johnson looked confused for a moment, then the penny

239

dropped. 'It wasn't Doulton, sir. It was Marion.'

'Marion!'

'Yes, sir. She'll . . . er . . . explain everything.'

'Marion came after me with a gun?'

'Sort of, sir, yes. Well, not exactly . . . '

'You were there for God's sake . . . '

'I'm sorry, sir . . . '

'But you can't tell me,' Jolley jeered.

''Fraid not, sir.'

'I see. Well, tell Marion I'm obliged to her and await her explanation with . . . eagerness.'

'Will do, sir.'

Jolley leaned back and closed his eyes. It must be time for Scotney's new pills, he thought. Marion had come after him, armed . . . What was he to make of that? Johnson cleared his throat. Jolley opened his eyes a crack.

'I'm afraid that's not quite all, sir. I have to ask you about last Thursday night as well, sir, if you feel up to it. The night of the murder . . . '

'What about it?' Jolley said, suspicious, something cold creeping into his stomach.

'According to information received, sir,' Johnson went on, visibly embarrassed, 'you went out between ten thirty and eleven p.m. and did not return to your home until approximately ten minutes to three a.m.. Inspector Lethbridge instructed me to ask you to account for your movements during that time.' His quiet, formal voice faltered. He looked down at his notebook, pen poised, a slight flush on his cheeks.

'I see. During which time, as far as we know, Dolores Bayger was killed.'

'The post-mortem fixes her death at between one and two a.m., sir,' Johnson said, without raising his eyes.

'I went for a drive, Constable. Write it down. I drove from Clifton Kings to Passington, via Oversleigh. Just outside Passington, I took the new slip road and drove on to Matsford. I parked the car beside the main bridge there and sat for a while. Then I got out and walked along the river bank as far as possible. You can only go so far. The buildings come right down to the waterside . . .  Then I turned back and walked up to the town square, wandered around the back alleys for a bit and then got back to the car. I sat for a while longer and then drove back. I used B roads, going via Seddington and Locksleigh, right through to Nusford, then back by the main road to Clifton Kings.'

'Thank you very much, sir. Did anyone see you who might be able to identify you or your car, sir?' Johnson's tone made it obvious that he had to ask this and did not enjoy doing so.

'No, Constable. I can't recall anyone who could corroborate my movements. I passed and was passed by a few cars, of course, but I was driving my own car, unmarked. If I saw anyone in Matsford when I was on foot, I can't remember it. I certainly spoke to no one. In short, I can't prove any of it.'

'I'm sure that won't be necessary, sir.'

'Are you? Then you're a damn sight more confident than I am.' Johnson closed his notebook. 'You haven't asked me why, Constable. You should.'

'Why what, sir?' His eyes, which flickered briefly to meet Jolley's, were troubled and embarrassed.

'Why I went walkabout, of course, or drive-about, rather.'

'No, sir. I presume you had your reasons.'

'Open your book and take it down, Johnson. I don't want Lethbridge saying you didn't do the dirty work properly.'

'Yes, sir.' He opened his notebook again.

'I'd had a conversation with my wife, shortly before leaving the house. A painful and personal conversation. The gist of it was that my wife believed I was having an affair with another woman. I assured her that I was not, at least not in the physical sense she feared and suspected. God knows, I had been unfaithful to her many times in my head . . . '

'Sir, I—'

'Shut up. I'm only going to say this once, so you get it down. I had been unfaithful to her in my head many times, but never in fact in the flesh, as you might say. I told her this and I also told her that my . . . infatuation was over. She did not believe this and I saw that she was right not to. It was because I realised this myself, after I'd been telling myself for some time that it was all over, that I walked out of the house and went for that drive. I wanted to think it all out, for myself. I was trying to free myself from what I felt for this other woman. I think I almost succeeded. But that's irrelevant now. You'd better add that the other woman was Dolores Bayger, and I want you to note, for the record, that I swear I never went anywhere near her or Chuters that night. I did not kill her.'

Johnson's pen scratched in the silence for a moment. Jolley closed his eyes tight. If he had gone to her that night, she might be alive today. His eyes pricked. He heard Johnson close his notebook and his chair scrape against the polished floor. She might have been alive today.

So, they thought he might have killed Dolores Bayger. It was the most unreasonable suspicion he had ever come across. What hurt was that it was bound to have originated with Teddy Tait. He did not blame Eileen. She would have been out of her mind with worry. Naturally she would turn to Tait – who else? – and naturally she would recall and mention his other, recent, unexplained absence. He had told her often enough that the only way to deal with the police, with a man like him, was to tell the truth, the whole truth. And in Tait's shoes he would have entertained the same suspicion. He had had the opportunity. Anyone who has the opportunity is automatically under suspicion. They had done to him no more and no less than he had done to Belle Smith and her mother, the Brimbles. Only like them he did not have a motive. Only Wilding had a motive and, at that time, apparently, no opportunity. No, he could not blame anyone for regarding him as a possible candidate and perhaps, in time, it would be good for him to know how it felt to be on the other side. How many men had he questioned and scared because they happened to have had the opportunity to commit a crime of which they were palpably innocent? That was the way it worked. He did not regret those hours of questioning, would do it all over again if he had to. Elimination was crucial because it swept a clear path to the real culprit. He understood their thinking, aligned himself with it. What he did not understand was why this taint of suspicion, for it was no more than that, hurt him so much. Of all the dreadful things he had seen over the years, none compared to that first sight of Dolores Bayger with her throat cut. He would never forget her voice and now it seemed he would never forget that last terrible sight of her. What hurt, perhaps, was his own rank foolishness, his loss of dignity and good common sense. What hurt was the fact that even now she did something to his heart and mind that stopped him hating and despising her.

Tears welled beneath Jolley's closed lids and slid silently down his face.

It was Wednesday afternoon before Jolley received another 'official' visit. He had spent the intervening time resting, sleeping and listening to cassettes. As a result, he felt better. Johnson's visit and the new perspective on the case it had given him had taken the edge off his curiosity. He still felt involved but not overlooked. He accepted, in a sense, that it was out of his hands. Even so, his heart quickened that Wednesday afternoon when, after the compulsory 'rest' period, Nurse Dawson swept back the curtains around his bed to reveal Marion Glade waiting in the centre of the room. He tried to lever himself up, disturbed his neck and had to submit to the indignity of being helped by the nurse, who settled him on his neatly arranged pillows.

'You look much better than I expected,' Marion said, coming towards him, a tired smile on her face.

'Which is more than I can say for you,' he retorted.

She looked like a woman who had snatched a few hours' sleep here and there for many days. Her hair was limp, dragged back in a convenient ponytail. Even her clothes had a crumpled, over-worn look.

'I'll get you a cup of tea,' Nurse Dawson said, giving him a look that could only be described as 'old-fashioned'. 'Would you like one, miss?'

'That would be lovely. Thanks, Nurse.' She pulled the visitor's chair out and sat gratefully, her bag on her knees. 'Simon warned me you were grumpy,' she said, opening her bag.

'Simon? Who's Simon?'

'PC Johnson. Here. I brought you a present.' She tossed a cassette on to the bed where it fell face down. Dutifully, Jolley picked it up and turned it over. *Callas: The Unknown Recordings 1957 – 1969*, with a picture of the *diva*, elegant and svelte in black, running down one side. He grasped it tightly and the old, generous smile broke out, transforming his face.

'That's truly just what I wanted. Thank you. How did you know?'

Putting her bag on the floor, Marion said, 'A little bird dropped me a hint . . . '

'The species Eileen, no doubt. Well, thank you. I appreciate it. Now you're getting in cahoots with my wife, are you?'

'She kept me informed of your progress.'

'Which is more than you've . . . ' He stopped himself, looked contritely at her pale and tired face. 'Sorry. I can see it's been rough. How are you getting on with Lethbridge?'

'OK. I couldn't have handled it without him. He's been . . . considerate. It would have been pleasanter with you, though.'

'Thanks,' he said gruffly. 'So what's the score?'

'We're asking for a remand in custody for psychiatric reports. Lethbridge's in court now.'

'Shouldn't you be with him?'

She shrugged. 'He doesn't need me and I thought it was

244

time I came to see you. I gather you've been threatening to burst a blood vessel.'

'I appreciate it. Really I do. And there's something else. I gather from Johnson, by putting two and two together mostly, that I owe you a big one. Apparently you saved my life.'

'That's putting it a bit dramatically, isn't it?'

'Considering I thought you'd shot me . . . or rather Doulton . . . '

She smiled at that, shaking her head. 'Poor Doulton. He nearly wet himself when he saw me pull the gun.'

'You'd better explain. Johnson was very cagey.'

'He was only acting on instructions. You gave him a hard time . . . '

'I'm a bad-tempered old invalid.'

'You're a frustrated police officer.'

'Well, a mixture of the two, perhaps. Ah, tea . . . ' They were silent while Nurse Dawson drew the tea from an urn and handed each of them a cup. Now that he was off the drip, Jolley took an inordinate pride in handling and drinking from a proper cup. He toasted Marion. 'What I don't understand is why you drew a gun in the first place. And who authorised it?'

'That's easy. They didn't. I took Dolores Bayger's gun from your desk.'

'Jesus Christ, woman . . . ' he said softly, his face growing pale.

'I know. I'm going before a disciplinary board next week.'

'I'll back you up. They'll have to let me out of here . . . '

'I've been lucky. The Super could have suspended me, had me demoted . . . Fortunately he needed me to help Lethbridge in your absence. The fact that he didn't do either will presumably help.'

'They can still demote you . . . ' She nodded. 'It was my fault, of course. I should have turned the bloody thing in when you told me to. Still, whatever possessed you?'

'I found it in the drawer and I just took it. Things were

looking black enough for you just then and I thought . . .
Well, I was going to turn it in. Then, well, everything
happened so quickly, it went clean out of my mind.
And when it came to it, when Simon got that door
open, I just had a feeling . . . No, I was convinced
Wilding was in there. It sounds crazy now, of course. I
can hardly believe it myself, but at the time it seemed
. . . likely.'

'What put you on to that idea?'

'You.' She looked at him, her blue eyes challenging him
to deny it. 'I tried to put myself in your place. I guessed
you'd gone to the house. I didn't know why. But where
else could I start? Then when we found the time-lock, it
suddenly came together. You'd locked the house up. That
didn't make sense unless you were expecting someone to
try to get away . . . '

'I might just have left and locked up after me, like
a good chap.'

'If I'd even considered that, the whole theory would
have collapsed and I didn't have any other. I guessed
you'd thought Wilding might be there, hiding out in the
studio. I still wasn't convinced. It just seemed something
you might think. I was more inclined to think that you'd
found nothing and got yourself locked in there or something. Then, at the last minute, as I stood there, waiting
for that damned door to open, I wondered what would
happen if you'd been right. So I pulled the gun.'

'Mm,' Jolley said, 'That makes sense to me. But why
fire it?'

'What would you do – given that you've got a loaded gun
in your hand – if you came face to face with a crazy-looking
bloke wielding a crowbar?'

'I'd rather not think. It's exactly that sort of admission
that makes me believe guns are more trouble than they're
worth. You'll have to tell the board something better than
that.'

'I know.'

'You could have killed him. Then what?'

'No.' She shook her head. 'I'm a good shot. I fired to miss. Over his head.'

'You're still a damned fool.'

'Maybe . . . '

'But I'll do my best for you. You can depend on that. And if we save your skin, don't you ever do anything like that again.'

'I won't. And you make sure you turn any firearms you find in straight away.'

'*Touché*. I'll have a word with Tait. This is one time I shall be glad to take advantage of his Mr Fix-it complex. Don't you worry.' She pulled a face. 'It'll be all right.'

'We'll see. Thanks anyway. Now you tell me, *did* you know Wilding was there? Is that why you locked up behind you?'

'Much like you. Yes and no. It occurred to me all right. The more I thought about it the more it seemed that he must be here, that Dolores had been lying all along— '

'Oh, she'd been doing that all right,' Marion interrupted with a note of bitterness in her voice that he had never heard before. 'Sorry, go on,' she added quickly, seeing the involuntary, pained expression on his face.

'It seemed preposterous but it niggled. You know?' She nodded. 'Then I thought, supposing he had turned up, killed her but not done a bunk? Supposing he was scared, overcome with remorse even . . . Or, more likely, that he wanted something, was looking for something. I thought of those photographs. Maybe there were copies, perhaps more. Where were they likely to be? In the studio. He could have got locked in or could have holed up there for a while. Either way I had to take a look at that studio. I should have done it before. It was on my conscience, if you like. But unlike you, when I came to it, when the door opened, I thought the whole thing was crazy. So I marched in there and got bashed on the head for my trouble.'

'And got tied up and God knows what else.'

'He didn't do anything else to me . . . ' He remembered Wilding's spittle on his face and wiped his hand instinctively across his dry skin. 'Nothing that mattered, anyway.'

'So was that why you locked up?'

Jolley tried to nod but could not. 'Yep. That was when I felt pretty certain of my theory. I thought he might try and break for it when the door opened. I wanted to make it difficult for him to get away.'

'Great minds . . . ' she said, 'or crazy ones. Anyway, we're going to charge him with assaulting and imprisoning a police officer— '

'What's wrong with murder?'

'It's a long story.'

'So, tell me.'

'It's complicated, difficult. If I wasn't so damned tired . . . ' She put down her cup. 'I feel like my brain's been bludgeoned.'

'So do I. So take it at your own pace. You can't go too slowly for me.'

'Wilding's not always lucid. He contradicts himself. Sometimes he's quiet and co-operative, seems quite willing to chat, tell you anything. Other times, he's just crazy. This'll make you laugh. We had to ask Arnolph to give him some heroin.' Jolley chuckled. 'You should have seen his face. He refused, of course. Gave him some sort of substitute . . . It made the whole procedure much more difficult.'

'What about the knife? Fingerprints?' Jolley interrupted, his tone clearly suggesting that he thought all she said was so much waffle, prevarication.

'A few smears only,' Marion sighed. 'We found a towel in the utility room with splashes of her blood on it. We reckon he wrapped the knife in that, perhaps to conceal it from her and then used it to wipe the knife clean. Or perhaps he wrapped the handle in it. Whatever, there are no conclusive prints.'

Jolley swore, disappointed.

'The point is,' Marion went on, seizing her chance, 'the man's a junkie, the worst I've ever seen. That's partly why we can't charge him. He's cunning. And Lethbridge is genuinely scared he'll be found unfit to plead. Hence the psychiatric reports. We've spoken to a psychiatrist who treated him in America. He's sending a full report. Until we get all that together, we can't push for a murder charge. Or, to be honest, we daren't. And then we're going to have to dry him out, I suppose, and no one knows what that'll do to his mind, his competence. You see you can't tell – I can't, anyway – what is genuine disturbance and what is the effect of his dependency. Is his mind damaged because he's been taking drugs for years or has that just exaggerated a natural condition?'

'I concede the need for psychiatric reports . . . '

'We're pinning a lot on the American guy, who's very co-operative and concerned.' She leaned back, rubbed her hand across her eyes. 'I'll try and piece it together for you, what little I know. It's difficult, because we get it all in dribs and drabs, and then he goes and contradicts himself . . . '

'Just do your best. Give me an outline . . . But tell me one thing first. Did he kill her?'

'Oh yes. Sooner or later, he was bound to kill her. The only really puzzling thing about it is why it took him so long. Why now?'


How and when Jay-Jay Wilding and Dolores Bayger met and formed what Marion called their 'unholy relationship' was still unknown. She was a rich, spoiled woman seven years older than Wilding. He was a drop-out from university, already dabbling in drugs. On his own admission he was besotted with her. She was the only person he had ever met who did not want to change him. According to the psychiatrist, there was a long history of parental conflict. His father was a small town, self-made, ultra-respectable man, who had built up his own butcher's business. He had three daughters whom he dominated and a son whom he saw primarily as his means of achieving everything he had missed out on. Jay-Jay was indulged as long as he toed the paternal line. When he dropped out of university, his father cut off all support and so forced him back home, where he was apprenticed to the butcher's trade. There he had learned the skills which, years later, had enabled him to cut his wife's throat so cleanly and expertly. It was, apparently, the only skill he learned during that time.

He ran away from home, went to New York, got more and more involved in drugs. He tried to be an actor and became a small-time model. Through this work, he met Dolores Bayger who, after several abortive and expensive attempts at a career, was working for a well-known fashion photographer. She had decided to become a photographer herself. At some point she and Wilding were married. She dabbled in photography, kept him supplied with drugs and they travelled, or rather drifted, from place to place. They never settled anywhere for long, had no discernible purpose. Eventually and inevitably, Wilding was arrested for possession and on suspicion of dealing in hard drugs. Dolores Bayger used her money and family influence to get him off. It was a condition of his release that he be 'cured' and receive psychiatric treatment. With his wife's connivance, he often reneged on this deal and was eventually detained under the American equivalent of the Mental Health Act. He made some progress, was weaned on to substitute drugs. His psychiatrist, the one to whom Marion and Inspector Lethbridge had talked, became convinced that the main block to his complete rehabilitation was his wife. He was dependent on her, completely dominated by her and she was, in the psychiatrist's view, intent on his complete mental destruction. She was forbidden to see him.

At this point, she came to England and bought the house in Chuters. When she was ready, she returned to America. Wilding was by then a voluntary patient. Dolores Bayger found him and had no difficulty at all in re-establishing their relationship with the aid of drugs which she liberally supplied. They came to England together and she brought him to Chuters. His dependence on her was total. He believed that, without her, and without obeying her every whim, he would be deported and incarcerated in a mental hospital, deprived of all drugs. Apparently for this reason, he agreed to live as a virtual prisoner in the studio.

'He was allowed as many drugs as he wanted,' Marion said wearily. 'She let him out at night, for exercise and fresh air. She trusted him. She could afford to trust him. She was totally sure of him. And when she felt like it, she photographed him. One of her little . . . games . . . was to withhold the drugs for days at a time and to photograph his reactions. We found hundreds of photographs. They're . . . disgusting . . . inhuman. But, he says, he never retaliated. I believe him. Or I think I do. I don't think he had any will or mind of his own where she was concerned. She was, according to the psychiatrist, mother, father, lover, wife, friend and the source of all authority as far as he was concerned. She was like a goddess, I suppose. All the influences and contacts the rest of us experience and make, the whole network of social interaction and behaviour, was concentrated in her. She was literally his world. And that, apparently, is what she wanted. A child, an animal, a man who wasn't a man. A creature she could mould and use at will.'

She paused, closed her eyes, fought back a yawn. Jolley thought that many a true word was spoken in anger, without any apparent rationale. Mrs Keene had called her a witch. He himself knew how powerful, how unbelievably attractive and plausible she could be. How one could want to please her, indulge her . . .

'There was just one thing he couldn't – can't – handle, apparently. He couldn't bear her being around other men. As far as we know, she had always been loyal to him. They had fulfilled each other's needs totally. But when she'd got him locked up, reduced him to a state of animal-like dependency, then, in a sense, she'd backed herself into a corner. She couldn't admit to anyone that he was there, imprisoned, drug-dependent. Maybe she got lonely. There must have been whole stretches of time when he was . . . useless to her. Perhaps she was even getting bored with him, now that she'd got him completely where she wanted him. And, of course, she couldn't keep him a total secret. Somebody was bound to find out about him.'

Jolley could believe that. All his old, irrational prejudices about Chuters and its inhabitants rose to the surface of his mind. Dolores Bayger had not chosen the setting for her bizarre life-style well. She had been fooled by the appearance of the place. She had underestimated the people.

Fred Smith had become suspicious. Then he became nosy. He kept watch and he saw Wilding in one of his 'exercise' periods. She used to let Wilding roam the village quite freely at night, knowing that he would come back. But he was seen, not only as a lurking stranger who frightened young women, but by suspicious, watchful men like Fred Smith.

'According to Wilding, in one of his calmer periods, that's why she killed Smith.'

'*She* killed him?' Jolley could not prevent himself interrupting. 'Surely he's lying?'

'I don't think so. She knew that Smith had seen Wilding. She must have known he was suspicious. Wilding knew he had been seen and he was terrified. Remember, he thought that if his presence was discovered, he'd be deported, separated from her, from drugs, from . . . well, what I suppose he had come to see as a kind of freedom. Even if he managed to escape that fate, there was always the possibility that she would punish him for being careless, for letting himself be seen. He was in a blue funk and the only solution, as far as he was concerned, was to kill Smith. Apparently Dolores agreed. She arranged to meet Smith. According to Wilding she told him to bring his gun. Some story about foxes threatening the ravens or something. He's not exactly clear on the details. And she shot Fred Smith with his own gun and made it look like suicide.'

'But how?' Jolley said, still not wanting to believe it.

Marion shrugged. 'She had extraordinary powers of persuasion . . . ' she said enigmatically, not looking at him. 'It's not difficult to believe that she could persuade him to give her the gun. After that . . . your guess is as good as mine.'

Jolley shuddered. The terrible thing was that he *could* imagine it. The promise in her eyes and voice, the way she had of making you want . . . want . . . 'And the others?' he asked, his voice hoarse.

'Corr-Beardsley, apparently. I don't think we'll ever know for certain. Wilding says Corr-Beardsley was too close to her. He thinks they were lovers. He was definitely jealous of Corr-Beardsley. He says he would have killed him if he had had the opportunity, but Dolores did it for him, to prove that she was faithful. A repeat performance, apparently, of the Smith incident. Another faked suicide. I don't know. It seems improbable, but why should Wilding make up such a complicated lie at this stage? He may be crafty, he may in some senses be "mad", but he knows his position, he knows we're on to him.'

'And the young lad, Brimble?' Jolley asked impatiently.

'No. That appears to be a genuine suicide and Wilding is very pleased to take all the "credit" for that,' she said bitterly. 'Brimble worked on the studio – apparently Bayger felt it wasn't secure enough – and he twigged someone was there. Inevitably, I suppose, they met. I can't work out how. Sometimes Wilding says Dolores let Brimble into the studio, sometimes he talks as though he was able to wander around in the daytime at that point. Anyway, he says they met. In fact – and this is an odd thought – apart from Dolores and you, Brimble is probably the only human being Wilding's spoken to in eighteen months or longer. Anyway, Brimble knew of his existence but was so . . . enamoured of Dolores that he promised to keep the secret. If it wasn't for the fact that this keeps on coming up, the influence or power she had over men, I simply wouldn't believe it. In fact, I can't believe it. I can't understand how she could seem so . . . adorable, I suppose.' Jolley said nothing. Marion sighed and leaned back again, stretching out her legs as though they were cramped. 'Anyway, Wilding was jealous of Brimble. He thought that Dolores was buying his silence by sleeping with him. Whether she was or not . . . ' Marion shrugged. 'It was enough that Wilding believed it. And he had access to Brimble. So he told him Dolores was dying. He told him she had AIDS and that she would have infected any-one— '

'Oh my God,' Jolley said. 'That's— '

'It's *all* disgusting,' Marion interrupted.

'But that means Brimble must have been her lover . . . '

'Unless the poor kid was so crazy about her he couldn't face the prospect of *her* death. Either way he killed himself and no matter how I look at it, I can't see how Bayger could have faked his death. Probably Brimble wasn't the brightest of boys but even he wouldn't let a woman put a noose around his neck . . . And besides, it was in his own back garden.'

'Yes,' Jolley said. 'I'd agree with you there. As for the rest, I don't know. Can we believe any of this?'

'It's up to you. We haven't got anything else. Maybe the psychiatrists can at least confirm or deny the possi-bility of some of it. Whether any court will believe the uncorroborated evidence of a man like Wilding, in his mental state— '

'They won't,' Jolley said adamantly, but did not know what he felt about this, whether he was relieved or angrily regretful. 'You say he denies killing Dolores. When he does, what does he say?'

Marion did not answer for a very long time. After a while, she got up and walked to the window. Darkness was hovering. Among the trees sodium lights were glowing into pale life. St Nicholas's steeple had become black and featureless against the sky, a two-dimensional silhouette.

'I suppose I can answer that for myself,' Jolley said at last.

'You were the last straw. You were a policeman as well as a rival. Dolores told him all about you. That was part of his subjection, I imagine. She exulted in the fact that you were a policeman. It added spice to a situation I'm convinced she was getting bored with. In fact, I think

254

she would have killed Wilding pretty soon, only he got to her first.'

'Go on,' Jolley said.

Marion turned and leaned against the window sill, her hands folded together, showing white against her dark skirt.

'You sure you want to hear this? There's no need . . . '

'Once. And from you. If you'll be so kind.'

'She used you and your job to frighten Wilding. She told him she would tell you about him, that you would protect her from any consequences of what she had done, while he would be deported, incarcerated, etcetera, etcetera. Sometimes she told him you were suspicious, that you were watching her, following her . . . All this so that she could threaten to have to cut off his drug supply— '

'Did you pick up Myers?' Jolley asked to buy himself a little respite.

'Yes. Passington Drug Squad are trying to trace his source of supply. He denies everything, but he's as guilty as hell. Apparently, he gets most of his antiques from Amsterdam. They're pretty sure that's how he got the drugs in, but they want to find the supplier. Thanks for the message, by the way. I should have said— '

'Go on with your story,' Jolley said, looking at his hands. In a minute a nurse would come bustling in to put on the lights, take his temperature, give him his pills. 'They'll be in in a minute,' he told her.

'That's it, really. Wilding insists you killed her, but he means— '

'I know what he means, Sergeant, thank you. I drove him to kill her. I was too big a threat. She went too far.'

'He says he watched you one night, when you left her. He was going to release the ravens one by one. He said he'd taken one out of the aviary and was holding it. He released it and it flew at you. You fell over— '

'I thought I'd imagined that,' Jolley said, his flesh creeping at the memory.

'Only then you stopped visiting her. He thought this

was all part of a conspiracy between you and Bayger. He thought he was in imminent danger— '

'So he killed her. Because of me.'

'Because he had to. The American psychiatrist says he had long feared that if Bayger didn't remove herself entirely, Wilding would turn on her. He says it was inevitable. In spite of everything, Wilding had a breaking point. Only Bayger didn't know that, or wouldn't recognise it.'

'Why the hell didn't the psychiatrist tell her that?'

'Oh, he did. He made a point of warning her.' Marion walked slowly back to his bed. 'It's possible that's what she wanted. She wanted to see how far she could push him, how far she could go with one human being before he retaliated. That could be the basis of the whole relationship.'

'Seems a bit far-fetched to me,' Jolley grumbled.

'Possibly. But it would explain why she warned you. Perhaps she knew that afternoon that Wilding had reached the end and perhaps she accepted it. There was no struggle remember . . . Anyway, I don't think we'll ever know.'

'But if I hadn't stayed away from her— '

'He might have attacked you, but that wouldn't have prevented him killing her, eventually. It was always on the cards. She was just using you. You were a— '

'Pawn,' he said. 'That would be a polite way of putting it.'

'An unwitting one.'

'And a very foolish one.'

'If you like. Maybe,' she said.

The door swung open and a nurse appeared, snapping on the lights.

'Give us a few more minutes, Nurse, please,' Marion said, turning to her. 'I'm a police officer. We've nearly finished.' The nurse hesitated a moment, then nodded and went out.

'It seems to me you've got enough to charge him,' Jolley said.

'Oh, sure,' Marion agreed, picking up her bag. 'But can we make it stick? Not unless we can get a cut and dried confession out of him. All I want is for him to say he

256

killed her, then we can go. But I'd have to put my money on his being unfit to plead.'

'Does it matter?'

'Personally, I think he's already been punished. However, that's not a professional view and certainly isn't how Lethbridge sees it. As long as he's put out of harm's way— '

'He needs help . . . '

'Of course. Though I sometimes think perhaps he's gone beyond that. Perhaps the kindest thing one can wish him is an overdose . . . However, there's no chance of that.' She swung her bag on to her shoulder, looking totally exhausted.

'We'll get you off the disciplinary board. That's a promise,' Jolley said. 'You had every reason to think Wilding was going to attack you. Everything you did was designed to help an endangered senior officer. They won't be able to ignore that.'

'Says you,' she smiled. 'You don't really think I'd admit to trying to save you, do you?'

He smiled back at her. It was good that she felt able to tease him. It did him good, too.

'You've destroyed nearly all my illusions this afternoon, Sergeant. Have the goodness to leave me that one at least.'

'All right,' she said, 'if you promise to take care of yourself and get back to work as soon as possible. A little of Lethbridge goes a very long way.'

'I'm sure. Now off you go and get some rest. That's an order.'

'Yes, sir. After all, you are the boss.'

# Afterword

It was Marion Glade's idea, but Eileen who put it into practice. Jolley put on his new surgical collar, an ugly, pink gauze-covered thing that fastened with Velcro, and took his seat, chin up perforce, beside Eileen in the car.

'We're only going out to lunch, dear,' she said, worn down by his sulking silence. 'A little celebration.'

'And what are we celebrating?'

'You getting out of that plaster collar for a start . . . '

'I don't know that this one's an improvement,' he grumbled.

'And then there's Marion's good news about the disciplinary thing. And now the fact that that man's been charged . . . '

She referred to the fact that, after a month's delay, Marion had received a severe reprimand and John James Wilding had been charged with the murder of his wife. He had been remanded to the hospital wing of Bainbridge prison, where there was a detoxification centre. Whether he would eventually be fit to plead remained uncertain. More reports would be made, his response to treatment would be taken into account, his mental state regularly assessed . . . Jolley sighed. He felt increasingly detached from the case. Deep down, he suspected, he did not care very much what happened to Wilding. He wanted to forget. He wanted to get back to work. He wanted to prove himself in some way he could not define. This long – to him interminable – lay-off bred a kind of lethargy which made him feel old and led him to doubt his continuing competence.

'I've asked Marion to join us,' Eileen informed him.

'You're getting very thick with her, aren't you?'

'I owe her a great deal, don't I? Besides, I like her.'

Jolley heaved himself round to look out of the side window. Mention of his narrow escape, Marion's part in it, filled him now with an awkward, over-emotional embarrassment. Scotney said it was shock, the inevitable depression that so often follows violence to the body, a long period of recuperation.

'I know it's difficult for you,' Eileen went on. 'I only wanted to cheer you up. And you do enjoy seeing Marion.'

'True,' Jolley admitted, mollified. 'You're right. We should celebrate. But if we're going to Seddington you've taken the wrong road.'

'We're not,' Eileen replied calmly, daring him to ask where they were going. He slumped in his seat beside her and pretended not to care.

It would be all right, he thought, when he got back to work, back into the routine and swing of things. It could not be long now. Scotney was irritatingly vague, but having the plaster collar off was a good sign. At least he could lie comfortably at night. Soon he would start to leave the collar off an hour at a time. Twice a week he did gentle exercises with a fierce young woman at the cottage hospital and he was down to two pain-killers a day. What more could a man ask?

'Oh no, Eileen. This has got to be some kind of joke.' He pushed himself up in the seat, frowning.

'Not at all,' she answered, slowing at the Chuters turn-off. 'The pub's under new management and the wife is French. The food is said to be wonderful.'

'But you know I hate this dreary place.'

'Anyone would think you were afraid of it,' she said, testing the waters she and Marion had discussed in private.

'Afraid? Don't be so stupid. It's just a place, after all.'

'Exactly, dear. And you'll have a good lunch no matter what.'

The trees were bare. The green in front of the pub was

stripped of its summer furniture. Incongruously, a string of coloured light bulbs outlined the façade of The Clouded Yellow. Their brightness seemed pathetically defiant, powerless against the grim atmosphere of the place. Awkwardly, because it was still difficult to bend his head even in this less rigid collar, Jolley got out of the car. Eileen fussed around him like a mother hen. He straightened himself and looked around. He saw nothing to make him change his view of Chuters. Even when it had been home to someone he had thought infinitely precious to him, he had not liked it. He was consistent, at least, he thought.

'What are you standing there for?' Eileen asked.

'Just seeing how many curtains twitch behind those dark windows. We don't want them to miss anything, do we?'

'As if anyone cares about you,' she said, taking his arm. 'Come along, it's cold.'

They'd care all right. Sight of him would bring it all back, start carrion gossips picking over her bones again. What rankled was that, without having any proof, they had been right about her. She was actually blacker than even they had been able to paint her. But he still could not forgive them.

Eileen led him into the dining-room and Marion waved to them from a table in the corner, near the fire. The place was transformed. There was a new, dark purple carpet on the floor, dried flowers in copper vases and pans, starched white tablecloths and a deliciously tempting smell of good food well prepared. Jolley felt all this but did not allow it to lighten his thunderous expression.

'It was my idea,' Marion told him as he sat down. 'You can blame me.'

'I don't know what you two are fussing about,' he said, reaching for the menu. They exchanged a look of complicity. 'But I don't want you getting too friendly,' he added.

'Your Lord and Master has spoken, Eileen,' Marion said, pulling a face.

'Take no notice of him, dear. He can't grumble about the place, so he picks on us. Funny, though, he never minded me being friendly with Dave Hughes.'

'That's because Dave Hughes would never form an alliance with you against me,' he said. 'Women are danger-ous.' He stuck his nose in the menu, ignoring their delighted laughter. Let them laugh, he thought. It was true. He had reason to know.

After duck à l'orange, profiteroles and two glasses of excel-lent wine, Jolley's mood had mellowed. He sat back and watched the two women who chattered together like old friends, not exactly excluding him but content to leave him to his own thoughts. Eileen looked terrific, he thought, the little green hat set saucily on her white hair, a wisp of veiling covering her forehead. Eileen and her hats, he thought, and smiled a little. And Marion had done something to her hair. He could not tell what it was but it framed her fresh, open face with a new and becoming softness. She had a healthy glow in her cheeks, a sparkle in her eyes.

'And what are you smiling about?' Eileen asked, covering his hand with hers.

'Just thoughts.'

'Coffee?' Marion asked.

'Not for Cy. It doesn't suit him after the . . . It gives him headaches,' she corrected herself.

'Well, then, let's just finish the wine,' Marion said, lifting the bottle and sharing it between their glasses.

'I thought I'd pop over and say hello to old Mrs Pasque,' Eileen said to her husband. 'You and Marion can go for a bit of a stroll and talk shop.'

'Why can't I come and see Mrs Pasque? I'm very fond of Mrs Pasque.'

'You can, dear. You can pick me up there later. I'm sure Marion has lots to tell you.'

'Have you?' he asked, fixing Marion with a suspicious stare.

'One or two things. And after that meal I could certainly do with a stroll.'

'That's settled then,' Eileen said, folding her napkin.

'Get the bill, Cy. I expect they want to close anyway.'

And so he found himself outside, in the dull, chilly afternoon. Eileen was already hurrying across the green in her unsuitable heels, one hand holding her hat. These days, he hated to see her walk away. Marion, hands in the pockets of her loose overcoat, was already walking up the lane, past the chapel. Shaking off his reluctance, Jolley caught her up. She glanced at him, smiled.

'You've got something up your sleeve,' he said.

'No.'

'So what's this all about?'

'We don't have to walk if you don't want to. The bar's open for half an hour yet, or you can join Eileen. I've got plenty to do back at the station.'

They wandered along in silence. Jolley kept his eyes cast down, aware that 'The Stables' was looming on their left.

'I meant what I said. When women get their heads together— '

'Eileen's worried about you. There's no conspiracy.'

'Eileen has been worried about me, about the children, about every pet we've ever owned and all the people we've ever known plus most of the rest of the world's population ever since she was seventeen.'

'Is that when you met her?'

'Yes.'

'She's a very caring woman.'

'What has she been telling you?'

'That you're feeling sorry for yourself, perhaps even guilty.'

'Don't I have reason?'

'Possibly. All right, yes. But perhaps it's not just your physical state. What about your mental attitude?'

Jolley stopped walking. Marion turned around, waited, looking up at him. From her expression he knew she intended to get an answer.

'You've spent too long reading psychiatrists' reports. You're supposed to be a policewoman . . . '

'What you've been through . . . it doesn't just stop like

262

that . . . ' She snapped her fingers. 'It takes time. The healing process is long and hard. Sometimes it needs a little help, a nudge in the right direction.'

'You're dangerously close to insubordination, Sergeant. My mental attitude— '

'You're on leave. I can say what I like to you.'

'But I won't always be on leave,' he threatened. She smiled, acknowledging the threat, turned around and looked at the house. Reluctantly, he followed her gaze. He felt nothing. 'What do you want, Marion?' he asked.

She held out her hand to him.

'Come and have a look at the studio,' she said, managing, almost, to make it sound like a sudden impulse, a whim. 'I'd like to. Will you?'

He considered for a long moment, fighting the impulse to turn and walk away. 'All right,' he said gruffly. 'If you want to.'

She let her hand fall to her side and went to the gate, opened it, crossed the neglected patch of lawn and pushed open the side gate. Jolley, trying to look nonchalant even if he did not feel it, followed her.

Workmen had repaired the aviary at the far end of the yard. New timber awaited a coat of preservative. The replaced wire mesh gleamed dully in the light. But the cage was empty.

'The one thing I feel really sure about,' Marion said quietly, standing by his side, 'is that Wilding felt something genuine for those birds. He really loved them. He still talks about them.'

'Probably thinks he's the Birdman of Alcatraz,' Jolley said gruffly.

'I think he felt a kinship with them. Wild things, impris-oned. Even though most of them were bred in captivity, they must know . . . Whereas he . . . His imprisonment must have been terrible for him at times. That's why he let them out.'

To settle on her window sill, Jolley thought, with a shudder. To observe her death.

*Dismal ravens crying*
*At the windows of the dying . . .*

It all swept over him then, the sound of the mezzo's wheedling tone, Dolores Bayger, smiling at him. Marion touched his arm gently. Only she was not Dido, as he had thought, magnificent in her fate, but the sorceress, summoning evil spirits. He had to remember that.

'Shall we?' Marion asked, moving towards the studio door. Jolley made his stiff little nod, all that the collar would permit. In for a pound, he thought . . .

There was a bright new hasp and padlock on the black door. He watched, impassive, as Marion produced a key from her pocket and opened it. She pushed the door wide and reached around the frame, fumbling with her hand. Lights flickered on.

'You've never really seen it, have you?' she said, walking into the room.

He followed her. The room was partitioned off at either end. Behind his back when he had been strapped to the chair was a door he had never seen. Like everything else, it was painted black. He looked at the sinks. Leaning against the opposite wall was a collapsed trestle table. Apart from that the room was empty. His footsteps echoed.

'I get it now,' he said, looking at Marion. 'Exorcism. That's what you've got in mind.'

'That's a big word, Inspector,' she said.

'But the right one. It's much smaller than I thought . . .'

'The real studio's through here.' She opened the door he had only just seen, but Jolley was staring at the wall opposite the main door. There was a neat black hole in it and the plaster showed pinkish where it had cracked with the impact of a bullet. He went close to it. It was about a foot above his head. Wilding was about his height.

'Didn't leave yourself much margin for error, Sergeant, did you?'

'I didn't have time, sir,' she answered, disappearing through the door, putting on more lights.

264

He followed her. This room was larger. Photographic lights, reflectors, tripods had been pushed to one end. There was a row of black filing cabinets against the wall. A black, leather-topped stool stood in the middle of the room. He knew what it was for, could almost see Wilding sitting on it, she angling the lights to show every line and twitch of his haunted face, twisting her lens to get the sharpest focus. He walked blindly over to the filing cabinets.

'Empty,' Marion told him. 'We took everything away. There are some things you don't ever need to see.'

Jolley leaned against the nearest cabinet, squeezed his eyes shut. 'How she must have hated,' he said in a dry whisper. 'Hated men, I mean. She must have been . . . filled with hatred.'

'There's no doubt she needed the psychiatrist more than Wilding.'

'Why, though?' Marion did not answer. She had no answer. She pressed her lips together, watching him, giving him time. 'I don't know how . . . ' he said, but could not finish the sentence. Perhaps it had no end. How could he have loved her, been fooled by her? Would he ever come to hate her? How was he to neutralise her, make her an incident in the past? 'You'd better show me the rest,' he said, pushing away from the cabinet and walking quickly into the central room. Her dark room, he thought, in all senses of the word.

Marion clicked off lights behind him, closed the door. 'This is where he lived,' she said, passing him and throwing open the other door. 'If you can call it that.'

The light dazzled from that door as it had when Jolley had been helpless in his chair. He walked towards it, into it, with a cold shudder tingling down his back. It was a tiny room. A shelf-like bed was built into the wall, just long enough to let a tall man stretch out. A frosted glass partition bisected the room laterally on his right.

'Shower and lavatory,' Marion said in answer to his questioning look. 'Somewhere to sleep, wash . . . Of course he had the run of the rest of the building.'

'Surely not the studio,' Jolley protested. 'Wouldn't he have destroyed the photographs?'

'She kept the cabinets locked.'

'The equipment, then?'

'Apparently not. Certainly not if she told him not to. You have to remember, he was dependent on her, physically, emotionally, mentally . . . He did as she told him.' Jolley turned away from the ugly, efficient little cell. 'There was only one way to defy her, to hurt her, to set himself free of her.' Jolley looked around him, turned his whole body round in a slow circle. 'And now, the biggest stumbling block we face is her absence. The euphoria's over for him. He's beginning to miss her, need her . . . '

'But *why* did he kill her?' Jolley demanded. 'Why, after years and years of indignity, all this . . . '

'Fear, I suppose.' Marion closed the 'cell' door.

'Of what she would persuade me to do?'

'More likely he just reached the end of his tether. Perhaps she found his breaking point. We'll never know, Cy.'

'You said, perhaps she wanted it,' he said, wonderingly. 'You said that's why she warned me that day at Brisestock. She knew it was going to happen. She knew it was going to happen and she did nothing to stop it. That's what I keep thinking now. Only why did she tell me?'

'I wondered when you'd ask that,' Marion said gently, walking towards the open door, the welcoming daylight outside.

'I suppose she must have wanted me to stop it somehow.'

'No. She said she didn't want you to think badly of her. You thought she meant gossip, that people would say she had it coming to her or something equally crass. What she really wanted was to make you feel guilty. She wanted to keep a hold on you, even though she was dead.' She stood in the doorway, waiting for him, the padlock in her hands. He walked out, past her and stood in the yard, watching as she locked the door. 'You're letting her. You're granting

266

her wish, Cy. Professionally, I'd say you're colluding with her. But you can stop, any time you want. You can break the spell, Cy. Only you can break the spell.'

Tears stung his eyes. He tried to nod his head, to show he understood but he could not be sure that he had seen.

'Well,' she said, sighing, 'I must be getting back. And Eileen'll be wondering where you've got to.

He walked to the end of the village and back, alone. Eileen was waiting for him in the car, opened the door for him. He got in beside her.

'I saw Marion. She had to get back.'

'I know.'

'You ready to go home now?'

'Yes.' He put his hand over Eileen's as she reached for the ignition. She turned to him, her face gentle, open. 'It's really over, Eileen. This time, it really is over.'

'I know, dear. I know it is.'

'And I love you.'

'I know that too.'

'And I'm sorry.'

'Of course you are, dear. But there's no need.'